Haunting and Homicide

Haunting and Homicide

A GHOST TOUR MYSTERY

Ava Burke

CROOKED
LANE

NEW YORK

Published in the United States by Crooked Lane Books, an imprint of The Quick Brown Fox & Company LLC.

Crooked Lane Books and its logo are trademarks of The Quick Brown Fox & Company LLC.

Library of Congress Catalog-in-Publication data available upon request.

ISBN (hardcover): 978-1-63910-928-9
ISBN (ebook): 978-1-63910-929-6

Cover design by Scott Zelazny

Printed in the United States.

www.crookedlanebooks.com

Crooked Lane Books
34 West 27th St., 10th Floor
New York, NY 10001

First Edition: January 2025

10 9 8 7 6 5 4 3 2 1

For William.
I think you'd like this one.

A Note to Readers

Although those native to and familiar with the Garden District in New Orleans will recognize many of the geography and landmarks in Haunting and Homicide, I have also taken some liberties. I hope you'll grant me some latitude with these changes.

Chapter One

Fifteen years ago

I heard my mother, but what I didn't do was listen. My act of defiance at the ripe old age of ten was to hide from her in the bramble of thorny rose bushes and shrubs, whose names I didn't know, at the back of my grandmother's yard. I knew I was prolonging the inevitable, but I wanted to make a stand, to illustrate how unfair it was to make me move away from everything and everyone I loved.

I navigated the thorns and tangles pulling at my dark hair and clothes until I came to rest on the little circle of flat stones in the heart of the bramble. It wasn't a proper hedge maze like you see in the movies, but Nan always told me the wild mazes were better, shaped by the hand of the fae. I'd never seen any of the fae, but my Nan told me stories about them, and I believed with all my heart and soul. I hugged my arms around my knees, closed my eyes, and asked them to hide me away.

"Surely you aren't asking what I think you're asking," came a male voice from somewhere behind me.

I stopped my whispered chant and held my breath, the damp scent of fallen leaves and dying blooms caught in my nose. I wanted to bottle that scent and take it with me, along with the leather and Old Spice cologne smell of PawPaw's favorite chair and the way Nan always smells faintly of honeysuckle.

"Lou," he said tenderly. I squeezed my eyes shut against the threatening tears.

I felt the air get cold around me as he came closer. I didn't know what about being dead caused the air to react that way, but spirits always bring a chill. I hugged my knees tighter, willing myself to be smaller, even though I knew I had no hope of hiding from a ghost.

"Lou," he said again. "Your mother is going to be furious if she has to come get you."

"I don't care. She doesn't care about my feelings. Why should I care about hers?"

"You know that isn't true."

"It is!" I fumed, opening my eyes and glaring at the misty figure seated in front of me. "You don't understand, Kenneth."

Kenneth's features filtered in and out of my perception as the mist or fog or whatever it was he used to take shape, swirled around. He was about my mom's age. Well, he was about my mom's age when he died. He wouldn't tell me what happened, no matter how many times I asked him, but he did say he had been on the grounds since before my Nan's house was built. I tried to look into the history of the area in the school library, but it was sadly lacking in obscure local history.

His hair was long and kind of shaggy, a circumstance he frequently complained about, that he'd died before getting it trimmed and was stuck forever with a manifestation that had a bad haircut. I'd known him my whole life. For reasons unknown to him, he was stuck where he'd died, so every visit to Nan meant a visit to Kenneth too. Although all the adults in my life called him an "imaginary friend."

The tears I'd been holding back all day—all week really—finally broke through my resolve and streamed down my freckled cheeks. I angrily wiped them away on the shoulders of my T-shirt. I'd hoped, in the way that only kids can manage to deny reality, believing the move just wouldn't happen, right up until the day my mother started loading the car.

"I don't want to leave," I sobbed, wishing I could hug Kenneth for comfort.

"Life is full of changes, Lulu Belle," he said softly. Normally, I would've bristled at his use of the nickname, but at the moment I loved hearing him say it. "This is just the biggest one so far. You're going to love it there."

"How do you know? You've only met Jared once." I spat out my mother's new husband's name like a sour grape. I didn't like him. He smiled too much and tried too hard, and he was forcing me to move away from my whole world.

"Because home isn't a place, Tallulah Grace Thatcher. It's in here." He pointed a wispy finger toward my heart. "You can make home wherever you are."

"But home is people too. Cady won't be there. Nan won't be there." My voice caught somewhere deep in my chest, snagged on the grief that had settled there. I took a deep breath and finally croaked, "You won't be there."

"But I'll be here." He smiled. "I'll be here every time you come and visit, and you can tell me all about your adventures."

"It won't be the same," I whispered back.

"Lou!" Mom's voice was getting closer.

Kenneth gave me one more sad smile and dissipated into the leaves. I wished I could draw the mist into a jar and take him with me like a genie, but I knew I couldn't. I'd tried to bottle him up and take him to school once, and he vanished about a block away from Nan's house.

I crawled back through the thorns and limbs, ignoring the tugs at my clothes and hair, even though it felt like even the shrubs wanted to keep me there. Kenneth was right; Mom was furious when I emerged from the bramble. I was right too. It wouldn't ever be the same.

Chapter Two

Present day

Kenneth's annoyance with me was clear, even though he wasn't fully corporeal. I looked back over the tarot card in my hand and hesitated to tell him I didn't have the foggiest clue what I was supposed to see there. If he hadn't been dead for more than a hundred years, and still had the lung capacity to heave a heavy sigh, I'm sure he would've done it. He'd spent most of the evening trying to teach me how to read those blasted cards, and we weren't any closer to a revelation than when we'd started.

"You don't have any idea what you're looking at, do you?" he asked, seeming as impatient as a thinly veiled spirit could manage. The modern cadence of his speech was always a little jarring given that his manifestation still looked like he'd walked out of a Dickensian scene.

I stared harder at the Moon card. One of the Major Arcana, the imagery varies depending on the particular deck of cards you use. Kenneth thought I would learn better with a basic, traditional deck. I was disappointing him more by the minute.

"What on earth does a crawdad have to do with anything?"

He was gone when I looked up from the card. My question had been the last straw, the final blow to his patience. I pulled out the accompanying book to the cards and flipped it open, learning that the crawdad is supposed to mean our fears and desires manifesting powerfully enough to crawl into the conscious mind from the deep, dark depths of the subconscious. I looked dubiously at the card again. I didn't think I would ever come to associate fears and desires with a freaking crawdad.

Maybe I just wasn't suited to read the rich and complex symbolism. When I look at a crawdad or a sword or a cup, it's all I see. Trying to train myself to see beyond the printed images was giving me a headache. I gathered up the cards, put them back into their velvet pouch, and put them on top of the interpretation book on the coffee table. The chill in the air when Kenneth was in the room had dissipated with him, and the warmth from the fire washed over me, causing me to yawn.

It was too early to turn in, so I stretched and made my way to the kitchen. My Nan's house had seemed like a mansion when I was a kid, with rooms upon rooms, and long, winding halls that seemed to stretch on for miles. As an adult, it was much smaller than I'd remembered, but it was still an impressive presence on Camp Street. Nan's property sits several blocks riverside of the famous mansions along St. Charles Avenue in the Garden District, but it's just as stately and regal in my eyes as the multimillion-dollar homes that line the scenic thoroughfare.

The main house sat at the front of the lot, flanked on the left by a large garden that Nan left mostly wild and the servants' quarters on the back right. The little cottage hadn't housed staff since the early 1900s and had been used as storage for most of the last century. The small back porch of the main house had expanded into a sprawling affair, accented with a swing and two bistro sets. Nan had added a gazebo, complete with brightly painted gingerbread trim, at the edge of the wild garden and had renovated the servants' quarters.

When I moved back home, she'd insisted I take over the little cottage for the harebrained business idea that had been cooking in my brain since high school. New Orleans was ripe with haunted history, and I'd thought a museum/memorabilia shop/guided tour would be a great way to honor the legacy. The problem was the city was already saturated with shops, museums, and tours dedicated to New Orleans and its various ghosts, haints, and boogeymen. It helped that I knew a good many local ghosts to help me iron out the history not captured in print or photographs, and it helped set apart my shop.

It had taken a while to make it match the picture I'd carried around in my head, but I was finally getting close to the store and tour home base I'd always wanted. I carried some touristy items like New Orleans T-shirts, key chains, postcards, and various knick-knacks. But the bulk of my store was dedicated to the town's haunted history and various occult items. Crystals, tarot cards, candles, cauldrons of all sizes, athames, and incense were placed strategically throughout the shelves.

The focus of the room was the main counter, dedicated to my ghost tours. Unfortunately, I was a latecomer to the business and didn't snag any of the most coveted routes along the most recognizable areas like Bourbon Street in the French Quarter or St. Louis Cemetery. My tour, however, was gaining some vital attention, and bookings had been solid for weeks. My success was due in part to dumb luck and in part to a very accommodating ghost named Mamie Haddock, who could produce the best orbs I've ever seen. And as long as I regularly shared the comments on guest videos of her handiwork, she was more than willing to keep dazzling my guests with them. The dumb-luck part was that my tour also took us past an old speakeasy where a perpetually sloshed ghost named Pete Grubbert stumbled out into view at least once a month.

I wanted to expand beyond the ghost tours, as much as I loved them. Attendance was affected by the weather since I couldn't yet afford a tram or bus. I felt like walking the streets added more ambience to the tours anyway. But having a backup source of income for inclement weather made good business sense. There wasn't any chance that my expansion would include tarot card readings, at least not if I was the one responsible for doing the reading. I hadn't nailed down any concrete plans. I had considered hosting Haunted History Cocktail Hour, but the logistics of getting a liquor license nixed that idea pretty quickly. The idea I was currently researching was using the shop as a venue for ghost-story author events, to keep with my general theme.

The kettle whistled in my ear, so I grabbed it off the stove and took it to my mug perched on the edge of the kitchen sink. As I dunked my tea bag, I stared absently out the window. That's when I noticed the light bobbing around behind my shop, and it definitely wasn't an orb. There was someone, alive, prowling around our yard. Funny how I would've been comforted by a ghost, but the thought of the living sneaking around my house made my heart race and the hair on the back of my neck stand on end.

Chapter Three

I left the tea on the counter; grabbed a flashlight; and, failing to find my pepper spray in a hurry, a can of wasp spray from under the sink. While I don't use pesticides and prefer to leave nature well enough alone, Nan doesn't share the same view since she has to carry an epinephrine pen in case of insect stings. I didn't turn the flashlight on right away, tucking it under my arm for easy access, since I'd hoped to sneak up on the intruder, but that plan was quickly abandoned when I hung my toe on a paving stone and nearly face-planted into a tall man concealed in a black hoodie.

"What are you doing back here?" I said aggressively as I raised the wasp spray. I quickly shoved the flashlight into my back pocket and pulled my phone out of my front pocket, my thumb hovering over the phone icon.

"Are you going to spray me with Raid?"

I recognized the voice right away. Adam Brandt. He runs a successful ghost tour company, employing guides that host both walking tours and trams. He had actively campaigned to keep me from opening my route and continued to look for any reason to file a complaint or interfere with my occupational license. My business was small potatoes compared to his, but he definitely took notice when my tours started trending on social media.

"I should," I growled at him, "since you're trespassing in the middle of the night."

"It's not even eight PM." I could hear the sneer in his voice, even though I couldn't make out his features in the dark. I could imagine the same smug look on his face, and the twinkle in his dark eyes that he always wore when he was accusing me of encroaching on his route or some other made-up complaint.

"The time doesn't change the trespassing part."

"You're hiding something, and I'm going to figure out what it is."

I put the wasp spray under my arm, pulled the flashlight out of my pocket, and clicked it on. Right in his face. He squinted and raised a hand between us. His dark brown hair was still neat, styled short and wavy, but he was sporting more than a five o'clock shadow. I'd never seen him with scruff. He was always clean-shaven and precise.

"I'm not hiding anything," I hissed. "Now get off my property before I call the cops."

"There's no way your nothing little tour is just stumbling onto that kind of paranormal activity. You're faking it, and I'm going to expose you for the fraud you are."

I glared at him. He couldn't stand the buzz my "nothing little tour" was getting online and by word of mouth. He resented that his reservations had fallen, even though I'm sure his numbers were still double, maybe even triple, what mine were, since he had several guides and ran back-to-back tours. My business was just yours truly.

"Bring. It. On." I gritted my teeth and raised the phone to my ear.

He held up both hands and took a step back. "I was just leaving."

I watched him make his way back across the lawn, hoping he wasn't trampling over any of Nan's plants. They would likely be okay, dormant for the winter even this far south, but I still resented that he wasn't using the walkway. Really, I resented him in general, how arrogant and entitled he always was. There was clearly enough business for both of us to operate in such a big city, and he had plenty of competition besides mine, but he tried to shut me down at every turn.

When I was confident he had continued down the street, I checked all the doors and windows in the shop. They were all secure. I was still fuming when I saw Nan's headlights pull into the back drive. I met her as she rounded the house.

"What on earth are you doing out here?" she squeaked as she shined a flashlight in my face, much like I'd done with Adam. "I nearly called the police."

"Adam Brandt was prowling around the shop," I said, pushing my dark brunette braid over my shoulder. "He thinks I'm faking the activity on my tours, and he's obsessed with trying to find evidence of the hoax."

She laughed, a deep, shaking laugh. "He'll be a ghost himself before he finds any evidence of that."

She gestured for me to follow her. "Come help me with the groceries."

"I thought you went to your book club?"

"Did. Stopped at Breaux Mart on the way home," she said, referencing our favorite locally owned grocery store.

I wasn't exactly sure how old Nan was, but basic deduction based on my dad's age, or rather the age he would've been if he hadn't gotten himself killed, told me she had to be, at the very least, seventy-two. My mom had told me she thought Nan was nineteen when she'd given birth to William Wesley Thatcher. But Nan and my mom had never been close, so it was just a guess. It didn't really matter. Nan was one of those people who managed to be sort of ageless. She didn't fit with many of the stereotypes of someone her age. She loves social media, and while it sometimes takes her a little while to learn all the ins and outs of new tech, she always gets there eventually. Faster than I do a lot of the time, if I'm being honest with myself.

Her bright blue eyes, though flanked by crow's feet, were mischievous and rarely missed a detail. She'd never dyed her hair as it started to gray, calling the streaks her "wisdom highlights." Her shoulder-length sleek bob was a silky silver now and framed her heart-shaped face in a flattering cascade.

After I'd helped her carry in and put away enough groceries for a small army, I reheated the kettle and poured us both a cup of tea. I joined her in what she calls the "sitting room," which is furnished just like the living room, minus the flat-screen TV. Nan's tastes run eclectic, and no one would ever accuse her of having hired an interior decorator, but it felt warm and comfortable.

I curled up in the chair that still smelled like PawPaw, a combination of Old Spice, sawdust, and leather. I still feel like it's a special magic that keeps the smell of him on his chair. After he died, she emptied out his study and positioned the pieces around the house. Some people hide away mementos when they lose someone. Not Nan. She wanted every reminder of him as close as possible. I don't know what causes some people, like Kenneth, to stay here when others move on, but neither PawPaw nor my dad had lingered. I'm happy about that, of course, because I can't imagine how hard it must be to get . . . stuck. But I also missed my PawPaw desperately and wanted to meet my dad.

"Don't worry about Adam Brandt," Nan said. She must've noticed I was deep in my thoughts.

"I'm not," I said truthfully. "He can stay mad about my success." I lifted my tea mug to toast that.

Nan clinked her mug against mine. We both fell silent. I don't know if she was lost in her thoughts, but I was certainly lost in mine. I don't know why, but in times of intense happiness or contentment, like sitting in my Nan's cozy house and enjoying a cup of tea with her, unpleasant memories tend to creep in and take hold. At that particular moment, I was remembering the time I'd come home with a first-place prize for my entry in the school drawing contest. I'd been elated. Jared, my stepfather, usually got home before my mom, who worked twelve-hour shifts as a certified nursing assistant, so he was the first to receive my enthusiasm. He promptly deflated that enthusiasm as effectively as if he'd stuck a needle into a balloon.

He'd taken one look at the little printed certificate and scoffed.

"It's great," he said with an eye roll.

"What?" I'd asked, crestfallen.

"Well, it's not like it was a prestigious honor or anything. I mean, they couldn't even spring for cardstock." He'd chuckled as he flicked the edge of the paper certificate.

I laughed with him, trying desperately to hide how badly he'd just broken my heart. But when I was alone in my room later, I cried until my eyes felt raw. I folded up the certificate, shoved it in the back of my diary, and never even tried to show my mom.

I hadn't been thrilled when Mom started dating him, and I'd rebelled when she'd married him. But after we'd moved and I'd settled into my new school and made new friends, I'd thought we could have a nice family. But then Mom got pregnant, and Jared had a child of his own, one that didn't come with a smart mouth and fear of abandonment. I spent my teenage years miserable. I guess it could be argued that the teenage years are intrinsically miserable for everyone, and it's true in the grand scheme of things I wasn't abused, necessarily. But I was forgotten, ignored. And when I wasn't over-looked, I was treated like I was in the way, a nuisance that just had to be dealt with.

Our house in Missouri wasn't even haunted, so I was alone most of the time. There was a nice ghost, Jane Blaylock, who haunted the railroad bridge three blocks behind our house, and I spent as much time with her as I could, but I still felt isolated in what was supposed to be my home. So when the opportunity arose, I jumped at the chance to move back with Nan, back to the place that truly felt like a home. Nan offered to let me stay with her while I attended college, to save on room and board. I'd started packing before we ended the call, and I've never left.

I shook off the unpleasant memories, kicked my shoes to the floor, and pulled my feet up underneath me. Nan's scruffy, one-eyed cat yowled from the doorway, kitty disdain clear on his scarred orange face. He hadn't always lived a life of luxury. Nan had picked him up in the grocery store parking lot, beaten up and dirty. After a few rounds of veterinary care, she'd brought him home, named him Fitzwilliam Darcy, or Fitz for short, and he'd settled into being pampered like he was born for it.

"What's the matter, handsome man?" Nan cooed. "Have you been neglected today?"

I smiled as he jumped into her lap and purred like a diesel engine. He circled a few times and then settled on her lap, doing his best impression of a loaf of bread. Nan stroked his tiger-striped fur and looked like she would purr herself if she could.

Chapter Four

Mornings have always been my least favorite time of day. It's not that I can't appreciate the beauty of a good sunrise, or that the awakening world doesn't hold a special kind of magic. I've just always been a night owl and a poor sleeper, so mornings simply come far too early for me.

I rolled over, away from the light streaming through the window, and snoozed the alarm on my phone for the third time. I needed to get up. I needed to get down to the shop and sort through the reservations that were flooding in. One of my tour guests had uploaded their orb video to TikTok a few days ago, and it had gone semi-viral. So far, my tours had only received buzz in local Facebook groups and an odd mention in a sub-Reddit dedicated to Louisiana hauntings. It made sense to figure out the logistics of adding a second tour each night, even if I wasn't sure how to accomplish it just yet. I already had a few nights here and there where I ran two tours a night, but I couldn't figure out how to do it full-time without bringing on more employees, and I just wasn't quite there financially yet. I wanted someone to keep the shop open while I was out with the group, and it would be even more important if a second group was gathering for an additional tour. But I only had one part-time employee who was willing to work for the pitiful wage I could afford, so I had to balance that with any potential income more tours might bring in.

I groaned and got up before the alarm went off again. I showered quickly and pulled my wet hair into a loose ponytail at the nape of my neck. It was such a dark brunette that it looked black when it was wet. I popped in my contacts, violet over my natural hazel today; dragged on some eyeliner and mascara to highlight my eyes a bit; and then stood in front of my closet, trying to decide how much of an effort I was going to make with my wardrobe. My clothes run the gamut from business casual to emo/goth. These days though, I tended to lean more toward comfort than any sort of statement, so I chose a loose plum-colored sweater over black leggings and finished it off with my Doc Martens.

About halfway down the stairs, I heard voices coming from the direction of the kitchen. My first thought was that Kenneth had forgiven my inability to interpret symbolism, and returned, but as I paused and listened more closely, it seemed to be an actual conversation, so that ruled out Kenneth. Nan couldn't see or hear him, but she sometimes narrates what she's doing. Kenneth can't resist talking to her despite her inability to hear him, so it makes for some interesting eavesdropping sometimes.

I don't know what is different in me that gives me the ability to interact with the dead. I've never had any major trauma, unhappy teenage years notwithstanding. I've never hit my head, nearly drowned, had anyone hypnotize me, or experienced any of the other ways people gain those abilities in movies and books. It's just always been a part of my life. Nan says all kids can see ghosts, but most people outgrow it as the magic of being a child gives way to the logic and reason that governs adults. And maybe that's the difference: I'm not very good in the adulting department. I don't guess it matters *why*. It's just who I am.

I continued down the stairs as I decided both participants in the conversation definitely had a pulse. But it brought up a whole round of new questions in my mind, starting with who might be causing Nan to giggle like that. I walked into the kitchen to find her swiping whipped cream onto the nose of a man who could double for a very tall, very buff Santa Claus.

"Oh, good morning, Lou," she said, still laughing.

"Um . . . good morning?" It came out as a question, and I couldn't seem to look away from the man who seemed to be quite at home in our kitchen.

"Lou, this is Ronald. Ronald, this is my favorite granddaughter, Lou," Nan said, taking the kitchen towel and smacking him on the hip with it.

"That's a technicality," I said. "I'm her *only* granddaughter."

"Pleased to meet you," he said, his voice low and growly.

"Likewise," I said. I don't know why I was suddenly so self-conscious. I knew Nan dated. She'd even had some serious relationships over the years since PawPaw died. It was just that I'd never met any of those men. She'd always kept that part of her life private—until Ronald, I guess.

I grabbed an apple out of the basket on the white tile counter and turned on my heel.

"Stay for breakfast," Nan said. "Ronald made a quiche."

"I've got a ton of work to do before I open this afternoon," I said, and left before she could argue.

I was aware that I was being rude, but the realization wasn't enough to make me stay for an awkward breakfast with Nan and her . . . boyfriend? It seemed like such a silly term for someone who had to be close to her age, but I didn't know what else to call him. *Lover* made me want to crawl out of my skin.

I took the short, paved path to the shop, and I noticed Ronald's black pickup parked behind Nan's little Jeep Renegade. My tiny Kia Soul was invisible behind it. I looked back once at the big kitchen window, and Nan was smiling as he fed her a bite of quiche with his fingers. I wondered how long they'd been seeing each other, because it seemed like they were plenty comfortable together. As I unlocked the door to my shop, my wonderful eclectic little haven, I tried to figure out why it bothered me at all. I wanted Nan to be happy. And she looked really happy.

I shook off the thoughts, made up my mind to just be happy for her, and decided I would grill her for details at supper. I took a deep breath as I crossed the welcome mat, which read "Doorbell broken, yell *ding-dong* really loud." I loved everything about my shop. Even the gaudy little touristy trinkets that occupied the shelves to the left of the door. I had New Orleans postcards, keychains, T-shirts, coffee mugs, tote bags, and more. The right side of my shop was dedicated to local history, with a special focus on the haunted parts, which admittedly, was *most* parts of New Orleans.

At the center of the display, above the shelves, was a framed photo of St. Louis Cemetery at sunrise. It is probably our most famous haunted location. Well, that and the fact that it is actually haunted. I don't like to go there, even though it's a treasure trove of sightings and activity. Ghosts, especially those who have been around for a while, don't get much chance to talk to anyone. And while I can understand the impulse to cling to anyone who can see and hear them, it's difficult to be around if my social battery is drained at all. I try to go and listen when I can, because they don't often get a chance to tell their stories, but it always leaves me exhausted for days. It's probably for the best that my walking tours are about three miles away.

The rest of the display holds the items for sale. My best friend, Cady, who, in addition to teaching online college classes, also happens to be a talented artist, drew a *Lord of the Rings*–style map of the Garden District highlighting all the haunted spots. We had them printed on sepia-toned, antiqued paper, and I included one for each person who took my tour, but I also offered them for sale, no tour required. Another local artist took photos of the haunted hot spots and paired them with the history, bound in a beautiful hardcover book. Some of the sites were actually haunted, and some were just plagued with local legends.

The hardwood creaked underfoot in the most pleasing way as I crossed the shop. The constellation-printed curtains were pulled back to let in the morning light, long streams of golden glow that seemed to collect in puddles on the floor. The air smelled of vanilla, which I had decided would be my shop's signature scent. According to scent marketing experts, vanilla evokes a sense of calm, warmth, and happiness. Given the potentially darker nature of my haunted-tour business, I wanted a contrast that would put my customers at ease.

I settled in behind the counter and opened my laptop. I was really thankful I had sprung for the reservation software before my bookings had blown up. Thankfully, the only thing I still needed to do manually was shuffle the wait list into the cancellations. I also tried to answer most of my emails personally, so I had to sort through them to find the ones that needed immediate attention versus the ones that could wait for a response or be answered by my part-time employee, Tess.

Tess wasn't due to come in until late afternoon, and she had proved to be absolutely invaluable. She splits her working time between my shop and my favorite coffee shop, Café Nate over on Magazine Street. I was initially drawn in by the clever play on the owner's name, especially when the chalkboard sign on the sidewalk said "Caffeinate at Café Nate!" I mean, how can you not love that? But I keep going back because it's just amazing coffee. My shop's name is much less clever: Haunts & Jaunts Walking Ghost Tours. It's a bit much to cram on T-shirts and swag, so most of the time I shorten it to simply "Haunts & Jaunts."

I'd just opened an email asking questions that are covered in the FAQ section of my website, when I got a text from Cady. It was a link to another video from one of my guests. I remembered her from a tour a few nights ago. She was quiet and hung back behind the crowd, which in itself is not odd or memorable. A lot of guests try to hide at the back. What was memorable was her T-shirt, at least to me. It read, "I'm the Velma of my group." As a lifelong Scooby-Doo aficionado, I kept meaning to ask her where she got it, but she slipped away before I could.

I watched Mamie's delicate orb floating in the top left corner of the screen. You could almost make the argument that it was a bubble or optical illusion, even though it was clearly moving against the wind, not with it. Well, at least you could try to make that argument until it turned into a diaphanous skull for a millisecond and then vanished with a faint scream.

Nice touch, Mamie, I thought to myself. She always amazed me with how she kept the sightings fresh and new. I couldn't wait to sneak back after the tour, when most of the neighborhood had gone to bed, to show Mamie the video of her handiwork. She was going to be so stoked. Especially at the number of people who claimed it was just really good special effects. She loved it when people commented on her skill. I continued to flick through the comments, enjoying the speculation squabbles about the video's authenticity. That part always amused me too.

How freaking cool! Cady texted again. *You're killing it!*

Thank you! I messaged back.

I clicked out of the video and started to text again, but I decided the encounter with Adam and finding a ripped Santa Claus canoodling with Nan was all too much for a message, so I called her instead. I punched "Speaker" so I could work on my laptop while we talked.

"Hey! I thought it might be easier to just call," I said as she answered.

"Well, that works out great because I need to talk to you too. But you go first." Cady's melodic voice filled the quiet space.

While I told her about Nan's new conquest and how aggravated I was at Adam Brandt, Cady appropriately commiserated and cursed Adam, in solidarity.

"What did you want to talk to me about?" I asked when I'd wound down.

"I need you to come to family dinner night. I really need a buffer between Dad and his new girlfriend."

I froze. I loved Cady. She is my oldest and dearest friend, not counting Kenneth, of course. But I have successfully avoided the rest of her family since I moved back home. Well, not her family exactly, but her brother specifically.

"Cady, I—"

"I know that wasn't the most enticing invitation, but I'm begging here," she said, and I could almost see her biting her lip the way she does.

I took a deep breath. It's not that I don't like Cady's brother. Quite the opposite, actually. He's been the subject of my teenage daydreams, my college actual dreams, and my adult guilty fantasies. Because Dylan Finch not only looks like he walked off the cover of a romance novel, with a chiseled jawline and carved abs, he acts like it too. He's funny, gentle, and oh so masculine, all rolled into a big ball of forbidden fruit. Dating your best friend's brother is a recipe for a disaster I'm not willing to start, even if it were a possibility. Which it wasn't. I'm not sure I even exist in Dylan Finch's world.

"When is family dinner night?" I asked, my voice cracking.

"Sunday," she said quickly. "And before you can argue, we can eat early, before you start your tour. Tess can cover the shop.

I sighed.

"I know it's going to be awkward. The woman is barely older than I am, which is why I need you. It's going to be as much fun as a root canal, and I can understand not wanting to come, but I really am begging here."

"Of course, I'll come," I said, and my stomach did a flip-flop at the thought.

Maybe this would be better than trying to avoid him at all costs. I could get it over with and move on from my stupid, childish crush. We talked on for nearly an hour while I made my way through the most important emails and funneled the rest into the "Tess" folder of the shop's email account.

The afternoon flew by, and before I knew it, I was gearing up for the night's tour. I didn't know if it was finding Adam skulking around my shop in the middle of the night, or dreading the dinner I'd just agreed to, but I was jumpy and uneasy, and I couldn't shake the feeling of dread.

Chapter Five

The tour went off without a hitch. Despite my continued impulse to look behind me and the feeling that someone was going to jump out of the shadows at me, things went smoothly. I didn't have a single skeptic, and everyone seemed to enjoy the walk and the history. The ghosts were quiet, but that was at my request. Too many occurrences and manifestations would draw suspicion and not just from Adam Brandt.

One of my least favorite parts of the tours was gathering back at the shop and answering all the follow-up questions. Much of the history I'd pieced together of the area was regarded as colorful fiction from locals and historians, and I'm okay with that. We all know tour guides embellish for effect. It had bothered me when I'd first started and would find myself arguing or insisting, but when you're the only one who can see and hear your only source for verification, you learn to let it go. But I still dreaded the times when *other* people wouldn't let it go.

"I've never heard of a speakeasy on Prytania Street." An older woman with silver-streaked blonde hair stepped in front of me on my way back to the counter.

"That'd be the point, though, wouldn't it?" a male voice behind me said.

I turned to look at him, but he didn't look up from the copy of *New Orleans: A Haunted History* that he was flipping through. His face was hidden in shadow, but he was tall and thin.

"Well, *someone* found out if she knows to include it in the tour." The woman turned her attention to him, and I took the opportunity to continue on my way to the counter. It was a cowardly move, honestly. I probably should have stayed to explain as best I could, but I ran away instead, leaving the two customers to battle it out.

A small line had begun to form, and Tess was busy helping another customer sort through T-shirts to find the sizes she needed. I felt another pang of guilt about not staying and elaborating a little, but I justified my escape by telling myself that my customers shouldn't wait long to pay out. I glanced over where the two were talking and it looked friendly enough. The woman, who was facing me, was smiling. The man, whose back was still toward me, seemed to be pointing toward Prytania as he spoke, or maybe it was just my imagination and they weren't still debating the veracity of my information at all.

I don't know how the debate about the speakeasy turned out, and neither the blonde woman nor the man purchased anything else before they slipped out unnoticed. At only fifteen minutes past our advertised closing time, Tess ushered the last of the customers out and locked the door behind them. She flipped the sign over to "Closed" and turned off the lights to the front of the shop. Her boots clacked on the hardwood floor as she made her way back to the counter. The quiet after closing was always somehow more quiet than usual after the space had been full of noise and voices.

"This was a good night," she said, straightening the brochures next to my point-of-sale iPad. Tess flipped her black braid over her shoulder and tapped the iPad to shut it down for the night. I looked around at all the reshelving and restocking that needed to be done and groaned. Success was a double-edged sword. I felt guilty that I hadn't yet incorporated her idea to have a cozy little nook tucked away in the corner where she could host her puppetry club. Coming from someone who sees ghosts, it's probably weird to be creeped out by puppets, but they give me the heebie-jeebies, so I hadn't exactly been excited about having them in the shop. I wanted to support Tess, though, so I vowed to get my butt in gear.

"It can wait till tomorrow. Go for your walk. I'll lock up here." She smiled as she followed my gaze toward the disorganized shelves.

Tess shrugged her knit sweater over her arms, covered in full-sleeve tattoos. I've always wanted a tattoo, but I'd never found anything I wanted to commit to my flesh. I admired hers, though. Her left arm was an homage to the women in her family with images that were special to them. She'd explained one day the dogwood blooms were for her grandmother, the crescent moon for her older sister, the rabbit for her younger sister, and the intricate vine that wove around and through all the other images was for her mother. Her right arm was an evolving mosaic of Tess's life. There were her favorite puppets (yuck, but to each their own); paw prints from her beloved childhood dog; her zodiac sign, the ram; and a beautiful rendition of the comedy and tragedy masks that celebrated her performing arts degree.

I'd convinced Tess that after an evening of being social and entertaining guests on the tour, I needed a long walk to destress and recharge. I'd learned as a kid that not everyone believes in ghosts, no matter how convincing I was at describing their great-aunt Ethel, so I don't tend to tell people anymore. As far as Tess knew, I was just an introvert who needed some alone time, not someone going to show a ghost her viral handiwork.

"I'm not going to want to do it tomorrow either," I said.

"Okay, let's knock it out together then." She shrugged, her black braid bouncing back over her shoulder with the movement.

"Thanks, Tess," I said, pulling her in for a hug. "I don't know what I'd do without you."

"Well, let's not find out."

We started by reshelving everything that had been moved around, so we could get an accurate idea of what needed restocking. T-shirts always needed refolding and reorganizing, and we'd sold a fair amount. That was good; my mark-up was a nice chunk on them and a few of the other popular items. Tess hummed as she worked, which I always found soothing. It would probably be more soothing if she hadn't been humming death metal. To be fair, though, without the screaming, the melody was pretty nice.

"Oh my gosh!" Tess suddenly whirled around, half-folded T-shirt in her hands.

"What?" I jumped, uncharacteristically for me. I usually had nerves of steel. I had no idea why, but tonight I was twitchy and apprehensive.

"I just about forgot to tell you the dad joke I heard the other day at the café," she said, grinning like the Cheshire cat. Tess was an avid collector of dad jokes.

"It was great." She'd already started laughing, an infectious, throaty laugh that caused me to giggle in anticipation. "This guy came in with his son. The kid was probably fifteen, and as he was staring at his phone, his dad elbows him, leans in, and says, 'Hey, what's the opposite of coffee?' The kid looks up at him, completely uninterested—like, I got the impression this guy has jokes for everything." She paused and laughed again.

"So," I prompted her, "what's the opposite of coffee?"

"Sneezy!" she said, and erupted in peals of laughter that shook her shoulders.

I couldn't help it. I joined in too. Even though the joke was terrible, it was her laughter that was contagious, and it did a lot to ease my jangled nerves. We finished in no time, and she reminded me again that she would lock up and allow me some peace and quiet.

"See you next shift," I said over my shoulder as I opened the door to the back. "Oh, who am I kidding? I'll be by the coffee shop before then."

She laughed. She often teased me about my addiction to all things Café Nate. In fact, I wished they were open at that very moment so I could grab an iced mocha on my way to see Mamie. The air had taken on a chill as the clock neared midnight. The sidewalk was well lit, and most of Camp Street was asleep. While the Garden District does have a decent nightlife, it's not on the same level as Bourbon Street, so I only passed a few people on my way.

Mamie's haunt centers around a small, two-story house that once served as a boarding house. Mamie told me it's been renovated and redone multiple times and that one of those renovations changed the height of the flooring on the second story resulting in her walking on the previous floor and causing her to look like she has no feet when she manifests on that level. She says she much prefers to roam outdoors anyway, because it was in one of those small rooms where she became ill with yellow fever and died. I can usually find her lurking in the shadows under one of the many oaks or magnolias or lurking near the Sixth Street entrance to Lafayette Cemetery No. 1, which also happens to be one of my favorite places in the entire city. The grounds are peaceful and iconic. Lafayette Cemetery No. 1 is where Anne Rice entombed her Mayfair witches and where numerous movies and music videos have been filmed. I don't love it because of the fame, though; I love it because it's one of the few places I've ever been where I feel completely at peace. It's probably all in my head, but I'll take a good placebo effect any day if it means I can forget the world for a while and just *be*.

I was in a hurry to get to Mamie's haunt, so I took the lower street. I was just about bursting with excitement when I passed the cemetery wall and darted through the alternating deep shadows and patchy light from the streetlamps.

"Mamie!" I said in a loud whisper, which would've been audible to anyone passing by anyway, so I probably should have just spoken normally.

I waited for her to appear. I pulled up the last two videos and readied them to show her, but she was still nowhere to be found. I waited for a moment and then ventured across the street, trying not to draw the attention of anyone who might be up at this hour or passing by on the street.

"Mamie?" I called again but it came out as a question.

I listened intently, and then I felt the air around me grow cold. I shivered involuntarily. I turned and was face to face with Mamie Haddock's spectral projection. Her delicate features hovered inches from my nose, fading into a fine misty fog at the edges.

"I cannot ever scare you," she said, disappointment clear on her ghostly face.

"In all fairness, I did come here to see you," I smiled.

"To be sure. But just once, I would like to surprise you," she said. And then noticed the phone in my hand. "Ooh! Did someone catch a moving picture?"

I grinned. Unlike Hollywood ghosts that are doomed to replay their deaths or perpetually stuck in the time period in which they died, most of the ghosts I encountered were just poor lost souls, still capable of learning and feeling emotion. None of the ones I've had the pleasure of meeting know why they're trapped in the earthly realm and why some souls move on. When I was a teenager, I tried to help Jane Blaylock, the ghost who haunted the train bridge by our house, resolve some of the things she thought might help her move on. Sadly, nothing worked.

I was able to show her that her daughter went on to fight for women's rights in the area and was instrumental in starting a women's college. We spent afternoons reading about the wonderful things her family was able to accomplish through the years and she promised me that I had brought her great comfort despite being unable to help her move on. I hoped she really felt that way and wasn't just trying to be gentle with a teenage kid.

There was one exception, however. Pete Grubbert. For whatever reason, he was perpetually staggering drunk as a ghost. He wasn't usually coherent enough to even remember he was dead. And maybe that was a blessing, in a way. I think that's also why he tended to be the most visible spirit I've ever encountered. He just stumbles out into view, a flask of whatever alcohol he was drinking the day he died sloshing out, slurring his "hellos" to whoever might be in his path before either blinking out of view or fading gradually away. I've tried to speak to him several times over the years, but he either tries to ask me out on a date or talk me into loaning him "a few bucks for a drink" before he vanishes again.

"Will you display the discussion?" Mamie asked, snapping me out of my reflection, an eager grin on her pale features.

I practically vibrated with excitement as I clicked the screen and started to read the comments to her. Learning to read hadn't been a skill she was able to achieve either in life or after her death. I read until I thought my voice would fail. Mamie seemed elated that her orb had generated so much online drama. I think she sensed I was exhausted, because she finally told me she wanted to save the rest for another day.

"Still want me to delay further exhibitions?" she asked as I clicked my phone off.

"I think we should let the buzz die down a little before we dazzle them again," I said. "We need it to be believable, but we don't want the place getting swarmed by internet ghost hunters and trashy reality TV producers."

She nodded solemnly and blew me a kiss. I pretended to catch it and she giggled as she vanished, a haunting melody that made the hair on my arms stand on end.

Nice, Mamie, I thought to myself. She was getting creepier all the time and I was there for it. It was hard to remember sometimes that Mamie was younger than she seemed. She'd died before she'd gotten to experience much of life, never fallen in love, never forged a life for herself beyond her little family. Scaring people was a game to her, one she enjoyed very much. She never meant any harm. She just loved it in the way siblings like to jump out and make one another scream.

I shoved my hands in my pockets as I crossed onto Coliseum Street. The night was clear and brisk, and the stars were bright enough to see even with the light from the city glowing well into the atmosphere. When I lowered my head to make sure I wasn't going to fall off the curb or walk into a tree, I stopped dead in my tracks. Freaking Adam Brandt was standing on the street corner looking right at me. No doubt he was following me again, trying to catch me doing something that would prove I was faking the manifestations on my tours. Anger boiled in my veins. I clenched my fists in my pockets and started toward him.

"Hey!" I yelled. We were going to end this once and for all, but he ducked around the corner and disappeared from my sight.

I broke into a jog as I followed in the direction he'd gone, toward the cemetery's main entrance. I caught sight of him, or at least I thought it was him, under a streetlamp near the wrought iron archway. I didn't take my eyes off him, but I didn't make it far. I hung the toe of my boot on something in the deep shadows, something very solid, and stumbled for several steps, dropping my phone out of my pocket as I pulled my hands out for balance. When I finally collected myself, I jerked my head back toward the entrance and Adam was gone.

Coward.

I turned around to look for my phone, and even in the oppressive shadows I could see what I'd tripped over. Or rather, *whom* I'd tripped over. It was Adam Brandt, and I knew he was no longer among the living even before I bent down and pressed two fingers to his neck to check for a pulse. I knew because he was standing beside his body, looking as horrified and confused as I felt.

Chapter Six

The police arrived in minutes, but it felt like forever. The shock of finding a body caused the air to feel colder than it really was, and I shivered in my thin jacket. The shadows were darker and seemed more sinister. The light from the streetlamps didn't seem to be keeping the darkness at bay like they had just a few moments ago.

I moved away from Adam's body while I waited, both because I didn't want to disturb any more evidence than I already had, and because I wasn't ready to let Adam know that I could see him. He would have all of the usual questions that the newly dead always have, and selfishly, I didn't have the emotional fortitude to deal with it. I had no idea if he'd met foul play or suffered some freak accident, but either way, he was definitely not prepared to still be in this realm. He circled his body, clearly trying to figure out his new condition. I couldn't hear him, but it looked like he was trying to wake his body up. My heart broke for him, and I was just about to try to gather my wits and go talk to him when a voice from behind me jarred me out of my thoughts.

"Lou?"

Oh god. I'd forgotten Dylan Finch might be the one who responded to my 911 call.

"Hi, um, the body is over there." I pointed awkwardly, silently wishing I could just disappear like Mamie does. "It's Adam Brandt."

Dylan stared at me for a moment, and I squirmed uncomfortably.

"I'm not sure how this works. I've never had to call the police before, much less found someone . . . gone. Dead. Deceased." *Good lord, Lou, just shut up.*

"I'll just need to ask you some questions. Did you touch anything?"

"No. I didn't need to. I recognized him right away."

I tried to keep my eyes on Dylan, but Adam kept diverting my attention. Dylan was wearing jeans, a button-down blue shirt, and a simple blazer. Cady hadn't mentioned that he'd been promoted to detective or anything. I had no idea what rank or designation allowed our local police to wear plain clothes or if he'd just come here in what he happened to be wearing. Truth be told, I didn't really know how anything in law enforcement worked.

"Walk me through what happened," Dylan said as he pulled out a little notebook from his breast pocket.

I glanced back over at Adam and his body. Two more uniformed officers had arrived and were stretching police tape around the scene.

Every time I started to tell Dylan that I had been out for my nightly walk when I stumbled over Adam's body, Adam would start yelling again. He followed the officers around and screamed in the general area of their ears. They couldn't hear him, but I sure could.

"Are you okay?" Dylan asked, leaning over to catch my attention from the scene only I could see.

"Yeah, sorry." I snapped back to attention and tried to ignore Adam's impassioned pleas that were falling on deaf ears.

"Do you always walk around in the middle of the night?"

"Most nights. Especially after a tour. I like to clear my head."

He scribbled something in his little notebook.

"How well do you know"—he checked his notes—"Adam Brandt?"

"We aren't friends, if that's what you mean," I said, more defensively than I'd meant to.

"But you recognized him right away?"

"Well, yeah," I said, trying to angle myself where I couldn't see Adam still frantically circling his body. "He runs another ghost tour business here in town. B&B Haunted Tours. The one that goes through the Barlowe. He accused me of faking my encounters." I don't know why I added that.

"So, you two didn't get along?" He raised an eyebrow. It was very subtle, but I caught it.

I didn't like where this was going.

"Well, no. But I didn't kill him or anything," I said with a laugh. I was trying to make a joke, since I wasn't sure how he'd died. I immediately felt horrible when Dylan looked at me like I was a monster for joking at a time like this.

"She may not have murdered me, but she's definitely responsible!" Adam roared. He'd apparently finally noticed us.

Well, that ruled out the unfortunate accident possibility.

Suddenly Adam was screaming in my ear. I shuddered involuntarily and then rubbed my arms, trying to act like it was the chill in the air that caused my reaction.

"You need to arrest her! If she hadn't been lying about everything, I wouldn't have been out here to begin with!"

Dylan nodded to another officer, but I couldn't hear what he said over Adam's yelling. I glanced sideways at Adam's ghost; his face contorted into a rage-fueled mask of horror. His frustration was almost palpable. He tried to swipe at Dylan, but his hand passed right through Dylan's chest. Dylan seemed entirely unfazed. I've always been fascinated with people who aren't sensitive to the things around them, and why I am.

I finally realized Dylan was speaking to me when he waved his hand in front of my face.

"Lou! Are you all right?"

"Yeah, sorry. I'm just . . . a little freaked out." That wasn't a lie. Adam's anger was unsettling, and I hated that I had been too selfish to try and comfort him before the police arrived. We weren't friends, but this had to be horrible for him, and I could have tried to help.

"What did you ask me?" I tried to catch up.

"I asked for the best number to reach you. And I was advising you to come in and make an official report tomorrow. We may have more questions for you."

"Yeah, sure," I said, unable to keep myself from watching Adam. He was getting more frantic by the minute.

I rattled off my phone number and was just about to tell Dylan that I would be happy to come by the station tomorrow, and that I wanted to help in any way I could, when Adam completely lost it. His spectral face contorted into something feral, unrecognizable. His screams were deafening, and I stumbled backward, my heel catching the curb. I landed in a heap on the sidewalk.

Dylan rushed to my side. Even in my distracted state, I expected him to be concerned, to ask if I was okay. But what he actually said was "Are you drunk?"

"What? No!"

"Drugs then?"

"Absolutely not!"

"Well, you're acting like a coon that's found the mash," he said as he helped me to my feet. I didn't appreciate the moonshine reference. Or the raccoon reference.

"I'm just not used to finding dead people on my nightly walks," I said a little too defensively. At least I wasn't used to finding *newly* dead people on my nightly walks.

He nodded, but his expression remained skeptical.

"Okay, well, I'm going to go home now." I cringed at my own awkwardness, but somehow, I couldn't keep myself from sounding like I was just discovering the ability to speak.

"You'll need to come in tomorrow and file a report," he repeated.

"Yeah, got it," I said over my shoulder, already walking away.

I pulled my jacket tighter around my shoulders as I hurried along the sidewalk. Walking around the neighborhood at night had never felt dangerous before. Now, there was a killer out there. Sure, there are murders in New Orleans pretty frequently, but they're usually gang or drug related, so if you're not engaging in that kind of criminal activity, it's easy to get lulled into a kind of false sense of security. It was easy to pretend you were safe, untouchable.

The shadows loomed around me, and the streetlights were of little help. I couldn't shake the feeling of impending doom, and I started to jog.

Chapter Seven

I hurried through the door, shutting it harder than I meant to, and promptly locked it behind me. I sprinted through the house to the back door and made sure it was locked before I went to my room upstairs. I still felt like I was being followed, which turned out to be accurate when I whirled around to face Kenneth.

"You look like you've seen a ghost," he said with a smirk.

"I think I told you once that never gets old. I was wrong."

"All joking aside, are you all right?"

"Not really," I confessed as I slumped down into my comfy, overstuffed reading chair.

"What happened?"

I took a deep breath and recounted everything, including that I had behaved like a crazy person in front of not just any police officer, but the one I'd had a crush on my entire freaking life.

"Oh dear," Kenneth said during the first break in my story.

"Yeah." I pulled my jacket tighter around me. I just couldn't get warm despite the usual coziness of my room. Even though Kenneth's presence brought the ambient temperature down a few degrees, it shouldn't be enough to chill me to the bone.

"I think I'm just going to go to bed," I said, suddenly feeling tired all the way to my soul. "I don't know if I can sleep, but I'm exhausted."

"Rest well, Lulu Belle."

I didn't bristle at my least favorite nickname. He moved closer and put a hand on my shoulder, and even though I couldn't feel it, it comforted me, nonetheless.

* * *

For a few blissful minutes the next morning, I forgot I'd found a dead body the previous evening. I forgot I had to go to the police department today and potentially face Dylan again, the man I was pretty sure suspected me of murdering Adam Brandt, and if his beliefs were not that drastic, at least he probably viewed me as being irreparably weird. I groaned and rolled over. I had a few minutes before I had to get up, so I took advantage of them and covered my face with the blanket. I wanted to stay there, in the cozy comfort of my bed, and forget everything that had happened.

When the snooze alarm went off again, I pulled the phone under the covers with me. I had multiple missed calls and texts from both Cady and Tess. I texted them back and let them know I would fill them in when I'd properly prepared myself to face the day and ingested enough caffeine to shake off the fatigue and anxiety. Cady promised to come by after lunch, and since that would be the time Tess came into work, I told them both we'd catch up then.

I was glad to find Nan was either sleeping in or was out for the day when I wandered downstairs for coffee and breakfast. It's not that I wanted to hide anything from her; I just didn't have the energy to recount everything yet. I slathered a bagel in cream cheese and gulped a homemade iced coffee before filling my travel cup with more coffee. I left a note for Nan, scratched Fitz's ears for a few minutes, and then screwed up my courage to get my trip to the police department over with.

Thankfully, it was a short drive to the NOPD Sixth District station, which services the Irish Channel, Central City, and the Garden District. The imposing red brick building didn't do much to put my mind at ease, but I guess a police department isn't meant to make you feel warm and fuzzy. I took a deep breath and a huge gulp of coffee and trudged inside. Turned out, my trepidation over seeing Dylan again was completely misplaced since he wasn't even there. I wasn't sure if that made it easier or worse. He'd left instructions with the desk officer to get a written statement and confirm my contact information. At least this officer didn't know how stupid I'd been at the crime scene.

It didn't take long for me to write out the events of the previous evening because there really wasn't that much to report. I'd taken a walk and found Adam murdered. I hadn't even recognized immediately that he *had* been murdered. I hadn't seen anything, and I had no idea who might want to kill him. When I got back to my car, I considered going to the cemetery to see if he was still lurking around. It's harder to talk to ghosts in the broad daylight, though, even in New Orleans, where talking to yourself on the street isn't exactly out of the ordinary. Most of the time, if I have to confer with Mamie or I'm trying to get a juicy bit of local trivia to spice up a tour, I just pretend I'm on the phone. But I figured my conversation with Adam might be a bit more extensive than I could hide with that pretense. I decided it would be better to find him after my tour and try to explain what I knew about his new condition, which admittedly wasn't a lot.

I grabbed some snacks and drinks for Tess and Cady and headed back to the shop. My mornings are usually spent shuffling reservations and cancellations, rescheduling, and answering as many emails and social media comments as possible. When I opened my social media apps this morning, however, I was bombarded with articles about Adam's murder. Most of them were scant on details, but my mind filled in the gaps. Images of his body on the sidewalk kept flashing through my thoughts. But one of the articles caught my eye: *"No Suspects in Stabbing Death of Local Ghost Tour Guide."* Stabbing death. I hadn't seen any blood. Weren't stabbing deaths . . . messy? I shook my head at the new flood of disturbing images my mind was dreaming up.

I shut the laptop and tried to busy myself opening boxes in the tiny stockroom behind the counter. I'd ordered some new Haunts & Jaunts T-shirts, and they did not disappoint. Tess had helped with the new design, which featured a Victorian-styled ghost and some of Mamie's more famous orbs. I couldn't wait to show her. Tess didn't know I actually see the ghosts that star in our tours, but she follows the videos that go semi-viral, and we dissect them for hours. I always feel somewhat dishonest when I don't disclose my abilities, but I can't bring myself to tell anyone either.

I managed to keep myself distracted, stocking and reorganizing, until I heard Cady yell, "Ding-dong!" and then giggle like she always does. She told me once that I could never change my doormat, that it was just too perfect.

"Hey! I'm in the back," I yelled in response.

"Girl! What happened?" she asked as she flopped her giant tote bag onto the counter. She flipped her long blonde shag over her shoulder. Her hair was always so shiny that it caught even the smallest amount of light. I'd always envied her gorgeous hair. Mine tended to lean more to the mousy side, both in color and texture, which is why I nearly always chose braids or ponytails.

"I don't know." I sighed. "I guess Adam was following me. I can't think of any other reason he would have been there. It's not like his tours overlap with mine."

"Did you tell Dylan that?"

"No. Not yet. I was a little stressed out last night, and he wasn't at the police department this morning. I didn't think to include it in my statement."

"I wonder who else would want him dead?" Cady stared off into the distance.

"Who *else*? He may have been super annoying, but I didn't want him dead," I said, not even bothering to try and hide my defensiveness.

"Bad choice of words." Cady reached over and patted my arm.

"I don't really know that much about him. I only met him when he was accusing me of faking encounters, or trying to get my tours shut down."

"It was probably someone he knew. It's usually someone the victim knows. None of the articles mentioned a robbery or anything."

"Have you talked to Dylan?" I asked, avoiding eye contact. I didn't exactly keep my stupid schoolgirl crush on her brother a secret, but I avoided acknowledging it as much as possible.

"No. He wouldn't tell me anything anyway. He knows I can't keep my mouth shut."

We both turned as we heard keys jangling in the back door lock. Tess came through the door like a tornado, slinging her backpack to the right and her lunch bag to the left before kicking the door closed behind her. She didn't even pause on her way to bear-hug me with a force that belied her tiny frame.

"I'm really glad you're both here," I said, my voice muffled against her shoulder. And for the first time since finding Adam's body, I let myself fall apart. Tess held me the whole time I blubbered about how awful it was, and she and Cady made me feel so warm, so loved, that I almost let it slip that it was also terrible to see Adam so lost and confused. I kept telling myself I would tell them someday, but I wasn't ready to do it just yet. There was always a part of me that was afraid they would think I was crazy, and stop being my friends.

"You might want to rethink wandering around at night alone," Tess said when we'd all settled onto the barstools I keep behind the counter.

"It doesn't look like a random murder," Cady said.

"Still." Tess looked doubtful. "There is a killer out there, regardless of their motivation."

"I'll be careful, and I'll start carrying my pepper spray."

"And you'll stop taking your walks until they catch this guy, right?" Tess pushed.

"Maybe." I smiled to try to lighten the mood.

We were all startled by a knock at the front door. Cady squeaked and Tess jumped like she'd been shot.

"Oh, it's just the lunch I ordered," Cady said breathlessly, clutching her chest. "I thought we could use some comfort food."

I could smell the po' boys from Joey K's Restaurant & Bar as soon as the delivery guy opened the door. My mouth started watering like I was one of Pavlov's dogs. It didn't take me long to dig into the delicious sandwich as Cady and Tess batted theories around about Adam's potential murderer. Cady was betting on a jilted lover, and Tess figured he was into something shady like drug dealing or some other criminal activity.

When it came time for me to share my theories, I had to admit that I didn't have any and didn't want to speculate. Cady seemed more disappointed by this than Tess did.

"Surely you have a suspicion." Cady popped a fried green tomato slice, whole, into her mouth.

"Not really. Like I said, I didn't know him at all outside work."

"But you have an impression of him, don't you?" she pressed.

42

"Yeah—he was a jerk," I said, and then instantly regretted it. Nan would tell me not to speak ill of the dead.

"So he must have plenty of enemies then, right?" Cady said in between mouthfuls.

"Who really has enemies, though?" Tess asked, reaching across to trade one of her fried shrimp for one of my onion rings. "I mean, plenty of people are jerks and they aren't getting knifed to death on the sidewalk."

I winced at the image. She must have read the same articles I had.

"Sorry," she said sheepishly.

"True," Cady conceded. "But people who don't have any enemies are certainly not getting"—she glanced at me—"killed in the street either. I'm just saying that it was probably someone he knew," she said, repeating her theory from earlier.

Tess nodded and we all fell silent for a while. The events of the previous evening were playing on a constant loop in my head when I finally blurted out, "I think Dylan might suspect me."

Tess and Cady both froze and stared at me. Cady was the first to speak up.

"There's no way he suspects you." She half laughed. "He's known you forever. And he knows I'd murder him, and then there would be two dead bodies."

"I was really upset, and I acted like an idiot."

"Of course you did!" Tess reached over and patted my arm. "No one can blame you for being a little odd after just finding something like that."

*Some*one *like that,* I thought, but didn't voice it.

I nodded, but I wasn't convinced.

"I have to run. I have a class this afternoon." Cady broke the tension.

I envied her online students. Cady is an empathetic and intuitive professor, and I know I would have loved to have had her teach any of my college courses.

"I'd better go fill Nan in on everything," I said with a deep sigh. "She'll never forgive me if she hears about this from someone else."

Chapter Eight

M y tour guests were milling around the shop as we waited for the last scheduled guest to show up. My policy, clearly stated on my reservation page and then emailed along with the confirmation, states that we leave promptly at the scheduled time, and anyone not present at the reserved time can reschedule once without paying the convenience fee. I learned early on that people will take advantage of a policy that's too lenient, but I hate to be too strict, in case there's an actual emergency.

I checked the clock one more time and then gathered everyone outside in front of the shop. I started my standard spiel about keeping the group together; gave a quick rundown of our route, which is outlined on the back of the tour brochure; and encouraged my guests to ask questions and take photos. It was an enthusiastic group, consisting of a young family with two children, several couples, and a fabulous group of women celebrating a divorce. They were delightfully rowdy, but not so much so that they disturbed the other guests.

We started down Camp Street, and I avoided overlapping with any of the other walking tours in the area. Adam Brandt hadn't been so courteous, and one of his trams had started encroaching on my route in the last few months. I pushed the thought out of my head and concentrated on telling the group some of the history of the Garden District.

Most of the area now called the Garden District was originally called Faubourg Livaudais, after the original Livaudais plantation, in 1832. The following year, it became the city of Lafayette, and it was finally incorporated into the city of New Orleans in 1852. The Greek Revival, Victorian, and Italianate architecture that the Garden District is known for serves as the perfect backdrop for ghost stories, and just like New Orleans as a whole, the Garden District is no stranger to the paranormal.

There's the Mansiòn Magnolia, which is considered one of the most haunted inns in New Orleans. Guests have reported hearing ghostly children unexplained sounds like metal scraping on metal, and belongings that have been moved around their rooms. My tour doesn't include the inn, but I liked to recommend it to my guests. Several of the more hardcore ghost hunters have tagged me in their reviews after staying there, and I'll take every bit of free advertising that I can get.

The Garden District was also home for a while to Anne Rice, one of my favorite authors. She lived in a sprawling Greek Revival home until 2005. When she was promoting *Memnoch the Devil*, she'd organized her own jazz funeral. She had ridden in a glass coffin, pulled by horse-drawn carriage, to the Garden District Book Shop, where she rose from the coffin for the book signing. It's just that kind of macabre pomp and circumstance that we're known for here in New Orleans, and personally, I'm here for it.

I found my thoughts wandering back to Adam with every story I told. The guilt I felt at not sticking around and explaining what little I knew about his situation ate away at my concentration, and I stuttered through my well-practiced presentations. I vowed to myself to load my pocket with my pepper spray, whistle, and spiky keychain and come back after my tour to talk to him. I didn't know if his haunt overlapped with any of the other Garden District ghosts, so I had no idea if any of them would be able to help orient him to his new situation. I also didn't know whether or not he could cross into the cemetery. Sometimes hallowed ground has funny rules.

As we rounded the corner and Lafayette Cemetery No. 1 came into view, I spotted and heard Adam right away. There was still steady foot traffic around the cemetery, and he was screaming at nearly everyone. Of course, no one heard him. A couple of people acted like they'd caught a chill when he passed through them, but that was the biggest reaction anyone had to his presence. I was pretty sure I was rambling off my standard spiel about the cemetery and my explanation for why we couldn't go inside on my tour; this included a friendly plug for Frank Beaumont's ghost tour, which did include the inner cemetery, once it opened back up to the public, of course. I fielded the usual questions about whether the guests could break away and go in on their own and why we couldn't alter the route to accommodate their curiosity. As I spoke, we continued to move along the sidewalk, getting closer to Mamie's haunt, where I would tell my guests about her personal history.

Mamie had been living in a two-story yellow boarding house on Prytania Street during the yellow fever epidemic of 1853. The house is a private residence now, and it's painted a pale blue. Mamie came to New Orleans from a farm north of the city, in the hopes of building a better life for herself. She found work as a maid in a local mansion and was stashing away a nice nest egg when the epidemic hit. She was one of the over nine thousand who had perished. Most people think I'm making her story up since there isn't much to support it. Mamie wasn't famous, and she doesn't appear to anyone but me. As far as I knew, there was just one mention of the address being a boarding house, in an obscure newspaper article from 1855, about a fire in a neighboring residence. But I didn't care. Tour guides are expected to embellish a little, so it was fine with me to allow people to think I was adding a bit to the local history.

I'd asked Mamie to hold off on dazzling anyone, but left any more subtle manifestations to her discretion. Sometimes I like to be surprised too. If anything changed, Mamie and I had worked out a set of code words. *Rabbit* meant she had free reign to do anything she wanted. *Owl's nest* meant that I needed her to hold off altogether. And *alley cat* meant that we needed a subtle, dialed-down approach to manifestations.

I was hopelessly distracted by Adam again, and while I watched him getting more and more frustrated that he was unable to get anyone's attention, he noticed my tour. As he watched us pause at the corner, to allow a couple of cars to pass, we locked eyes with each other. The recognition that washed over his face was unmistakable. He knew I had seen him. I quickly looked away, but it was too late.

"Are you all right, dear?" an elderly guest with fantastic pink hair asked. She was one of a small group of women, all wearing matching T-shirts that read "Granny Ghost Hunters," which was about the best thing I'd ever seen. Under different circumstances, I would have already asked all about their adventures.

"Sorry—I'm good," I lied. "Just a little extra distracted tonight."

"Is it the ADHD?" another of the Granny Ghost Hunters asked. She was tiny and slightly kyphotic, but her eyes were bright and lively. "My grandson has the ADHD. Bless him, attention span of a gnat, that one."

"Yes," I said before my brain kicked in. "I mean, no. Well, not entirely."

I stole a look toward Adam, who was still watching me with an intensity that made my skin feel hot, even in the cooling air.

"Are you feeling a presence?" the pink-haired lady asked, practically vibrating with excitement.

"No," I said honestly, because I wasn't feeling a presence; I was *seeing* a presence. And I was avoiding making eye contact with that presence as he crossed the road and made his way toward our group in disjointed, jerky movements, like he hadn't quite mastered the art of moving without a corporeal form.

"If you'll all just follow me." I waved my arms, flight-attendant style, trying to usher everyone out of Adam's haunt.

"The brochure says that even though we don't go through the cemetery, we will learn about some of the famous sightings." The skinny young man speaking pushed his glasses back up on his nose and held the brochure at a better angle, to catch the light from the streetlamp, before he continued. "And we are 'encouraged to visit the grounds on our own after the tour. While the cemetery isn't open to the public, much can be seen through the gates, and the cemetery hosts tours of their own.'" He hooked the fingers of his unoccupied hand in air quotes.

"Sure, sure." I nodded frantically as Adam wove through my group, never taking his eyes off me. "The brochure is a little outdated. The cemetery is closed to the public right now, for renovations."

I opened my mouth to start my spiel about the cemetery history, but before I could speak, Adam closed the distance between us. He opened his mouth wider than any human form should be able to, like a snake unhinging its jaw, and screamed into my face. The sound that filled my ears and rattled my brain was primal, guttural, full of rage and frustration. Ignoring him and pretending I couldn't see and hear him was futile. I gasped, clapped my hands over my ears, and stumbled backward. If it hadn't been for the massive oak at the edge of the sidewalk, I would've landed on my backside. Instead, I plowed into the rough bark with a thud that knocked the wind out of my lungs.

"Oh my gosh, dear!" The pink-haired lady grabbed my upper arm and steadied me.

"You can hear me, can't you?" Adam screamed in my face again.

I did my best not to react to his tantrum.

"I'm so sorry, everyone," I said, trying to laugh casually, but it sounded more maniacal than relaxed. "You know, they say Louisiana mosquitoes can carry you off."

There were some nervous chuckles from the group, and the pink-haired Granny Ghost Hunter still held onto my arm.

"We're just going to take a small detour from the printed route, but we will circle around and hit the hot spots as promised."

There were some murmurs in the group, but I didn't catch anything specific, and they followed as I motioned for them to hurry down the sidewalk away from the cemetery.

"Don't you dare walk away from me!"

Suddenly Adam was directly in front of me. I paused for a second before my brain caught up and realized I could just walk right through him. As I did, he bellowed again, but this time it was a cry of anguish and defeat.

"I'll come back when I'm finished with the tour," I said as loudly as I dared. The Granny Ghost Hunters were following more closely than the rest of the group.

"I knew it! You can hear me! And I'll bet you can see me too. *Do not walk away from me!*"

I instinctively ducked away from his booming voice, and I'm sure the group was beginning to think I'd completely lost my mind. I hurried as fast as I dared away from the cemetery, hoping that whatever keeps ghosts tethered to the general vicinity where they died would kick in soon.

After what seemed like forever, Adam's yelling finally started to sound distant, and I stole a glance over my shoulder. I could just make out his general form trying to pass whatever invisible boundary exists for ghosts. Passing through the boundary would cause him to dissipate into nothingness, only to reform once he was inside the barrier again. Unable to accept that any better than he'd accepted his death, he would find a slightly different spot and try again.

I noticed the members of my group watching me nervously and whispering to one another.

"So sorry about that," I said as I turned to face them. "We can get back on track right here." I gestured to the brick house behind me. The newly renovated two-story house didn't quite fit the general aesthetic of the Garden District, but its history sure did. I told my group about the house's stint as a notorious speakeasy and how locals often catch a glimpse of an unfortunate ghost who appears perpetually sloshed and sometimes asks passersby for the time before stumbling off into the street and vanishing into thin air.

Thankfully, the rest of the tour went more smoothly, and by the time I brought the group back to the shop, they'd relaxed and no longer looked at me like they were afraid I might go off the deep end at any moment.

Tess guided them through purchasing souvenirs, and made recommendations for other tours in the area. I'm always ready to send a paranormal enthusiast to other tours, and I know a few that do the same for me. By the time the last guest shuffled out the door, I was exhausted. Tess turned the lock into place just as I looked up from the, point of sale iPad, and I caught a glimpse of someone looking through the side window.

"What?" Tess asked as she whirled around in response to my gasp.

"There was someone at the window," I said, feeling silly since it was probably one of the guests who had just left. I did a quick scan of the shop for coats, wallets, cell phones, or anything else someone might have come back to retrieve. That didn't really make sense, though, because why wouldn't they just knock on the door?

"I don't know why it startled me so much," I said aloud, trying to calm myself down.

"You just found a dead guy. Of course you're jumpy," Tess said as she looked both ways out the window where I'd seen the face. When she found nothing there, she shrugged and dropped the blinds.

I grabbed the flashlight from under the counter and pulled my pepper spray out of my bag.

"Don't go out there," she said in a loud whisper.

"I'll be right back," I said quietly. "If not, call the police."

"Lou!" she whisper-yelled as I ignored her and opened the back door.

I swept the yard with the powerful LED flashlight but didn't see anyone. I descended the two small steps and continued to scan the yard. Nothing. I listened intently, but all I could hear was traffic and the sounds of the city. I turned around to tell Tess all was clear when a head poked out and then ducked back behind the shop.

I palmed the little canister of pepper spray and rounded the corner. I flipped the flashlight into the prowler's face and leveled the pepper spray even with his eyes.

"Bryce?" I squeaked as I realized I was looking at the terrified face of my little brother.

Chapter Nine

"What are you doing here?" I asked as I lowered the light.

"I needed someplace to go," he said, and shoved his hands in the pockets of his bomber-style jacket.

"Our mother is probably worried sick," I scolded. I was honestly less concerned about our mother than I was about *why* my sixteen-year-old brother was suddenly on my doorstep in the middle of the night. Alone.

"She probably doesn't even know I'm gone." He shrugged and looked at his feet, causing his wavy red hair to fall in his face.

"How did you get here?"

"I took the bus."

"The bus stop is nearly two miles away! How did you get *here?*"

"I took an Uber," he said, like it should have been obvious.

"Why wouldn't she know you're gone?" I asked skeptically. I know our mother isn't perfect, but I was sure she would miss her favorite child.

"I'm supposed to be spending the weekend with a friend. I thought that would buy me some time."

"Some time to what? Run away? Get kidnapped and sold on the black market? What exactly was your plan here?"

"I don't guess I have a plan." He shrugged again.

"Everything okay?" Tess called from the doorway.

"Yeah," I yelled back. "We'll be right in." I turned back to Bryce. "Get your butt inside."

Bryce hesitated for a moment, then trudged inside like he was marching to certain death. He hovered behind the counter while Tess looked from him to me, and then back again.

"Tess, this is my little brother, Bryce, who makes really stupid life decisions and takes a bus cross country to show up unannounced in the middle of the night. Bryce, this is my friend Tess."

"Hey." Bryce barely glanced up. He pulled his hand out of his pocket long enough for an awkward little wave and then shoved it back in his jacket.

Inside in the light, I could see he was the spitting image of his father, my stepfather, Jared. Same deep red hair, same Benedict Cumberbatch jawline and grin. I hoped Jared's rugged good looks were all he'd given my brother, keeping for himself the selfishness and indifference about anyone he deemed less than worthy.

"Nice to meet you," Tess said, and then looked back to me, mouthing the words "What's going on?"

I mouthed back, "I don't know," and shrugged.

"So, are you going to call Mom, or am I?" I moved around him to grab my phone off the counter.

"Please, Lou, don't make me go back."

The pleading in his voice made me stop in my tracks. I took a deep breath and rubbed my eyes. I'd found a dead body, and now I had a sixteen-year-old runaway on my doorstep. I wasn't sure how much more I could handle.

"Why don't you want to go back?" I asked when I'd gained my composure again.

Bryce picked at a spot on the floor with the toe of his tennis shoe.

"Bryce," I said a little more loudly.

"I don't know," he said.

"Okay, I'm not playing games with you. It's late and I have to finish up here. You can stay tonight, but we are going to call Mom in the morning."

"I can't go back. You don't understand."

I was prepared to scold him again, but when he looked up, tears were welling in his pale blue eyes. His sandy hair fell in wavy layers around his face, longer in the front than in the back. His lower lip quivered.

"Bryce, what's wrong?" I pulled him in for a hug, and surprisingly, he didn't resist.

"There's this bunch of guys at school, Lou. They're making my life miserable. It just keeps getting worse." His soft words turned to sobs, and he buried his face against my shoulder.

"Want me to make some hot chocolate?" Tess offered.

"I'm going to take him to the house, get him settled in, and I'll be right back to help with closing," I said, and then mouthed, "I'm sorry." I felt bad for keeping her later than usual. She waved off the apology.

When we got back home, Nan must have already gone to bed, so I hastily scrawled a note and left it on her door. I hated for her to wake up and find a random kid wandering around in the house. I showed Bryce to the guest bedroom, although he remembered where it was from the few times Mom had brought us for visits.

"Thank you," he said as he took his backpack off and slung it on the bed.

"Have you talked to them about what's going on?"

"Of course I have," he snapped, the first sign of anger since I'd found him.

"What did they do?"

"Nothing. Dad just says I need to 'man up' and Mom says she won't go against what Dad says."

"What about the school? Teachers? Counselor? Principal?" I asked, even though I was furious with Mom. Of course, Jared would be a jerk about it. I wouldn't expect anything else from him, but I had hoped that Mom would've handled it better.

"I'm not an idiot, Lou." Bryce crossed his arms and stood up straighter. "I talked to them. I talked to everyone, and nothing has changed. If anything, it's worse. You don't know what it's like. They put dog crap in my locker. They smeared rotten food in my hair. They make these stupid videos about me and share them with everyone. I can't take it anymore."

"I'm so sorry, Bryce, I really am. But Jared is never going to let you stay here," I said, my heart breaking for him.

"Yeah, I know," he said, and all traces of anger were gone from his voice, replaced by defeat and grief. "But maybe this will get his attention."

I crossed the room and wrapped my arms around him. He was as tall as I was, and I tried to remember if he'd been this big the last time I saw him. I felt guilty for not visiting more often, even though I FaceTimed with him at least once a week.

"Get some sleep. We'll deal with this in the morning."

* * *

Tess had nearly everything done by the time I got back to the shop. The only things left to do were the end-of-day tally and getting the cash deposit ready for the bank.

"Is he okay?" she asked after I'd finished putting the deposit in the envelope.

"Yeah, I think so. He's getting bullied at school. My jerk stepfather told him to 'man up,' and Mom is just following along." I rolled my eyes.

"That's awful," she said.

"I need to clear my head," I said as I rubbed my eyes.

"I hope you're not planning to go on your nightly walk." Tess was suddenly at my side.

"I had hoped to, yes," I confessed. "Especially now."

"You do not need to go out in the middle of the night, alone, with a killer on the loose," she said forcefully.

"I promise, I will be careful and extra vigilant." I held my fingers up in a mock Girl Scout oath.

"I'm serious, Lou."

"I know. And I appreciate your concern very much. But we all know that crime isn't exactly unheard of in our fair city." I smiled at her stern expression. "We're lulled into a sense of security because we're blessed to live in a quiet neighborhood, but you watch enough crime documentaries to know it can happen anywhere at any time."

"You're right. I watch enough crime documentaries to know that when you do stupid things, sometimes you get murdered." She crossed her arms over her chest and glared at me. "What if a serial killer is targeting ghost tour guides?"

I chuckled and she glared at me harder.

"That might be a stretch." I pulled out my pepper spray and my cat keychain that doubles as brass knuckles, with spiky ears I would definitely not want to get punched with. "I'm going to be careful."

"I can go with you," she offered half-heartedly. She knew I wouldn't take her up on it. I can't talk to ghosts with an audience, so I've always told her that I need the alone time after being forced to be "on" and social during the tours. She took one look at my face and then added, "Okay, I give up. But if you get murdered out there, promise me you'll put on a good paranormal show for the tourists."

I winced.

Tess held her ground, and the expression on her face dared me to argue with her, so I didn't.

Tess and I said our goodbyes on the porch as I locked up. She went around the shop to get into her yellow VW Beetle, and I started down the sidewalk in the opposite direction.

I don't know if it was all the talk about murderers or if I was just rattled by everything that had happened, but I felt jumpy as I headed back toward the cemetery. It was a sense of general unease that I just couldn't shake.

Chapter Ten

I hurried down the street and glanced behind me frequently. Actually, I tried to look everywhere at once and tried to be aware of alleys and deep shadows. By the time I reached Lafayette Cemetery No. 1, I was a nervous wreck. Even at the late hour, there was still a lot of foot traffic. All of the area tours had ended hours ago, but people still milled around outside the gates. I scanned the area for Adam but didn't see him attempting to harass any of the pedestrians.

I circled to the back entrance and found Adam lurking in the shadows there.

"What do you want?" he asked as soon as I came closer.

Instead of the rage that I'd witnessed earlier, he seemed defeated.

"I told you I'd come back after my tour," I said softly. There was no one very close, but I pulled out my phone and held it up to my ear, just in case.

"Who are you talking to?" He gestured to my phone with one hand and waved his other in front of my face. I instinctively took a step back.

"You. I act like I'm on the phone, so it doesn't look like I'm talking to myself."

59

A look of dawning recognition washed over his diaphanous features.

"You do that all the time, don't you? Every time I saw you talking on the phone in some alleyway or out of the way corner, you were talking to a . . . someone like me."

"Wait, what? Every time you saw me?" I screeched louder than I meant to, and quickly looked around to see if I'd caught anyone's attention. "Were you stalking me?"

"Call it whatever you want to. It doesn't matter now."

"Of course, it matters!" My voice rose another octave, and a couple walking across the street turned to look at me. "I came here to help you, but I'm second-guessing that impulse now."

"Yeah. I was stalking you."

My mouth hung open as I stood there trying to process the fact that he'd just admitted it. I guess he figured he had nothing to lose. But the admission still floored me.

"Okay, I'm done. Good luck in your afterlife." Anger bubbled up like acid, and I could feel my face burning with fury. How dare he follow me? *Stalk me.* And I was equally furious and horrified that I hadn't known. Hadn't even had a clue. I hated the feeling of vulnerability and the idea that I could be that clueless, that *blind*.

"No! Wait!" Adam lurched forward, reaching for me, but his hand passed through my shoulder.

"You freely admit to stalking me and then expect me to be . . . what? Happy about it?"

"Please, I'm freaking out here," he pleaded, and for the first time since I'd known him, he sounded genuine. Honest.

"I know now that I'm . . ." He hesitated, and I think if ghosts could shed tears, they would have been welling up in his eyes.

"Dead," he continued. "But I don't know why I'm still here or why I'm stuck in this area." He gestured a wide circle.

Despite still being furious at him, compassion burned in my chest, along with the anger, and a lump formed in my throat. I couldn't truly imagine how awful it must be.

"I'm so sorry, Adam. I can't offer you those answers either. I don't know why some souls stay and others don't."

"But you see ghosts, right?" Desperation crept back into his voice.

"I do. But none of the ghosts I've spoken to know the answers either."

The look on his face was so heart-wrenching that I wished I could hug him, even if I was still fuming about him stalking me.

"So, I'm just stuck here forever?"

"I don't know. Some of the ghosts I've seen died a very long time ago. I've tried to help, but nothing has worked."

"Please don't let them brush my murder under the rug," he said quietly.

The shift in focus threw me for another loop. "What?" was all I could manage as my brain fought to catch up.

"I heard the police talking while I . . . my body . . . lay there getting cold. They think it was some random mugging. It wasn't. I was targeted."

"Do you know who killed you?" I couldn't help but look around. If I hadn't known Adam was stalking me, then I probably wouldn't know if someone else was too.

"No. I didn't see anything because I was watching you." He spat the words at me like I was the one in the wrong.

"Oh, well—so sorry your stalking got you killed." I instantly regretted saying it, but it was too late to take it back.

"You're a lot more cruel than I initially took you for," he said, moving away from me a few feet.

"And you're a lot creepier than I initially took you for." I doubled down, pushing the guilt away and embracing the anger. "*You* were following *me*, not the other way around."

He stared at me for a long time, long enough to make me squirm with the awkwardness of it.

"You're right," he said finally. "I was just so convinced that you were faking those encounters. I mean, no one on any of my tours has ever gotten so much as a suggestive shadow, and you have viral videos all over the internet. Now I know why." He laughed a humorless laugh that made the hair on the back of my neck stand up.

"Mamie." I smiled as I said her name, happy for the more pleasant change in subject.

"Who?"

"Mamie Haddock. She died of yellow fever right over there." I pointed down the street. "You can't see it from here, but there's a little house over there that used to be a boarding house. She can make the coolest orbs you've ever seen."

"I'll be damned," he said, and then a look of horror washed over his face. "But I guess I already am."

"I'm really sorry."

"I meant it, Tallulah. Please tell that detective friend of yours that it was not a mugging."

"He's not my friend," I scoffed.

"Okay, whatever. But you *do* know him."

"He's not going to listen to me. I'm pretty sure he thinks I'm the one who killed you."

"Well, you can't let him pin this on you, then," Adam said with a devilish smile.

"Who would want you dead?" I asked. I sighed and used my free hand to rub my eyes. I was suddenly very tired.

"Besides you, I don't really know." He chuckled.

"Okay, if you're not going to help, I'll just go home." I turned on my heel, but he was fast, impossibly fast, and he blocked my path. I knew I could just walk right through him, but I stopped in my tracks anyway.

"Please. I'll cooperate." He put his transparent hands up in a gesture of surrender. "I honestly don't know who would want me dead. I don't have enemies."

"Have you considered that maybe it really was random?"

"I would think that too, but they said something." He hesitated for a moment. "I didn't recognize the voice because they whispered, but they said, 'This makes us even.'"

"That seems personal," I agreed.

"I couldn't twist around and get a look at them either. I think they were male, just based on how strong they were and how easily they—well, you know."

"Do you remember anything at all that might help identify them?"

"They were wearing a black hoodie, or at least I think it was a hoodie. The arm was all I could see."

"That doesn't narrow it down much. I mean, I'm wearing a black hoodie."

"That wasn't lost on me," Adam said with a wry smile.

"Funny," I said, and glanced around again. I still felt uneasy that someone had followed me for days and I'd never been the wiser.

My phone, which I was still holding to my ear, rang loudly, and I screamed before I could stop myself.

"You're awfully jumpy for someone who's used to seeing ghosts," Adam said with another mocking grin.

"Yeah, well, I am most certainly not used to finding out I've been stalked," I snapped back before answering the call.

"Hello?"

"May I speak to Tallulah Thatcher?" a professional-sounding female voice asked.

"This is she," I said. I always feel awkward saying that phrase, but I can't think of a better response either.

"Your grandmother, Elizabeth Thatcher, is here in the emergency room."

My stomach dropped, and I must've gone pale, because Adam suddenly looked concerned.

"What's wrong?"

"My grandmother, she's in the ER," I said breathlessly. "I have to go. I'll come back."

I don't know if he responded. I was already sprinting down the street.

Chapter Eleven

I burst through the visitor's entrance at the hospital, like I was in a scene in some dramatic movie. The volunteer at the front desk looked up from her magazine and put on a weary smile.

"Elizabeth Thatcher, please," I said, still out of breath. I'd felt like I couldn't breathe ever since the nurse told me Nan was in the ER.

"Yes, she's in trauma room four." The lady pointed to the set of doors to her right.

I tried not to cry at the name of the room: trauma room four. I also tried not to think about worst-case scenarios as the volunteer buzzed me through the locked doors. I found the nurse's desk first.

I gave Nan's name to the first person who made eye contact, and I didn't bother to hide how frantic I felt.

"I'm Mrs. Thatcher's nurse," came a voice from behind me.

I turned to find a woman about my mother's age, with her long auburn hair in a single braid that cascaded over her shoulder. Her pale pink scrubs and calm demeanor settled me a fraction.

"I believe there may have been a misunderstanding," she said as she gently put her hand on my shoulder and steered me toward a room. "Your grandmother is stable. Her injuries were relatively minor, we think."

"You *think*?"

"Well, examining her has been a challenge since she won't give up the puppy," the nurse said, as if that made sense.

"I'm sorry—the *what*?" I felt like I had walked in during the middle of a movie and had no clue what was going on.

She opened the door to reveal Nan, reclining on a hospital stretcher. Her right arm was elevated on a pillow with an ice pack, and her left arm was wrestling a very wiggly puppy.

"Nan, what happened?" I said, the tears that I'd managed to keep contained on my way to the hospital finally breaking loose.

"Oh, it's nothing." She tried to wave dismissively, but the little dog took the opportunity to bound onto her chest and try to lick every inch of her face.

I stepped forward and scooped the little fella up in my arms, and after a brief look of *"What the heck just happened?"* he started trying to lick every inch of *my* face.

"That little rascal came out of nowhere, and when I swerved to miss him, I lost control. My poor car is still in the ditch unless that nice officer at the scene called a tow truck," she said, smiling up at me.

"Now that your granddaughter is here to take care of your little friend, can we get those X-rays?" the nurse asked from behind me. I'd forgotten she was there.

"Oh yes, of course."

I took a seat in the corner and tried to contain the wagging, wiggling, whining puppy that had caused all this. He looked to be mostly beagle, with little black floppy ears and the standard brown and white beagle markings. It took another couple of hours for the ER staff to get Nan's X-rays, have them interpreted, and get the doctor in to splint her broken wrist. By the time we were climbing into my car, we were all beyond exhausted, including the dog. I'm not even sure how I made it home, as I had no memory of the drive back.

We didn't speak as we staggered into the house like two zombies. Fitz greeted us with a steady meowing as he trotted up to Nan. He hissed and growled the second he noticed the wiggly puppy in my arms.

"Sorry, Fitz," I said, and attempted to let him smell the new addition, a gesture that he took great offense to. He hissed again and bolted out of the room.

Nan sighed and frowned.

"Poor Fitzwilliam. He's never had to share his house before."

"I'll get you settled in your room, and then I'll walk this little beast," I said, and then nuzzled his little head. He really was the cutest thing.

"Nonsense." She shook her head as she bent to scratch Fitz's ears. He still hadn't stopped glaring at the puppy in my arms. "I can settle myself."

"You were just in a horrible accident, and you have a broken wrist," I protested.

"Believe me, I know, but I can manage."

"Let me help you."

"Okay, you go walk that little fella—he's bound to need to go by now, and I'll go upstairs and do what I can do on my own. You can help me with the rest when you get back."

When I hesitated, she added, "I will be fine."

I nodded and turned back around, stopping when I realized I didn't have a collar or a leash for my squirmy little buddy. I detoured through the kitchen, confident that I could find something that would work in the junk drawer. I rifled through everything that had no other place in the house and found a random hoodie drawstring and an old, braided leather men's bracelet. I didn't want to think too much about where the bracelet came from as I fastened it around the puppy's little neck. It took multiple tries because he was in constant motion, trying to lick and chew on me.

Poor little guy was going to need a trip to our vet very soon. His hair coat was rough and dirty, and his distended belly paired with his skinny body told me he was probably wormy. He had no idea what being leashed was all about, so it took forever to get him to stop chewing on the makeshift leash and do his little business. Once he finally did, I told him what a good boy he was and scooped him up to go back in the house.

Nan had managed to get mostly undressed and mostly into her nightgown, but the button on her jeans was more than she could manage through the pain. I helped with that last bit and arranged her throw pillows next to her so she could elevate her arm as the nurse had told us to do, all while the puppy chewed on my shoes and anything else he could reach.

"I'll take him to my room," I said as I captured the little beast again.

"He's here because of me—I'll take care of him."

"He's hard to manage with two good hands. We'll be fine, won't we?" I bent down and snuggled him again.

"Oh my gosh," I said as it finally dawned on me. "I almost forgot to tell you. Bryce is here."

"Bryce?"

"Yeah, it's a really long story, and I'll fill you in on all the details tomorrow."

"Give me the abbreviated version, then."

"He's getting bullied at school. Mom and Jared are jerks, and he ran away from home to get them to listen to him for a change," I replied.

"Hmm." She frowned and pulled the covers over everything but her elevated arm. "Well, you tell that boy he can stay here as long as he needs to."

I smiled at my wonderful, generous grandmother. She was always ready to take in strays, no matter if they were cats, puppies, or kids.

"You know Jared is going to blow a gasket." It was my turn to frown.

"Let him," she scoffed. "Right now, though, I need to get some sleep. Good night, sweet girl."

"Love you," I said as I closed her door.

I decided that a bath was in order before I could finally crash. Little dude smelled like straight-up sewage. I didn't even wait for him to dry. I just curled up with the damp puppy and went to sleep as soon as my head hit the pillow. Kenneth was kind enough to keep watch over Nan, and promised to get me if she needed anything, so I slept like a log. It was a good thing too, since the puppy's tiny bladder woke us both up before the crack of dawn. I dressed at lightning speed and ran him down to the back lawn, where he didn't waste any time finding the perfect spot to go.

I'd been mulling the possibilities of names over in my head, but only one felt like it fit. He just looked like a Toby to me. I stared off toward the shop while *Toby* finished up, catching sight of a shadow moving near the back door. I wished I'd brought a flashlight out, but I only had the sad little light on my phone.

"Hey!" I yelled, and the shadow froze.

"What are you doing here?" I yelled again. I was getting really tired of finding people prowling around our yard.

I dialed 911 and hovered my thumb over the "Send" button.

The shadow hesitated for another second and then sprinted off down the street. I caught the briefest glance of a human shape in a brown coat as he passed under a streetlight. It was definitely time to get a security system. I led Toby over to the shop and found everything locked and secure, with no obvious attempts at a break-in. I pocketed my phone since there was nothing to report.

I was still outside at sunrise, playing a rousing game of chase the puppy, when Ronald came tearing into the back drive. He jumped out of his truck so fast that he had to double back and close the door.

"How is Lizzie?" he asked in his deep, gravelly voice. "I came as soon as I got her voicemail."

"She's doing fine. Broke her wrist and bruised up some, but otherwise all right."

"That's what she said too." He let out a sigh. "I thought she might be downplaying it, though."

"She probably is." I nodded. "But the ER doctor said she would be okay, so I'm more inclined to believe her."

"Appreciate the update," he said as he turned toward the house. "I'll see if she'll let me be of any assistance."

His grin told me he knew Nan better than I'd given him credit for.

I watched him go inside, and the little puppy strained at the end of the drawstring to go with him. He couldn't be a bad person if a puppy liked him, right? Nan had good judgment when it came to men. My grandpa had been the best man I've ever known. Me, on the other hand—well, that was a different story.

"Come on, little guy, we need to go get you a proper leash and harness," I picked him up and suddenly remembered that I'd promised Adam I would come back last night.

I cursed aloud and hurried into the house. Ronald was doing his best to help Nan down the stairs while she gently protested the entire time.

"I need to run and get puppy supplies. Are you all good here?" I asked Nan, with a little nod toward Ronald.

"I'm fine." She smiled warmly up at him with a look that I'd only ever seen her give my PawPaw. My stomach twisted a little at that look. Of course, I want Nan to be happy, to be in love again and share her life with someone; but selfishly, I can't imagine her with anyone but PawPaw. I shook my head and tried to refocus on the issues at hand. I really did need puppy supplies, and I needed to go back and talk more with Adam, like I'd promised.

"I'll be back as soon as I can." I grabbed my bag off the hall credenza. "Oh, if Bryce wakes up before I get back, just tell him we'll call Mom together."

"Take as long as you need. I've cleared my day," Ronald replied, never taking his eyes off Nan. "Who's Bryce?"

"Coffee first." Nan patted him on the shoulder. "Then explanations."

Chapter Twelve

It took much longer than I'd anticipated to make it through Pet-Cetera. By the time I'd loaded up the counter with puppy food, bakery treats, a new collar, harness and leash, a puppy bed, and a tiny little T-shirt that read "We don't hide the crazy, we parade it!" which I just couldn't resist, I'd spent the better part of an hour in the store. In my defense, people did keep stopping to pet his sweet little head and that slowed me down a bit.

I put the little guy in the back seat of my Kia Soul and loaded the supplies in the hatchback.

When I climbed in and started the car, he whined from the back seat. I realized I'd mentally been referring to him as "Toby" all morning, and finally gave up and decided that's what I was going to call him. Initially, I'd hesitated to name him, but the sweet girl behind the counter at PetCetera confirmed my suspicions that he was wormy and neglected, so I was less afraid that someone would claim him.

"What's wrong, Toby?" I turned around to see if he was doing the unmistakable puppy pee dance and he wasn't, so I tried to ignore his impassioned pleas for attention as I wove my way back toward the cemetery. He'd started howling as I navigated into a parking spot underneath a huge oak on Prytania Street. The white brick wall of the cemetery seemed too bright in the daylight despite the weathering and moss. The domed crypts visible over the wall, many also covered in moss, loomed over Toby and me like sentinels as we took to the sidewalk to find Adam. I had no idea where he might be lurking. I finally found him trying to get a reaction from the tourists gathering at the main gate.

He noticed me right away, and I indiscreetly motioned for him to follow me. Interestingly, Toby seemed to be able to see him too. I've always known that cats can see the dead because of course they can. I mean, they're cats, after all. But I've never been one hundred percent sure about dogs. Sometimes I thought they could see spirits, or at least sense them, and other times, it didn't seem like they could. Maybe it depends on the dog. Maybe they don't all have the ability to see, like humans. As we rounded the corner, away from the group at the front gates, Adam ran through me, looming before me while he screamed.

I stopped in my tracks, and Toby yelped and strained at the leash to get away, solidifying the fact that Toby, at least, had the ability to see spirits. Adam's words could only be described as a roar, and he was terrifying my puppy. I tried unsuccessfully twice to get Toby contained, before I completely lost my composure. I whirled around, threw my free hand in Adam's face, and yelled *"STOP!"* at the top of my lungs. I didn't even care that I drew attention from everyone on the sidewalks because whatever I had done sent Adam flying backward through the cemetery wall. I was finally able to pick Toby up and cuddle him when a middle-aged woman with a classic "Karen" haircut power walked up to me from across the street.

"You should never yell at a puppy like that," she scolded, waggling her dagger-manicured finger at me. "You shouldn't even have pets if that's how you treat them!"

Something in me snapped like a glowstick, and I glared at her. In that moment I didn't care who knew my secrets.

"Lady, I'll have you know I wasn't yelling at Toby. I was yelling at the ghost who was scaring him."

The range of emotions that washed over her face was numerous and varied, but finally landed on horrified, and she gave me a wide berth as I passed her.

Adam climbed back through the cemetery wall with what looked like a great amount of effort. Like I said, hallowed ground can be funny.

I walked right up to where he seemed to be stuck about halfway through.

"If you ever scare my puppy like that again, I will leave you here, by yourself, from now on," I said through gritted teeth.

He stopped struggling and looked up at me. Toby squirmed and buried his little face under my chin.

"I'm sorry," Adam muttered quietly. When he stopped fighting the wall, he kind of slid through it, like icing melting off a hot cake.

He shifted in that way ghosts do sometimes that looks like a cross between a mirage and a stop-motion film, and stood in front of me. People passing on the sidewalk were no longer paying any attention to me, which honestly makes a lot of sense. When you live in a city known worldwide for its eccentricities, my behavior probably didn't even register on anyone's radar.

"You should be," I scolded. "Did you act like this when you were alive?"

"Honestly, yeah. But not this bad. It's like losing my body caused me to lose control too."

I wasn't sure how to respond, so I just glared at him.

"I know I have no right to ask, but please make sure they take my case seriously. I don't know who did this, or why, and I'm scared they might go after Mia." He must've registered the confusion on my face because he added, "Mia is my wife. If they targeted me for some reason, I don't know if she will be safe."

I softened at his concern. If he was still worried about his wife's welfare after death, then he couldn't be all bad, despite the angry outbursts. I wasn't about to let him off the hook that easily, though. Dead or not, he needed to respect some boundaries.

"Let's get something straight," I said, Toby still wiggling under my chin. "I'm not going to tolerate any more of your outbursts, so you better figure out a way to contain yourself pretty quick. I'll do what I can with Dylan—um, the police."

"So, you do know him," Adam managed to twist his ephemeral features into a smug sneer.

"I never said I didn't know him. Do you want me to help you or not?"

He held his hands up in surrender.

"Let's start by seeing where your haunt borders are," I said as I gingerly set Toby down on the sidewalk.

"My what?"

"How far you can move in each direction. I have no idea why or how it works, but ghosts are kind of rooted to the general area where they died."

"Oh yeah." He nodded somberly. "I've already done that."

"Perfect. Show me while I walk Toby."

I pretended to be talking to someone on my earbuds while Adam showed me the perimeter of his haunt. He did overlap with Mamie a bit. I wondered why she hadn't shown herself to him. I decided not to mention it to Adam as we finished our walk back to my car.

"So, you'll talk to your friend? Dylan?"

"I will. I'm going there as soon as I leave here." I tried to hide the stomach-churning dread I felt at the thought of talking to Dylan.

It was stupid. I was an adult, not some lovesick teenager, but it didn't matter. I felt like a lovesick teenager.

"Lou," Adam said as I turned to get in the car, "you need to be careful too. I don't know if the killer—my killer—saw you that night."

I'd had the same thoughts, but hearing Adam voice them made me shudder.

Chapter Thirteen

I sat outside the police station for a stupid amount of time before I worked up the courage to go in, Toby tucked under my arm. The desk officer took my name and seated me in the most uncomfortable hard plastic chair I'd ever had the displeasure of sitting in. I assumed the accommodations weren't meant for comfort. I was in the process of squirming around and removing Toby's little hind leg from the waistband of my pants when Dylan appeared in front of me. Because of course, I would be in the most awkward position possible the minute he walked up. Of freaking course.

"We don't need another statement, Lou," he said as he eyed Toby. "And we don't really allow pets in here either."

"I'll keep him contained." I instinctively held the squirmy puppy a little closer. "I need to talk to you."

He seemed to be considering something, kicking me out maybe, and then suddenly said, "Follow me."

He led me down a narrow hallway. I initially assumed he was taking me to his office or, if he didn't have an office, to a conference room. But he took me into an interrogation room. It looked like something out of *Law & Order*, and I jumped as the door shut behind me.

"Is anyone listening?" I looked toward the camera in the corner.

Dylan laughed and my cheeks burned.

"No one is listening," he said when he saw the look on my face. "What did you need to talk to me about?"

"I'm hoping you can tell me about the investigation into Adam's murder," I said as I took the seat across from him. Toby had just about had enough of being still and was starting to squirm in earnest.

"Adam?" Dylan leaned back and cocked his head slightly to the side. Good lord, that was unnerving. The harsh LED lighting didn't wash out his tan or make his blue eyes any less piercing. I was wondering if he had any idea how gorgeous he was, when he leaned forward and stared right into my eyes.

"You called him 'Adam.' You said you didn't know him that well. I believe you said you weren't friends."

I snapped back to reality pretty quickly as I realized I was being interrogated in the interrogation room.

"I *didn't* know him that well. And his name was Adam, so what else would I call him?"

"Most people refer to people they don't know that well by their last names. 'Mr. Brandt,' for example."

I sighed as I worked to calm my nerves jangled both from sitting across a tiny table from the man who haunts my fantasies, and because he was treating me more and more like a suspect every time we met.

"Okay. Can you tell me anything about Mr. Brandt's murder investigation?"

"What do you want to know?"

I was getting more exasperated by the second. Dylan might be smoking hot, but he was acting like a jerk.

"Do you have any suspects?"

"We do."

I waited. He didn't continue, just kept staring at me with an intensity that made me squirm like Toby.

"I understand you might not be able to give me details," I said as I tried to figure out how to tell him that Adam was worried about his wife, without telling him I see dead people. "But I know, statistically speaking, the murderer is usually someone the victim knows. Do you think Ada—*Mr. Brandt's* wife and friends might be in any danger?"

"Statistically speaking," he scoffed, "why would his family and friends be in danger?"

I did not like the smirk that was plastered across Dylan's face.

"You're not taking this seriously," I said, feeling defeated. Adam was right.

"On the contrary, I'm taking this very seriously. And you should too."

Something about that last sentence put me on edge.

"What do you mean?"

"Exactly what I said."

The cold horror of realization washed over me.

"Oh god, I'm a suspect!"

It had been obvious he thought I'd acted strangely at the scene, and to be fair, I had. And I'd jokingly told Tess and Cady that I thought he suspected me, but in truth, I hadn't really thought I was an official suspect.

Dylan leaned back in his chair and regarded me again, his expression unreadable.

"We haven't ruled anyone out yet. We will follow the evidence, wherever that leads."

"But you do suspect me?" I meant it as a statement, but it came out as a question.

"Lou," he said, his voice softening ever so slightly, "you are the only one so far who has motive, means, and opportunity, to borrow an overused phrase."

"What? How?" I sputtered, and Toby began to whine as he tried to wiggle out of my arms. "I don't have any of those things!"

"You were in the middle of a disagreement with the deceased." He held up a hand as he ticked off the points one by one. "He was killed by a dagger that's sold in your shop, and you have hours and hours of every day that aren't accounted for."

I gasped. The decorative daggers I had just put on the shelves last week flashed into my mind. How many had I sold? Were there any missing?

"You can't possibly think I did this." I still felt breathless, like I'd just run a mile. Uphill. "You've known me forever. And how do you know the dagger is one of mine? I buy most of my stuff wholesale, so it could have come from anywhere."

"Which is exactly why I can't let our connection blind me. The evidence will speak for itself."

"You didn't answer my question."

"It still had the Haunts and Jaunts sticker on the handle. We will need to see your sales records for the daggers. We can get a warrant, of course, but it would be better if you just brought them in."

I felt myself hyperventilating as my vision narrowed to a tunnel. Toby pulled against me, sensing that something was wrong.

"Lou, take a deep breath." Dylan shook my shoulder. I don't know when he got up and moved to my side, but his voice finally reached me through the fog.

I did as he instructed and tried to slow my breathing. The world crept back into focus, and I felt less like I was going to pass out on the floor.

"Do you need some water?" Dylan asked as he pulled his chair around to sit beside me. He gently took Toby, who tried to wash his entire face, wagging his little tail enthusiastically.

"No, I just need to get out of here." I snatched Toby back so suddenly that it startled both the puppy and Dylan. My little dog recovered quickly and resumed his licking, this time on my neck.

"Lou, if you're innocent, you don't have anything to worry about."

"If?" I snapped.

He put on an innocent look, which I'm sure was part of his whole "good cop" spiel.

I turned on my heel and left, and didn't look back until I got into my car. I still felt shaky and breathless, but I was also flaming mad, and unlike the panic I'd felt earlier, I could do something with mad. I could channel it into finding who actually had murdered Adam.

Chapter Fourteen

I was furious as I blew through my emails at the shop. When I got home, I'd gone straight inside to check on Nan and found her asleep in her recliner, Ronald keeping a close eye on her. I thanked him for being there since he clearly cared for her, and he assured me he would be there as long as we needed him.

"Bryce up yet?" I whispered.

"He came out long enough to eat and thank Lizzie for letting him stay here, and then retreated back to the guest room," Ron whispered back, although his whisper was more like a growl.

I nodded. I took a quick detour upstairs and knocked on Bryce's door.

"Entrez," came a muffled voice from within.

Bryce was hunched over his laptop on the floor beside the bed.

"There's a whole desk, right over there." I pointed across the room.

"I'm good."

"You know we have to call, right?"

"Yeah, I know."

I sat down beside him, and Toby bounded out of my arms and licked Bryce's face all over before he could stop him.

"Who is this?" Bryce laughed.

I told him how we'd ended up with little wiggle butt while I pulled up Mom's contact on my phone.

"Hello? Lou?"

"Hi, Mom," I said. I understood her surprise at seeing my number. I don't call her. I answer once in a while when she calls me, but I don't call her.

"Is everything all right? Is every*one* all right?"

"Everyone is fine. Look, I'm calling because Bryce is here."

"What? No, he's at his friend Derrick's this weekend. We dropped him off."

I glared at Bryce. "I don't know about any of that. I just know I'm looking at Bryce right now. And he told me why he came, so we need to talk about that."

There was a long pause.

"Let me speak to him," she said angrily.

"You're on 'Speaker.' Talk."

"I would prefer to speak to my son privately." There was a cold edge to her voice.

"I'm sure you would. But he's here now, and I'm part of this, so we need to figure this out together for a change."

"What is that supposed to mean?" she snapped.

"Please don't start fighting," Bryce interrupted. "Mom, I don't want to come back. I can finish out the year down here. Then I can get a summer job and pay for private school tuition."

"Oh Bryce, not this again. You just have one more year. Surely you can put up with a little teasing for one more year."

"Oh my god, Mom, it's more than 'a little teasing,'" my voice rose in anger despite my trying to stay calm.

"I'm sure he's told you all sorts of things."

My heart broke at the look on Bryce's face. I knew how bad it felt to have that woman ignore your feelings. I took her off "Speaker" and stood up.

"I am not about to sit here while we debate what you believe and what you choose to ignore—"

"Tallulah, you don't know the whole story," she interrupted.

"I know that my sixteen-year-old brother rode a bus for over twelve hours to escape a situation you're choosing to ignore," I said through gritted teeth. "And I don't give a flying fig how you feel about that. What I care about is how we're all going to support what's best for Bryce. And if that means me petitioning for custody, then you better lawyer up."

"Tallulah!" she gasped about the same time Bryce did too. "You can't do that!"

I took a deep breath. I couldn't let myself get into a battle over the phone with that woman.

"Tallulah!" she squawked in my ear again.

"Mother," I replied quietly, "I think we can agree we both want what's best for Bryce, right?"

"What's best for him is to come home. This is insane," she snapped. "Just wait until Jared hears about this."

"Mother, I'm an adult. I'm not afraid of getting grounded anymore. But we need to discuss how to proceed."

"There isn't any discussion. We will come get him. We're out of town this weekend since we *thought* Bryce was at a friend's house, and I don't know if Jared can get off work." She spoke rapidly, almost absently like she was talking through this with herself rather than with me. "No, *you* should bring him home. You can just close your little tour or whatever for a couple of days."

"No. I can't. I have reservations." I pinched the bridge of my nose between my eyes to try to stave off the stress headache that was threatening to take hold. "I tell you what, we can talk either later tonight or tomorrow. But nothing is going to happen that doesn't include a plan to address the bullying he's been dealing with. Bryce can either stay here and finish out the year, or we have a concrete plan, in writing, detailing what you're going to do to keep him safe."

I'm not even sure what she started screeching in my ear because I just removed the phone and left her to it. When the shrill noise died down, I put the phone back to my ear.

"I've told you what's going to happen. I'll talk to you again soon." And I ended the call.

I took another deep breath and sat on the edge of the bed. No court in the world would give me guardianship if I was a murder suspect.

"Did you mean it?" Bryce asked while he fended off Toby's latest assault.

"Yeah, I meant it. We'll make sure you're safe, one way or another."

He reached over and squeezed my foot and wiped his eyes on his sleeve.

*   *   *

Back at the shop, however, my anger boiled back to the surface. I pulled all the decorative daggers off the shelf and shoved them in a box in the back room. I pulled up the original order, since I needed to provide the records to the police anyway, and found I had purchased ten of them. I had seven left. I searched through invoices and found that we had sold two of them, both cash sales, so there was no identification attached to either of them. And that left one unaccounted for completely. Since I had no way of knowing what happened to that tenth dagger, I channeled my frustration into work. In between bookings and answering questions, I searched social media for Adam's wife and business partner. Adam might not believe those closest to him would want him dead, but I'd wager a lot of victims felt that way until it was too late.

Mia Brandt's social media was filled with condolences that she hadn't responded to or acknowledged in any way. Her last Instagram post had been two days before Adam was murdered. She'd posted a selfie outside a salon where she had apparently had high and low lights added to her jet-black hair. She was stunningly beautiful; her pale skin and red, pouty lips made me think of Snow White. I switched over to Facebook, but it was more of the same.

Damian Boyle, Adam's business partner, was largely absent on social media. He had a personal Facebook page where he shared business posts and the occasional fishing photo proudly displaying his latest catch. I couldn't find him on Instagram or Twitter—or rather, X, or whatever Elon Musk is calling it now.

I also searched for a family law attorney, narrowed my search to two, Greg Dannemaker and Elaine Hastings. Mr. Dannemaker didn't have any available appointments for two weeks. Ms. Hastings was able to get me in for a consultation right away. I booked the appointment and tried not to think about what would happen if I got arrested.

I heard Tess's keys jingling as she unlocked the back door.

"Hey," she called as she used her foot to close the door behind her.

"Hey, you." I pushed the iPad away from me on the counter and stretched as I slid down off the stool.

"What is all this?"

"I'm hoping to put the finishing touches on some of the puppets for the show this weekend, in between customers, if you don't care," she said as she pulled out a fuzzy monster puppet.

I fought the urge to shudder and frown.

"I don't mind." I plastered on a smile that I hoped looked like I was supportive and not like I wanted to run away from the creepy things.

"Thanks!" She beamed. "Oh my goodness! Who is this?"

She bent down and scooped up Toby, who took the opportunity to try to lick every inch of her face and neck.

I told her about Nan's accident and the latest development with Bryce, and she cooed over Toby the whole time.

"Well, he's definitely a stray with that skinny little butt." She bent down to kiss his little round head.

"Yeah, I don't think he's had much in the way of care or nutrition."

"That'll change now, won't it?" She sat on the floor with him and rubbed his ears.

"Oh my gosh! I didn't even ask how Nan is!" Tess cupped a hand over her mouth.

"She's doing okay." I instinctively looked through the window toward the house. "Her boyfriend is staying with her."

"Her what?" Tess looked incredulous. "I mean, good for her. Get it girl, and all that. I just didn't know she was seeing anyone."

"I didn't either. Not until two days ago anyway. His name is Ronald and he seems . . ." I struggled with what to say, which was stupid since he had been nothing but perfectly nice.

"It's got to be weird for her to be dating someone," Tess said sympathetically.

"I want her to be happy," I said more to myself than to Tess.

"Of course you do, honey, but it's okay to feel your feelings too."

I was momentarily taken aback by the validation, so naturally, I just stood there with my mouth hanging open.

"Oh, before I forget," Tess said as she got to her feet, Toby tucked under her arm, "we are completely out of both printer paper and receipt paper. I put the last roll in last night."

I glanced at the clock. "I can go grab some before we start getting much traffic."

"I'm sorry—I meant to tell you yesterday, and then I thought I would text this morning, but I'm so distracted right now." She gestured toward the puppets.

"You don't need to apologize. I should know when we're getting low." I glanced around the counter. "Will you run through the reservations and make sure nothing is urgent? I'll do a quick run through and see if we need anything else."

"I think I can manage that." She grinned and plopped down on the floor with the shop laptop.

"Hey, before I go, can you look at a couple of photos and see if you recognize anyone?"

"Sure. Why?"

"Because Adam was killed with one of those stupid decorative daggers we just got last week."

She gasped and cupped her hand over her mouth.

"I checked the sales receipts. We sold two, and one is missing. Whoever took it would have flown under the radar, but I was hoping maybe you would recognize them if they were milling around in the shop before they took it."

She went pale as a sheet as she nodded slowly.

I pulled out my phone and loaded Mia Brandt's profile picture first. Tess shook her head. "Who is that?"

"Adam's wife. And this is his business partner." I pulled up Damian's photo next.

"I don't remember seeing him either," she said quietly. "It's really freaking me out that a murderer was in here."

My first impulse was to tell her that most people interact with more than thirty murderers in their lifetime and never realize it, but I decided it wasn't much comfort.

"I'm so sorry. If you want to stay away until this is all over with, I completely understand."

"Oh absolutely not!" she said with mock indignation. "I am *not* going anywhere."

"Well, I understand if you change your mind."

"Not gonna happen."

I hurried through my supply check and made a list, even though there weren't many items we needed. I was hopelessly distracted, and I didn't want to forget anything. I shoved the list in my bag and headed for the door, when I was met by a group of law enforcement officers, both uniformed and in plain clothes. One of the plain-clothes officers leading the pack was a middle-aged Black man with more salt than pepper in his hair.

"Good morning, Miss Thatcher," he said with a broad smile.

He handed me a thick packet of folded papers. "We have a warrant to search the premises, so we'll need you and your employee to step outside please."

"What do you think you're going to find here?" I asked while people filed in on either side of me.

"Everything is outlined in the warrant."

"Lou, what should I do?" Tess was suddenly beside me.

"Let's go to the house," I said, glancing back as we left strangers to ransack the culmination of all my hard work.

"Miss Thatcher," the plainclothes officer called after me, "you'll find that your residence is also included in the warrant."

"Are you saying we can't go to the house?"

"No, not at all. I just wanted you to be aware that there will be officers going with you."

Begrudgingly, I allowed two uniformed officers to follow Tess and me to the house. Tess kept glancing over her shoulder at the cops trailing behind us. I opened the door awkwardly and everyone followed me inside. Nan and Ron were still in the kitchen. After I explained what was going on, Ron pulled a pair of reading glasses from his breast pocket and went over the warrant. When he was finished, he addressed the two officers.

"The warrant limits the scope of your search in the house to Tallulah's room," he said, one eyebrow raised.

"That's correct," the shorter of the two replied. "Would one of you show us to her room?"

"I'll take you," I said. "I don't have anything to hide."

After showing them to my room and fighting the awful feelings of having both of my safe spaces violated, I warned Bryce about the intrusion.

"Are the police here because of me?"

"No, not at all. They're here because I found . . . someone who was hurt . . ." I struggled. It's not like he was a little kid, but I wasn't sure how to say it gently either.

"I don't understand. Why are they here?"

"I found someone . . . murdered. They have to rule me out as a suspect so they can find out who really did it. The victim, Adam, and I had history. He tried to get my business shut down, so we weren't exactly friends."

"Wow. I don't know what to say."

He looked wide-eyed, and I hoped I hadn't freaked him out.

"I'm sorry," I said. "I know this is a lot."

"You don't have to apologize. You didn't exactly plan on me being here."

"Come down and get some breakfast."

He shrugged on a hoodie over his T-shirt and followed me downstairs. We joined Nan, Tess, and Ron in the kitchen. Or at least I thought we were joining them. Ron was gone when I got back downstairs.

"Where's Ron?"

"He went down to the shop to make sure that they stick to the warrant there too," Nan said. I could see it in her smile that she was swelling with pride. I had the distinct feeling that Ron was going to be sticking around. She was taking the arrival of the police remarkably well, but I still felt guilty.

"I'm so sorry about all of this," I said, hugging her tightly.

"Nothing to be sorry for. It'll all blow over."

"Now, what are we going to feed you, growing boy?" Nan ruffled his hair with her good hand. Her warm smile was infectious, and Bryce beamed at the affection.

"Just anything. I'm not picky."

I wished I shared Nan's confidence. At least they were serving the warrant during the day, so maybe I could clean up their mess before customers started filing in that evening. At least I hoped that was the way it worked. I'd never been the subject of a police investigation before, so I had no idea how long it would take them to complete their search. I felt bad about the house being invaded, not only for Nan but also because I was sure that Kenneth was miserable with this many people in his space. He'd probably already retreated to the attic.

"I can go get the stuff on the list if you want me to," Tess offered.

"No, I'll go. I don't want to watch this, and I need to do something else anyway," I said.

"Okay, then. I'll work on answering emails and confirming reservations." Tess pulled her laptop out of her bag.

We all looked at the ceiling as we heard a crash and a thud coming from my room. I hoped I had a room left when they were finished.

Chapter Fifteen

I t didn't take me long to get the few office supplies, even though another customer took huge offense to me shopping with Toby, and I had to dodge her multiple times while I gathered my items. I sat in the parking lot of the big box office supply store, staring at my phone while Toby curled up to sleep in the back seat. I searched for Adam's business page, and my thumb hovered over the "Call now" button.

Who was I kidding? I'm not a detective, and Adam's business partner would have no reason to talk to me. I had nothing to use as leverage and no authority to compel him. I shoved the phone in my bag and pulled out of the parking space. Images of being arrested and hauled off to jail flooded through my mind. I shook my head and told myself I was being ridiculous, so I pulled into another parking spot and dialed the number.

"B&B Haunted Tours, how may I help you?"

"I need to speak to Mr. Boyle, please." I tried to sound self-assured and confident.

"May I ask who's calling?"

Crap. Why didn't I think this through a little more before I called?

"Um," I stammered, and looked around my car for any ideas. "It's floor . . . um . . . Flora. I'm Flora. I need to speak to Mr. Boyle."

I inwardly cringed.

"He has some availability next week. What is this regarding?"

"I need his signature on an invoice. Today."

"You can bring it by the office, and I will have it available for you this afternoon."

"Can I just wait there?"

"Mr. Boyle is out of the office this morning."

"Okay, thank you."

She gave me the particulars for dropping off my nonexistent invoice and then ended the call.

I sighed, disgusted with myself for messing that up so badly. I cursed myself as I pulled out into the road, and ran through all the scenarios in my head where I didn't just act like a complete idiot. I must've been on total autopilot because when I came back to reality, I was pulling into a parking spot at B&B Haunted Tours.

"What do you think you're doing?" I asked my reflection in the rearview mirror.

Toby yawned and stretched and then whined pitifully in the back seat. I connected his leash and got out to walk him in the little patch of grass next to the brick building. When he'd finished and sat wagging as he looked up at me with the adoration only dogs can manage, I smiled at his sweet little face.

"Come on, Toby. Let's see if we can find out anything in person."

I walked through the doors, Toby tucked under my arm, and was greeted by the voice I'd just heard over the phone.

"Hello, I'm Lou Thatcher," I said. I'd already decided that since deception had gotten me nowhere, I would try with a bit of honesty sprinkled in. "I wanted to offer my condolences to Mr. Boyle."

"Thank you." Her smile faded to a somber frown. "It's all been very . . . hard."

"I know Adam and I weren't the best of friends, but I am so very sorry."

"Mr. Boyle is at the Barlowe. As you can imagine, we are having to adjust tour schedules and move some reservations around."

"I'll try to catch him another time, then."

She nodded and I left without looking back. My heart was pounding as I got back into my car. Nothing I'd done was dangerous or necessarily wrong, but I felt like I'd just pulled some sort of caper, which was stupid of course. I hesitated as I started to pull out into the street. What could it hurt? Nothing. It wouldn't hurt a thing if I headed to the Barlowe Hotel to try to catch Damian Boyle. At least it wouldn't hurt anything if I could stay far enough away from the hotel itself to keep the ghosts from screaming at me so loudly I couldn't hear anything else.

Chapter Sixteen

The Barlowe Hotel and its surrounding garden take up most of the block. It's an imposing three-story brick and iron building, smaller than the Hotel Saint Vincent but just as commanding. It was flanked on either side by massive oaks, Spanish moss hanging in their branches like bridal veils. The Barlowe was quintessential Garden District charm. It was also one of the most haunted places in all of Louisiana, although sightings for anyone but me tend to be few and far between. They're usually pretty impressive when they occur, though. Like the now analyzed-to-death video a guest captured in the servant hallway of a wisp of smoke shaped like a young woman. She looks back at the camera and then disappears through the wall. The entire encounter is a little over three seconds, but the clarity of the shot, and the fact that it hasn't been satisfactorily debunked, keeps people coming for a chance to capture more.

I don't like to go there. The ghosts there are very angry. In the 1920s, the hotel, which was an elite spa at the time, caught fire. The guests panicked, fearing that the staff would be competition for the elevators. Investigators would later say that someone wedged a candelabra under the staff door, and twelve people perished. Four of them are still there, and while I fully understand their anger and anguish, it's difficult to be around. I try to go and listen when I can, because they don't often get a chance to tell their stories, but it always leaves me drained for days. The ghost captured in that video is one of the four, Anna. She was a young maid trying to earn enough money to help her family get out of debt. She asked me once to try to find any information about them, but I wasn't able to find much of anything except some birth and death dates. She's really the only one of the four who has moved on from the circumstances of their deaths. The others hold onto their anger like an anchor.

It didn't occur to me that I didn't know what Damian Boyle's car looked like until I was circling the parking lot. Lucky for me that he had a B&B Haunted Tours sticker on both front doors of his silver GMC SUV. I picked a spot where I could watch his car and the front doors. I hoped I could pull off a "chance meeting" and get him to talk to me a little. I felt silly as I thought that through. It wasn't like he was going to confess to murder, to a complete stranger, in the hotel parking lot. But maybe I could get a feel for how much he was or wasn't grieving. If he was happy Adam was out of the picture, that might tell me something, wouldn't it?

I got out of the car and let Toby stretch his little legs. He sniffed every tire and meandered through the cars while I watched the front entrance of the hotel. I tried to ignore the constant moaning and screaming of the ghosts within. I was overdue for a visit, and although I didn't personally owe anything to the spirits trapped there, I still felt a responsibility to them. I didn't know anyone else who had my abilities—not that I'd asked for the ability to see and hear the dead, but I still benefited from it. And if I could at least listen to their anger and frustration, I felt like maybe that could help. I hoped so, but it also takes a lot out of me, and I'd been putting it off.

"I'll come back when Nan feels up to watching you," I told Toby as I bent down and scratched his ears.

When I straightened up, I caught sight of Damian Boyle descending the front steps of the hotel. He was Adam's polar opposite. Adam had always been impeccably groomed and had worn what a lot of the locals called "hipster" clothes. Damian looked like he would be more comfortable in the swamp than on the steps of an exclusive hotel. His thin, scraggly hair kind of floated around his head, and he wore overalls over a faded Grateful Dead T-shirt. He clutched a wad of papers in one hand and several file folders in the other, which he dropped as he descended the last step. The papers that had been inside scattered out across the pavement. I hurried to help him, thinking this was the perfect way to casually bump into him.

"Here you go," I said as I handed him a stack I had hastily gathered up. I wasn't trying to snoop, but I'd noticed that some of the documents appeared to be insurance paperwork related to Adam's death.

"Thanks," he said, and took them rather roughly.

"Damian Boyle?"

"Who wants to know?" He had a faintly Cajun accent, which I always found endearing since my PawPaw's thick accent had been such a comfort.

"I'm Lou Thatcher. I'm so sorry for your loss."

"Are you?" he scoffed.

I was taken aback. I hadn't expected him to be overly friendly, but I didn't think he'd be openly aggressive either.

"I am," I said softly. "Adam doesn't deserve this."

"Of course he didn't." He turned away from me with a sneer.

"I was hoping to ask you a few questions," I said to the back of his fuzzy head. His baby fine, graying hair continued to float around his head in erratic waves.

"What could you possibly have to ask me?"

The severity in his voice and the speed with which he whirled around on me made me jump back a step. "Adam knew you were faking your encounters to undercut our business, and he was determined to prove it. Maybe I should have a few questions for you."

His face reddened as spat the words at me.

"You can ask me anything you want," I said as I tried to settle my frayed nerves.

He took a step closer to me, and I wanted to shrink away, but I made myself stand my ground. He just shook his head, so I blurted out my question before he could leave.

"Who would want to hurt Adam?"

"Besides you?"

"What did *you* have to gain from his death?" I snapped, and instantly regretted it. Being confrontational and openly accusing him of murder sure wasn't going to make him give me any useful information.

He rocked back on his heels and looked me up and down. I resisted the urge to squirm.

"If you contact me again, if you even come within a hundred feet of me, I'll call the cops and file harassment charges so fast your head will spin." His voice was low and menacing.

I was using all my concentration to keep my jaw from falling open when he added, "Do you get that? Is it sinking in?"

I fought to regain my composure.

"Look, I didn't mean to get off on the wrong foot. I just want to find out what happened."

"You think you can do better than the police?" He laughed. "No. You know what? I don't even care. Just get lost and stay lost."

He turned, walked away, and then looked over his shoulder.

"I meant what I said. Contact me again and I'll go straight to the cops."

I watched him go, and Toby whined at my feet, tugging on the leg of my jeans. When I looked down, he wagged his skinny little tail. I picked him up and held him close as the feeling of defeat washed over me. It would be really hard to imagine that encounter going any worse than it had.

I pulled my phone out of my pocket and clicked Cady's contact in my favorites.

"Hey, you. What's up?" I could hear the smile in her voice.

"Do you know anything about Damian Boyle?"

"Who?"

"Adam's business partner. I thought it was a long shot, but since you've lived here your whole life, I thought maybe . . ." I let my voice trail off.

"New Orleans is a big town, Lou," she said, laughing.

"Yeah, but The Garden District is a small town." I chuckled too.

"Point taken. Let me call Aunt Sugar, and I'll get back to you."

"Perfect! Thank you!"

Cady's Aunt Sugar pursued gossip like it was an Olympic sport and if Damian Boyle had any skeletons in his closet, she would know.

"Excuse me."

I became vaguely aware that the barely audible "Excuse me" was directed at me. I turned around and found a tall, very thin man with long arms and legs, who subtly reminded me of a stick insect. The feeling was enhanced by his slightly bulging eyes.

"I never liked him," he said quietly.

"What?"

"Damian. I never liked him. Adam trusted him, but I always thought he was a jerk." He shrugged.

"Oh," I said, and the confusion must've shown on my face because he took a step back and put his hands up.

"I'm so sorry. I just overheard part of your conversation with Damian, and I wanted to offer my support." He smiled nervously and ran his hand through his stringy dark hair.

"Thanks?" It came out as a question, but he didn't seem to notice.

"No problem. Damian is the reason I lost my job here." He hooked a thumb back toward the hotel.

"What happened?"

"He accused me of messing up their reservation schedule. Which did *not* happen, I can tell you that. I would never do anything like that. I'm always careful about details. Adam was supposed to talk to him for me, but now he's . . . well, you know."

He fidgeted from foot to foot while he talked.

"How well do you know Damian?" I asked, relaxing a little.

"Not well at all. Just what little I'd interacted with him at work and then through Adam." He smiled nervously again.

I nodded.

"I'd like to help, though." He shoved his hands in his pockets and then pulled them out again like he wasn't quite sure what to do with his long limbs while he spoke. "I'm Lucas. Lucas Wells."

I looked at him skeptically.

"I know you don't know me," he continued, "but if he was involved in any way in Adam's death, I'd love the opportunity to make sure he pays for it. Especially after what he did to me, so I guess it's a bit selfish. But Adam was my friend, and even if Damian is innocent, I want to do one last favor for him. He was always really good to me." He took a deep breath.

There was something very endearing about his awkwardness.

"I really have to get back to work, but you can reach me here just about any time." I pulled a slightly worn business card out of my back pocket and handed it over. "That's my cell number on there."

"Great! I'll talk to you soon, then." He saluted and then blushed like he wished he hadn't. He turned and walked away, looking back one more time to wave as he wove his way through the parked cars.

Chapter Seventeen

The police were gone when I got home, which surprised me. I'd expected them to be there all day, or longer. I went to the house first, where I found Nan, Ron, and Bryce gathered around the dining room table, playing a game of Monopoly.

"Watch out for this one," Ron said as soon as I entered the room. "He's a ruthless land baron."

Bryce laughed and called Toby over. He slid off his chair and joined the puppy on the floor.

"Can I borrow you for just a minute?" I asked Nan.

She nodded and followed me to the kitchen. I quickly told her everything I'd left out about Bryce earlier. I told her I'd made an appointment with a family law attorney and fully expected her to try to talk me out of it. Instead, she told me that she would go with me if I wanted her to, and she would be happy to help in any way she could, adding, "Bryce is a good kid. If he ran away, there was good reason for it, even if it *was* stupid." I had to agree, but given my rocky history with my mother, it was nice to have someone else confirm it.

"I'd better get back out there before those two start plotting against me."

"Cutthroat game?"

She laughed. "You wouldn't believe how devious."

Back at the shop, I tried to focus on work, tried to make myself concentrate on juggling reservations and orders, but I kept finding myself scrolling through Damian and Mia's social media accounts. What I was looking for, I have no idea. I was interrupted when a text notification popped up on my phone screen.

Hey! It's Lucas. Now you have my phone number too. It included several smiley face emojis and ended with a thumbs-up.

I wasn't sure how to respond, so I just texted, *Thanks!*

I was still in a weird mood when my tour guests started to gather in the shop. Tess assured me she didn't mind keeping Toby, but I felt bad leaving her with a puppy. That was definitely above and beyond her job description, which she was quick to correct.

"I'm no longer interested in job descriptions that don't include puppies."

"Apparently, you're in the right place then."

When the shop clock chimed the hour, I called for the guests to gather around while I gave them my standard greeting and advised them to stay with the group. One guest, a short man wearing a bright orange jacket, scoffed or grunted multiple times while I was trying to speak. Experience had taught me to ignore that kind of behavior. In the early days of my tours, I'd attracted a lot of skeptics for some reason, people who wanted to argue with everything I said or those who demanded I produce proof of paranormal activity. Funnily enough, once Mamie's orbs started going viral, those kinds of guests became less frequent, and they nearly stopped altogether after innitforthespirits's great video of Pete Grubbert stumbling into the mortal realm in his perpetual state of drunkenness. So, I was a little out of practice in dealing with hecklers, but I knew better than to engage with him.

As we started down the sidewalk and I started talking about the rich history of the Garden District, how the area had evolved from plantations to affluent Greek Revival homes dripping in Victorian elegance, my orange-clad heckler took a phone call. He loudly discussed what sounded like a fantasy football league. I tried to talk when he paused, but that became more difficult as he stopped pausing. I finally gave up, stopped the tour, and stared pointedly at him until he got the hint. He nodded and ended the call.

I resumed my talk about massive columns and intricate plaster-work, to ease my guests into the discussion of the darker history and the ghosts left behind. I had just paused at a particularly stately home, with giant oaks in the front yard, when Mr. Heckler piped up from toward the back.

"Is this a history lesson or a ghost tour?"

"I just provide a little background before we get to the haunted hot spots," I said through my plastered-on customer-service smile.

"That's a bit of a stretch, isn't it?" He took a few steps through the group so that he stood in front of me. "Your little tour doesn't really go through any haunted hot spots. You don't go through Lafayette Cemetery. You don't go through the Barlowe. You don't even hit the Mansion Magnolia."

"Then why are you here?" one of the other guests asked from the back of the group. I couldn't see her, but she sounded young.

"All the good tours were booked," he snapped back.

"Well, I hope you'll change your mind after the tour," I said trying not to sound like I was speaking through my gritted teeth.

He laughed.

"Or you can head back to the shop for a refund. Your choice." I dropped my attempt at placating him but stopped just short of completely losing my cool.

"Can't handle being challenged?" He held up his hands as if in surrender.

"I want all my guests to have a good time, so if you're not enjoying the tour, you're welcome to get a refund and find something you might like better."

"Sounds like a great idea," the female voice from the back of the group piped up again.

"Fine, fine." He held up his hands again. "I'll keep quiet and not point out how this tour is crap and we're all getting robbed."

"Dude, seriously." A young man with long blond hair, at the front of the group, stepped forward. "Either go get your refund or stop acting like a douche. It's pretty simple."

At that, the heckler threw his hands in the air and stalked back off toward the shop. I pulled my phone out to text Tess.

"Pardon me for just a moment," I told my group.

I typed out a message as fast as I could, warning her of his arrival and authorizing the refund, and then returned to my tour. Even though he was gone, I spent the rest of the evening feeling inadequate and self-conscious, and then hating myself for feeling that way. Thankfully, the rest of my group were very kind, and everyone seemed to enjoy the experience. Mamie, never one to disappoint, planted some very nice, subtle orbs for them to discover along the way. And even Adam behaved as he'd promised. I was feeling a little better by the time the last of our customers filed out into the night.

"What a night," I said as I flopped on the floor behind the counter to play with Toby. "I hope this little monster didn't give you too much trouble."

"Actually, he slept nearly the whole time." Tess shrugged. "And traffic was light, so I got a lot of work done."

I suppressed a shudder as she gestured toward the pile of puppets on the back table. There was one blue thing with yellow eyes that looked like it wanted to eat my soul.

"Sorry about that jerk," Tess said as she straightened the brochures on the counter.

"It's fine. I just need my nightly walk to decompress."

"Do I need to remind you again that there's a killer out there somewhere, and I think it's a really bad idea to go for your walk?"

I opened my mouth to argue, but she waved me off.

"I know, I know. You're going to go anyway."

"I love you for worrying about me," I said, and turned my head sideways to give her a silly grin.

"And I'd like to smack you for making me worry." She playfully shoved me with the toe of her boot, which Toby took as an invitation to attack said boot.

It took us longer than usual to straighten up and close down since we both had to navigate the little ankle biter, who seemed to be everywhere at once. After Tess loaded her creepy puppets and said her goodnights to both Toby and me, I went to check on Nan. She was curled up on the sofa, covered with one of the quilts she'd made herself. Ronald had pulled Nan's recliner over next to the sofa, and his hand rested on her arm while she slept. I tried to back silently out of the room, but Ronald stirred enough to register that I was there.

"Hey, kiddo," he whispered.

"Sorry," I whispered back. Toby's little tail thumped against my rib cage. I'd initially bristled against the pet name, but now I ignored it. He had given me no reason to resent him, other than not being my PawPaw. "I didn't mean to wake you up."

"It's okay. She's pretty conked out on those pain pills, but I think she's doing all right."

"Thank you for being here," I said, and tried to smile warmly.

"I wouldn't be anywhere else."

Unlike my attempt, his smile was beaming with warmth, making his cheeks round out and giving the impression that he was an off-season Santa all over again.

"Your grandmother is pretty special, you know?"

"I know." I looked over at her. She was faintly snoring, and her face was so slack it was forming a sort of puddle on the throw pillow, a fact that would horrify her if she knew it.

"Your brother went to bed earlier," Ron whispered in that low growl of his. "He's a good kid."

"You mean aside from running away from home?" I frowned.

"He's sixteen. His brain ain't finished cookin' yet. Lord knows I made some pretty stupid decisions at that age. Sounds like he felt cornered and couldn't find any other way out."

"Did he talk to you about it?"

"Yeah, some. That dad of his sounds like a real gem."

I snorted. Everyone could see Jared for the jerk he was except dear old Mom.

"I'm going to walk the puppy and clear my head. It's been a long day," I said, holding Toby up a little higher to illustrate my point.

"No problem. Just be careful out there."

I nodded and headed back out into the night.

Halfway back to the cemetery, I couldn't shake the feeling I was being watched. I kept checking behind me that there was no one following me. There weren't a lot of places for anyone to hide, even if they were following me. Of course, I hadn't noticed Adam following me either, so for all I knew, there could be ten stalkers lurking in the shadows around me. In an attempt to keep my wits about me, I chalked it up to my stupid nerves, which had been on edge ever since I'd found Adam's body.

I knew Adam would be waiting for me, so I took a detour to circle around his haunt. I wanted to talk with him, but I wanted to visit with Mamie first. I found her watching a family through their living room window. She'd never voiced it, but I wondered if she'd wanted that kind of life for herself at one time. I called her over to the sidewalk, and she immediately went to Toby.

"He is cute as a button!" she said as Toby tried to figure out why he couldn't lick her face.

I told her about how I came to be taking care of the little mutt, and once I'd assured her that Nan was mostly okay, she returned to cooing over him.

I heard something rustle in the leaves behind me and jumped like I'd been shot.

"Are you all right?" Mamie floated up to eye level.

"Yeah, I'm just super jumpy lately."

She cocked her diaphanous head sideways and studied me. It was a little unnerving, especially because when she is really still, she fades in and out of focus, and her eyes are a light honey brown. I don't know if that was their color before she died, but the glow of her pale eyes is very unnerving, a fact she would love.

"You are not usually unnerved," she said. "No matter how hard I try." She added a playful wink.

"I just feel . . ." I tried to figure out exactly how I felt, why I was suddenly jumping at every shadow. "I don't know. Everyone keeps reminding me that there's a killer on the loose, and I think I've let it get to me."

"But there is always a killer on the loose," Mamie said, shrugging her transparent shoulders.

"Gee, thanks for the pep talk."

"My apologies." She smirked. "I'll check around and make sure there is no one lurking at the moment, so we can relax and look at the discussions."

"I'm sure it's fine."

"You will feel better if I make sure it is safe."

"Be careful."

She turned and I was momentarily fascinated with the fact that her ghostly skirt twirled like fog around her.

"Lou," she said, her features giving the impression that she was deeply concerned, "I'm already dead. Why would I need to be careful?"

"Okay, valid point. I just mean I care about you."

"I care about you too, my friend."

And with her parting words she dissolved into a fine mist that dissipated into the night.

I was just pulling up the latest round of comments on the video of Mamie's orb when she materialized again beside me.

"Nothing appears to be amiss," she said quietly, still looking at me like she was concerned about my mental health.

I ignored it and waved her over to go through the comments.

By the time Toby started to whine, we had scrolled through hundreds of comments. If ghosts are capable of beaming with pride, Mamie was doing it.

"I'm so sorry to run, but I still need to go talk to Adam, and this little guy is getting tired."

"Lou, be careful. Even though I found nothing to cause alarm tonight, that does not mean you should ignore your intuition."

I laughed nervously. "I'm not sure I have any intuition."

"You see ghosts. You have more ability than most."

Chapter Eighteen

I finally found Adam lurking near Commander's Palace restaurant. It had been closed for hours, and the pedestrian traffic was isolated to a few late-night dog walkers and one jogger that I met heading toward Prytania. When Adam noticed me, he rushed toward me in a blur. What was odd was that it disturbed the leaves on the sidewalk. I hadn't known a ghost who could manipulate the physical world. Sure, Mamie could produce orbs, but a constant source of frustration for her is the fact that she cannot influence anything beyond them. Of course, we've all heard stories about physical manifestations, cupboards being opened, doors being slammed. I'd just never experienced it myself.

The lingering scents of seafood and po' boys made my stomach growl. The off-brand prepackaged breakfast bars I'd scarfed down before my tour had long ago run out of steam.

"You can't leave me alone that long," Adam said as he stopped in front of me.

"Adam," I said, my heart breaking for him, "I can't be here all the time. I'm so sorry. I can't imagine the isolation—"

"No! You can't!" he roared.

Toby flinched and I picked him up as I turned to walk away.

"I'm sorry! I'm sorry. I won't do it again. I can't control anything!" Adam was kind of flickered in and out of my sight. "I'm trying, I really am."

He looked truly desperate.

"I wasn't kidding when I said I won't tolerate that kind of behavior," I said quietly but firmly.

"I know! I just can't seem to keep myself . . . level. It's like everything is amplified, anger, sadness, loneliness—it's all just more . . . intense."

"I'm sorry you're lonely, Adam. I truly am." I don't know if it was exhaustion or stress, but tears began to well in my eyes. "But I can't be responsible for your happiness. I didn't ask for this either."

"I know," he said miserably.

I sniffled, fighting back the tears that burned my eyes.

"I want to help you, or I wouldn't be here. I don't want you to be isolated either. Let's just take it one step at a time," I said as I put the squirming puppy back down. He immediately started chasing leaves as far as the leash would allow.

"I talked to Damian, and he was . . . less than helpful."

"He can be kind of blunt, but he's a good guy."

I nodded, trying to figure out the most diplomatic way to tell him that his business partner was a jerk.

"Was he able to help at all?" Adam asked as my silence dragged on.

"No, not really." I shrugged. "But, in his defense, I may have suggested that he killed you."

"Why would you do that? He didn't kill me!"

"You don't know who killed you," I countered. "How well do you know him?"

"I know him well enough to know he didn't do it."

"I caught him outside the Barlowe, and he had insurance documents. I couldn't tell what they said, but I did see your name on them."

"Yeah, I was insured. So is he. We didn't want the business to fail if something happened to one of us. We worked too hard for that."

I nodded again. It made sense.

"He kind of accused me of killing you too," I said sheepishly.

"Oh good lord."

I couldn't be certain in the dim lighting, but I'm pretty sure he rolled his eyes.

"There's no delicate way to ask this, so I'll just come right out and say it." I bent down to pet Toby since he'd started whining again. I really had to get home and let the poor baby go to bed. "Was there any trouble in your marriage?"

"No," he said coldly. "We're not doing this."

"Adam, if you want me to help, I need to look at every possible suspect."

"Damian and Mia aren't possible suspects, end of story."

"Did you ever watch any true crime shows? Listen to any podcasts? Ever catch an episode of *Dateline*? The murderer is usually someone the victim knows—more often than not."

"I don't care. There's no way that either of them had anything to do with this."

The angrier he became, the less he kept his human shape. What little form he had flickered and danced like flames.

"I need you to look at this logically. If they're not involved, we can rule them out and move on," I said with more confidence than I felt. The more I tried to convince Adam to let me look into his wife and business partner, the more I realized I was completely in over my head. I had no idea how to conduct an investigation, save for what I'd learned from my addiction to true crime stories, and no authority to make anyone talk to me. I'd already botched talking to Damian, so even if he was the killer, I had no way to prove it.

"You know," Adam said quietly, barely more than a whisper as his appearance became more stable again, "I had this stupid idea that when you die, you move on and gain some sort of great cosmic wisdom. What a joke."

"Most do move on. Ghosts are pretty rare in the grand scheme of things," I said, and then instantly regretted it when he looked like I'd punched him in the gut. "I just mean that—"

"You just mean I have the worst luck possible."

"No, that's not at all what I meant."

"Well, it's true. I'm dead—well, sort of. I'm still here with all the issues and problems I've always had, but without the ability to *do* anything about any of it. No one but you and dogs can see me, and maybe that one kid earlier today. No one can hear me. Yeah, I'd say my luck is about as bad as it gets."

My earlier doubts about my ability to investigate his murder crept back into my thoughts, but I pushed them down. I couldn't help him move on; at least I'd never figured out how to help any of them move on, but I could sure do everything in my power to help him with this. And helping him would be helping myself too, since I seemed to be the only one the police were looking at seriously.

"Humor me," I said, sitting on the curb. "Tell me about your wife. Mia? Is that right?"

"That's right."

He joined me on the curb, but the skepticism was clear on the parts of his face that were in focus. Toby toddled up between us and barked playfully at Adam. Clearly, he wasn't holding a grudge about Adam's outburst. Unable to pet him, Adam settled for moving the leaves for him to chase again. I wanted to learn more about this ability, but I didn't want to derail the progress I'd made in getting him to open up about his family and friends. That discussion would have to wait for another time.

"Look," Adam said without looking at me, "I didn't want to talk about Mia because you will immediately think she's guilty."

He turned to face me as Toby became fascinated with the fact that he could run through Adam's form and cause him to swirl like smoke with the disturbance.

"Okay . . ." I said while trying to will myself to remain objective.

"I need you to know that we had already worked through it. We were back in a good place."

My mind raced with possibilities, and no matter how hard I tried not to speculate, my imagination was in overdrive.

"Mia cheated on me." Adam looked away again. "We just drifted apart. I'd spent all of my free time building the business, and we lost sight of each other for a while. She found comfort with someone else. But then she decided our marriage was what she wanted after all. She confessed and I forgave her." He slumped as though the weight of the situation still caused him to hardly be able to bear it. "I have had a more difficult time forgiving myself."

I had no idea how to respond to any of it. I opened my mouth twice to say something, but nothing seemed appropriate in the face of such a raw, honest admission.

"Adam, I'm so—"

"No, don't do that." He stiffened. "I don't want sympathy. I just wanted you to understand that we reconnected, and she wouldn't have wanted to hurt me, because she *chose* me. She didn't have to, but she did."

"Do you know who it was? Do you know who she . . . found comfort with?" I tried not to think about the possibilities . . . Damian, for instance.

"His name is Jace Klein."

"Is he someone you both know?"

"No. He works for a landscaping business. She met him when he was working on the neighbor's backyard."

"Do you think he would want you out of the way?"

"No." He stared off into the distance again. "Maybe. I don't know. Mia said it was just casual between them, but I think I saw him watching the house a couple of times."

Now, *that* was interesting.

"I don't think it was like that, though. I never got the impression he wanted anything serious from her. He's a playboy, and I think that's just the way he likes it."

"But you don't know that for sure, right?"

He glared at me.

"How long ago did she break it off?"

"A few months ago."

"Would you recognize him if I pulled him up on Facebook?"

"Yeah."

It was ridiculous how many men are named "Jace Klein." After we scrolled for several minutes, Adam identified a very tan, very buff man in his mid-twenties, with a short mullet. He posed shirtless in his profile photo, axe in hand, one leg propped up on a stump. Somehow, even with the prominent six-pack and flannel tossed over a pile of chopped wood, the lumberjack vibe didn't quite hit the mark. His face was too clean, too pretty to pull it off completely, at least in my opinion. I looked through his page, which appeared to be set to public.

I scrolled through too many selfies to count, check-ins all over New Orleans, and numerous photos of the various fish he'd caught. Most of the people in his friends list were women, and most of the comments were from women as well. His whole page was set up as a thirst trap. I didn't find any connection to family or anything more personal than the fishing posts. Maybe he had a second profile for personal stuff, or maybe he was just that superficial.

"You *think* you saw him watching your house, or you *know* you did?" I asked as I tired of scrolling through more shirtless selfies.

"It was definitely him the second time." Adam nodded as he said it. "I'm pretty sure it was him the first time, but I can't be certain about it."

"How long ago was it?"

"Two days before I got a knife in the back."

Chapter Nineteen

I left Adam with a renewed sense of focus. His wife's lover was as good a place as any to start, especially since I'd messed up so badly with Damian already. Toby was as exhausted as I was by the time we got home. Nan was still asleep on the sofa, Ronald snoring softly in the recliner next to her. I managed to sneak past them on my way to my room, but Kenneth met me at the top of the stairs.

"Do we like that man?" he said, gesturing vaguely toward the living room where Nan and Ronald were sleeping.

"I don't really know him very well yet," I said while Toby tried to put his little paws up on Kenneth's legs. "But he seems nice enough."

"Hmm."

"Why?" I asked, suddenly suspicious.

"No particular reason."

Kenneth didn't always bother to make himself completely visible, and tonight he was a vaguely human-shaped swirl of mist. It was hard to read the mist's expression, but I got the impression he was deep in thought.

"There must be something." I continued down the hall to my room, Toby toddling along next to me. "You've never said a word about any of the others."

"None of the others ever stayed the night."

"True. But this isn't a social visit. He's keeping an eye on her."

"I can keep an eye on her," he said in a low growl.

I stopped in my tracks and turned to stare at what parts of him I could see. "Are you jealous?"

"Of course I'm jealous!" he hissed, like it should be obvious. "It's just been the three of us for a long time. I'm not ready for anyone to replace Otis just yet."

I'd had much the same feeling about my Pawpaw but definitely hadn't explained it that succinctly, even to myself.

"I know," I said. I opened the door to my room, and Toby made a beeline for his little doggy bed and started circling. After a few rotations, he settled in with a groan. "But we both want Nan to be happy, and let's face it, she's not getting any younger."

"That's not funny."

"I didn't mean it to be funny. It's just a fact. I understand how you feel, and I've been arguing with myself about it all day. But Ronald seems very nice, and he seems to care for her very much. She deserves to be happy."

Kenneth made a noncommittal sound.

I was just about to tell him I was exhausted and ask him if he would make sure Toby didn't wake up and eat my entire room while I showered, when he pulled himself into a more corporeal form and floated through the doorway.

"What's going on with you? You're out later than usual tonight."

I gave him a quick rundown of the latest developments. When I finished, he looked worried.

"Are you sure you should get involved? Someone *killed* him. They could come after you if you get too close to the truth."

"To be honest, no. I'm not sure. But I'm also the one the police are looking at, so I *have* to get involved if I want to stay out of jail."

"Do you think that Lothario fellow did it? Seems he would just move on to the next one if Mr. Brandt's wife became too complicated. Those types don't stick around for *complicated*."

I smiled at his usage of the outdated word. He usually made an effort to keep his vocabulary updated, even using the word *yeet* recently, but every once in a while, old habits snuck back in.

"I thought that initially too, but Adam said he caught him watching the house a few times. Maybe he became obsessed with her. It happens."

"Do you think the widow would talk to you about it?"

"I don't know. I haven't figured out a way to approach her yet."

"Are there any dead in the area?"

"What?" My exhausted brain came to a screeching halt.

"Are there any dead nearby that you could speak to first? If they can corroborate Mr. Brandt's account, then there might not be a need to speak to his widow. You have the ability: use it."

"That's actually a great idea."

"I'm full of great ideas."

I resisted the urge to tell him he was full of *something*, opting instead to suppress my juvenile urges to give him a hard time every chance I got. I managed to talk him into watching Toby for me while I took a quick shower. And as I ushered him out of my room so I could sleep, I talked him into keeping an eye on Bryce for me as well.

* * *

I'd honestly expected Toby to wake me before my alarm went off, but I knew he'd given up on me the minute I yawned and took a deep breath. He was pawing at the edge of the bed and whining for me to pick him up, when I looked over the room and saw the extent of his multiple accidents. I pulled him into the bed with me, fended off his many attempts to lick the entirety of my face, and enjoyed some cuddles, and the occasional needle-toothed attack until I could no longer ignore the unbearable stench.

After cleaning and deodorizing my room, I hovered outside the guest bedroom, only to be met by Kenneth's head poking out the door.

"He's still asleep. If he repeats his schedule from yesterday, he won't get up until closer to noon."

I thanked him. He rolled his eyes and disappeared back through the door. I knew he didn't approve of letting my brother sleep that late, but Bryce would have to get back into a routine soon enough. I was going to let him sleep in while he could. I crept down the stairs to check on Nan. I heard voices in the kitchen as I neared the bottom. I found Nan perched on a stool at the counter, and Ronald sporting her floral apron at the stove.

"Good morning, Sleeping Beauty," Nan said brightly.

"Sorry—I was up late."

"How about pancakes?" Ronald plated the ones he'd been flipping on the stovetop.

"That sounds amazing." I was pleasantly surprised by how comfortable it felt to find them, smiling and happy, when I got up. "How are you feeling today?" I looked back at Nan.

"Oh, it aches a little." She made a dismissive gesture. "But a good night's sleep helped a lot." She bent down and scratched Toby's little head with the hand not in a cast. "How is this little fella? I'm sorry I stuck you with him."

"We're getting along pretty well." I omitted the morning's incidents. That really hadn't been Toby's fault. "I'm going to take him out for a minute, and then I'll be right in to help."

"Not necessary." Ronald beamed as he plated more pancakes. "I've got it all under control. You just bring your appetite. Should we wake Bryce?"

"I'll let him sleep a little longer."

Toby circled the yard for what felt like hundreds of times, but was really probably closer to ten, before he found the perfect spots for his little number one and number two. After I'd settled him in the kitchen with his breakfast, and plowed through a stack of the fluffiest, tastiest pancakes I'd ever put in my mouth, I headed out to see if there were any ghosts in the area around Adam's house.

Ronald insisted that they keep Toby while I ran errands. Apparently, he had cleared his schedule all week to help Nan around the house. When I left, Nan was playing tug-of-war with Toby on the sofa, with an old piece of rope. I'd only had the little monster for a few days, and I already missed him.

I pulled up to the curb outside the house at the address Adam gave me. I don't know what I'd expected, but the modern tiny house with its huge front windows and harsh angles wasn't it. From the sidewalk, it looked like there were maybe four or five hundred square feet. There were no signs that anyone was home. No lights on inside. No car in the driveway.

I got out of my car and scanned the area. The few pedestrians all appeared to be alive. They were wearing contemporary clothing and appeared to have solid form, neither of which is a guarantee that someone isn't a ghost, but the chances are less. I started strolling down the sidewalk, trying to will myself to look inconspicuous. It was a nice neighborhood. It was quite a commute to his business, though. It made me thankful that my shop was essentially in our yard.

I'd wandered to the end of the next block before I finally gave up and started back in the other direction. I was momentarily distracted by a small house that sat back from the sidewalk. At first glance, it wasn't remarkable. The yard was fenced in chain link, and the house was a nondescript white ranch style. I stopped and realized what had unconsciously caught my attention. An elderly woman was watching me from what appeared to be the living room window. I thought she might be a ghost, so I waved to signal that I could see her. If she *was* a ghost, then she was not impressed by my ability because she flipped me off and pulled the curtains closed. I chuckled to myself as I walked away. I probably wouldn't have reacted quite *that* way, but I'm sure I wouldn't appreciate some rando staring at my house either.

I scanned the area again, and deciding that I was wasting my time, I headed for my car. I'd only taken a few steps down the sidewalk when someone sprang out from behind a huge oak tree and yelled, "Gotcha!"

I screamed some guttural, animal-like noise and jumped into the street. Thankfully, there was no traffic, or I would have been toast. I collected myself to see an elderly man nearly doubled over in laughter. His white hair was cropped short, and his small, dark eyes shone behind dark-rimmed glasses. He was much shorter and rounder than me and was laughing so hard he wheezed.

"That wasn't nearly as funny for me," I said as I joined him on the sidewalk.

He immediately stopped laughing and looked at me like he was the one seeing ghosts.

"What?" he said with a little cough. His well-lined face pulled into a worried grimace.

"It's okay," I said, trying to reassure him I wasn't going to call the cops or anything. "You just scared the thunder out of me, that's all."

"You can see me?"

"Oh my gosh!" I clapped my hands together, and it was his turn to jump, causing him to fade out of sight for a second with the sudden movement.. "I can. I'm sorry, I hadn't realized you were a ghost. I was about to give up, when you jumped out and scared me."

"Give up?" He still looked slightly horrified.

"I was looking for someone like you," I said delicately. I'd inadvertently offended some spirits by calling them such, and I hoped my use of the word earlier hadn't already done any damage. "I'm trying to find out some information about something that happened here recently, and you're more likely to have seen something."

He looked around like he might bolt.

"I'm sorry. I'm sure this is a shock since most people can't see you." I tried to be as nonthreatening as possible. I'd encountered ghosts who want nothing to do with the living, and I hoped he wasn't one of them.

"Yeah." He chuckled nervously. "I was just having a bit of good-natured fun. I would never hurt anyone. It's just fun sometimes to give people a little jolt, but now that I say it out loud, it sounds a bit silly."

"I'm not mad, especially now that my heart rate has returned to normal."

"There's no reason to banish me." He put his hands up in surrender.

"What? No. I won't do that." I shook my head. I wasn't even sure I *could* do that. "Why are you afraid I want to banish you?"

"Just happens sometimes when the living find out."

"I have no intention of banishing you. I just wanted to ask you a few questions, if it's okay."

He looked up and down the street—I assumed, it was to make sure I was alone.

"Yeah, okay," he said, though he still seemed plenty nervous about it. "What kind of questions?"

"I'm Lou Thatcher. It's very nice to meet you." I wanted to jump right into my questions, but I didn't want to be rude.

"Albert Fortier," he said, still eyeing me skeptically.

"You see that tiny house over there?" I pointed to Adam's house. I decided to skip the small talk. I wanted to get to it before I scared him off.

"I have not haunted that house!"

"That's not what this is about," I said as he moved farther away from me. "I promise, this isn't about you at all. The man who lived there, Adam, was murdered. I'm trying to find out who's responsible, and I was hoping you might know if someone had been watching their house recently. A young man. I have a picture, if you wouldn't mind looking at it," I said everything as fast as I could because I got the impression he was about to disappear on me.

He looked from me to the house and back again.

"I promise, this isn't about haunting."

He seemed to consider it for a few more moments before saying, "I know who you're talking about. He was out here a lot, lurking around."

"When was the last time you saw him?"

"I don't know exactly. I don't have a great sense of time."

"I want to hear everything you know about him," I said, taking a seat on the curb. I pulled out my phone to take notes.

Chapter Twenty

My mind was still racing when I pulled into the driveway. Nan sat in the porch swing, bundled up in a quilt with Ronald, while Bryce played with Toby in the yard. I wanted to get all my thoughts out on paper, organize my notes, and figure out what to do next.

"You ready for me to take over again?" I asked as I got out of the car.

"I doubt you can talk Bryce into giving him up right now. They're like two peas in a pod."

I looked wistfully at Toby, who at that moment decided to bark his shrill little puppy yap and lunge at Bryce's ankles. Toby finally noticed my approach and came over to attack my shoelaces. When he couldn't dislodge them right away, he gave up, bounded up the steps, and began his assault on Ron.

"I'm going to make a grocery run later." Ronald ignored the fact that Toby was pulling at his pant leg. "I can bring him to the shop when I leave."

"Okay, that'll be great."

"You doing okay?" I asked Bryce, who'd joined us on the porch.

"Yeah. Mom has called about a hundred times." He looked at his feet while he spoke.

"Have you talked to her?"

He nodded. "She's really mad. And Dad won't speak to me."

"I'm so sorry."

He shrugged it off, but I knew he was upset. How could he not be? His whole world had been turned upside down because the people who were supposed to keep him safe blamed him for not being able to deal with his bullies on his own. Mom might be mad, but I was too. And if she wanted a war, I would give it to her as long as it meant Bryce would have a chance to be happy.

"I'm going to go make a list of the things we need," Ron said, and then leaned over and kissed Nan on the forehead. Bryce grinned and I tried to look anywhere but at the two of them.

After Ron got up, I took a place beside Nan on the porch, folding my legs underneath me. She reached over and stroked my hair like she'd done when I was a kid, and I leaned into her hand.

"How are you feeling?" I asked quietly, lulled by her comforting touch.

Toby gave up trying to get me and Nan to play with him and went back to attacking Bryce's shoes. Bryce sat on the porch steps and they played tug-of-war with the sleeve of his hoodie.

"I'm doing all right, Lulu Belle."

"Are you sure? You don't have to play tough for me."

She laughed her soft, melodic laugh. "I'm not playing. I'm achy and sore, but I'll be fine. It'll take more than a cracked bone to keep me down."

"I know how strong you are, but you don't have to be. I'm happy to take care of you for a change."

"I'm fine. Go do what you need to do." She patted me gently on the head and then drew her arm back under her quilt. "I have Bryce and Ron if I need anything."

126

I pulled myself to my feet and then bent down to kiss her fore-head. I glanced back a couple of times as I crossed the yard on my way to the shop. Bryce and Toby both seemed to be having a great time, and Nan looked amused watching them. It didn't take me long to run through the reservations and emails, so I went back to cyber-stalking Jace Klein. I'd already seen enough of his Facebook and Instagram pages to know that I wouldn't find anything useful there. His Twitter—now X—account was just reposts and a few off comments on some online gaming discussions.

I swiped over to TikTok and searched for him there. Jackpot. He posted there a *lot*. Daily. Sometimes, multiple times a day. And his most recent video, dated yesterday, was from his new jobsite at Coliseum Square Park. I glanced at the clock in the upper left corner of my phone. Since he was working so close, I had plenty of time to pay Jace a visit.

* * *

I wasn't expecting to miss the little monster as much as I did, so the jolt of happiness I felt as Ronald passed an exhausted Toby off to me on the way to my car caught me off guard. Having a puppy with me would give me a great excuse to walk in the park where Jace was work-ing. He curled up and went to sleep in the back seat almost as soon as I put him down. He was so freaking cute I could hardly stand it. One of his little floppy ears covered his eye, and the other one stretched out beside him on the seat. I felt a pang of guilt that I hadn't gotten him a doggy car seat yet and vowed to remedy that today.

I pulled into a parking spot near Coliseum Square Park and debated doing some of my drive-through errands so Toby could sleep, but he popped up as soon as the car came to a stop. Puppies: recharged after only a few minutes of sleep. I gently wrestled him into his harness and clipped on the leash. Smart little guy had already figured out that the harness meant he would get to go exploring, and his tail was wagging a mile a minute. I kissed his round little head before I put him down on the sidewalk.

I couldn't wait to show Toby the fountain in the center of the park. It was a little too chilly for him to play in it, but I could imagine him splashing around in the sweltering summer months. As it turned out, Jace Klein's company was working on the fountain and a stretch of the path near it. The rim at the edge of the fountain had been cracked and crumbling for some time, and I'm sure the pathway had similar issues.

It took me several minutes to spot Jace amid the workers. Once I picked him out, I started casually making my way toward him. I mentally cataloged the things I wanted to ask, and told myself that I wouldn't screw it up this time. Toby found a myriad of interesting scents and examined them all with great gusto—and the attention span of a goldfish. He trotted along, his little hound dog feet flopping with every step. We finally made our way to the orange net barrier, and I positioned myself near Jace Klein. After a few moments, he noticed me watching him.

"Good morning," I said with a chin lift when I was sure he was looking at me.

"Do I know you?" he asked with a crooked grin, and leaned on the handle of his shovel. I could definitely see what women saw in him. His piercing blue eyes twinkled with mischief, and every inch of him rippled in muscle. I'm not sure I've ever seen anyone as absolutely *buff* in real life as Jace Klein. He looked like the cover model from a bodice ripper.

"No, not exactly." A nervous laugh escaped despite my intense effort to keep my cool. "I was hoping to ask you a few questions."

The smile fell from his face like it had never been there. Jace dropped the shovel and took off at a speed that would make Olympic sprinters jealous.

Chapter Twenty-One

I watched Jace disappear down the street, and stood there cursing myself for messing up yet again. One of the other workers glanced up in the general direction Jace had gone, but otherwise, no one paid any attention. It made me wonder how often he bolted away from a jobsite. I waited around for a few minutes to see if he'd come back, and when he didn't, I wandered back to my car.

Since my interview—and I use that word loosely—with Jace took a lot less time than I'd planned, I had plenty of time to run errands. I started at the pet store, to get a doggy car seat, opting for a model that was too big for Toby currently but should fit him as he grew. He only jumped out of it twice on the way to the bank, then three more times on the way to the post office, before finally curling up and falling asleep just in time to get back to the shop. He woke up the minute I turned the car off. As I carried him out into the yard to do his business, my phone dinged with a text message.

I pulled it out of my pocket and expected Cady or Tess, but I was faced with an unknown number instead. The message made my breath catch in my chest.

If u keep sticking ur nose where it doesn't belong ur going 2 regret it just like adam did.

My first thought was *How did Jace get my number?* My hands shook as I typed back.

Who is this?

The message was green on my iPhone, meaning the person on the other end either wasn't using an iPhone or didn't have iMessage enabled, so there were no little dots showing me someone was typing back. I didn't have to wait long for a reply, though.

Just a concerned citizen. U need to back off.

I took a deep breath to steady my nerves. I couldn't stop myself from looking around to see if I could spot Jace Klein watching me from the shadows somewhere. Toby whined at the end of his leash, snapping me back to reality. I picked him up and carried him into the shop since he still hadn't gotten the hang of being leash broken just yet. He trotted over to his bed, circled several times, and then curled up again. Poor little guy was all tuckered out.

"Oh hey," Nan said as she came out of the back room. I forced myself to sound normal and not like I'd just received threatening messages.

"What are you doing here?"

"I'm happy to see you too." She smirked.

"Sorry, I just meant why aren't you resting?" It was going to be harder to report this to Dylan with her here, and I debated whether or not to tell her. I didn't want to upset her, but I considered the fact that it might be a good idea for both of us to be worried.

"My wrist is barely broken. The doctor used the word *crack*. I'm not going to just sit around."

"Where's Ronald?" I'd felt better knowing Nan wouldn't be alone. "And Bryce?"

"He's still grocery shopping. I'm a little afraid he's buying out the store. Bryce is holed up in his room. Apparently, he'd made arrangements with his school counselor, and they're letting him complete most of his work online so he doesn't get too far behind."

I was impressed by his initiative. I'd considered the fact that he might get behind, but I hadn't done anything about it. I wondered if Mom or Jared had any clue what a good kid he was. Probably not. Jared couldn't comprehend anything outside his own orbit. And Mom—well, she never did seem to care much about anyone but Jared.

"Have you been cleaning?" I looked around the shop, and everything was spotless. The T-shirts were all folded perfectly, and not a single trinket was out of place.

"I fussed around a little." She shrugged. "A couple wandered up into the yard when they found the door locked. They wanted to make a reservation, so I let them in, sold them some souvenirs, and gave them a brochure."

"Wow. Good job." I rounded the counter and gave her a big hug.

"I think I'd like to do this more often," she said as she snuggled into my embrace.

"Work here?"

"No, break my arm." She rolled her eyes. "Yes, work here."

"I'd love to have you here more often, but I can barely afford Tess. Reservations are up, though, so maybe—"

"Lulu Belle," she said, cutting me off. "You would *not* pay me. I just want something to do, and I really enjoyed talking with that couple about your business. I don't know why it never occurred to me before."

"I don't know what to say." I smiled at her. Having her here would make things so much easier since Tess was only able to commit to part-time hours, and sometimes even fewer, depending on her theater schedule. When she couldn't staff the storefront, it meant I had to lock up when I was out giving tours. Even though I always

131

put up the sign about how to book online and when I would return, I'm sure I lost business, especially on in-store sales.

"Nothing to say. I'll come to work here, and you'll promise that if I get in the way too much, you'll send me packing. I want to help, make things easier, not complicate matters."

"You're hired!" I hugged her again.

"Perfect! I think I figured out how to use that"—she indicated my point-of-sale iPad—"but you better check and make sure."

It didn't take long for Nan to pick up on all my processes and programs. I was just finishing up showing her the inventory when someone burst through the front door, sending it banging against the wall with an angry crash. It was a miracle it didn't break the glass. Nan and I both jumped. I only relaxed a little when I realized it was Dylan. But I tensed again when I noticed the fuming expression on his face.

"What the hell were you thinking?" he boomed as he crossed the distance between us in a few long strides.

"I'll thank you to adopt a more respectful tone, *Mr. Finch*," Nan said between gritted teeth. I noticed that she didn't bother with his official title.

"Forgive me, Mrs. Thatcher, but it would seem Lou has done something really stupid." He tipped his head to Nan and then glared at me.

"What are you talking about?" My voice was certainly stupid. My words came out in a squeak.

"Did you tell Jace Klein that you were a *police officer*?"

"What? No!"

"But you did show up at his worksite and question him?"

"No! I mean, I was there, but—"

"He came to the station with his attorney, Lou. He thinks that because he was having an affair with Mia Brandt, we consider him a suspect. He thought you were the police, which is quite frankly, a little insulting."

I ignored the barb. "I never said I was—"

"They're threatening to sue us for harassment."

"Well, since it *wasn't* the police, you should be fine," I countered.

"That's not the point!" he roared.

"Dylan Finch! You *will* use your inside voice, young man," Nan said in that distinctly Southern way that does not invite discussion.

He closed his eyes for a moment and took a deep breath.

"I apologize. I just want to effectively convey how important it is for Lou to stay out of this investigation."

"Well, I would if you were considering suspects other than me."

"None of this is personal, Lou. We are following the evidence, that's all."

"It *is* personal! I just got this," I opened my phone and shoved the threatening text in his smug, aggravating face.

To his credit, he did read it. But he didn't look the least bit concerned.

"This is just another really good reason why you need to stop playing detective."

"So threatening *me* doesn't mean anything to you?"

"If you feel like it's a legitimate threat, then you need to come by the station and file a report."

"A *legitimate* threat? Do you think I sent this to *myself*?" My face was getting hot with anger, and I'm sure my skin was blazing red, another perk of having such a pale complexion.

"Just come by and file a report," he said with a grimace, and then turned to Nan, "Good day, Mrs. Thatcher. I hope to see you under more pleasant circumstances soon."

She gave him a tight-lipped nod. I opened my mouth to say everything that was on my mind, but Nan put her hand on my shoulder to signal me to keep my mouth shut, which I did. Grudg-ingly. I watched Dylan leave. He didn't look back.

"You didn't tell me any of this, Lou," Nan said with a frown.

"I didn't want to worry you." Guilt mixed with my anger.

"That's a crap excuse, Lou."

"You're right. I'm sorry."

"Okay, apology accepted. Now, tell me everything."

She pulled the desk chair over to the counter and patted the stool seat next to her. I swallowed, even though my mouth felt dry. I wished with all my heart that I could tell her the whole truth.

Cady breezed into the shop just as I was finishing up my run-down of the last few days with Nan. Nan greeted her with the same warmth she would for a member of the family, which Cady practi-cally was. I was thankful for the distraction, because Nan was less than thrilled with me for keeping so much from her and, like Dylan, for sticking my nose "where it doesn't belong."

After some quizzing about what happened and how Nan was feeling, Cady dug around in her bag and produced a thermos of dark roast from Café Nate and her amazing homemade scones.

"I talked to Aunt Sugar," she said after popping a bite of blue-berry scone in her mouth. "She said she knows Damian Boyle's sis-ter, Margaret. Apparently, he has a habit of blowing every spare penny in various casinos, but his favorite is the Diamond Deck. He's borrowed money from Margaret off and on over the years, but his spending has been extra reckless lately, and she cut him off recently."

"You've dragged Cady Anne into this?" Nan frowned at me again.

Cady, looking panicked, choked a little on her scone. "I don't know about 'dragged.' I volunteered."

Nan turned the scowl on Cady, and she visibly shrank in her seat.

"I can't just sit around and let them pin this on me," I said quietly, not meeting Nan's eyes. "Not only that, but I can't let myself even be named as a suspect. Mom would have a field day with even an accusation if things get ugly with Bryce."

I was also mentally cataloging the information that Damian Boyle had a great reason to murder his business partner, especially if he was named in the insurance policy and he no longer had to share business profits.

Chapter Twenty-Two

I almost wished Adam had been murdered closer to the shop, because traipsing down to the cemetery every time I needed to talk to him was getting old. And then, of course, I felt guilty for even thinking that. To my surprise, I found a convenient parking space with no trouble at all. I was just getting ready to get out when Adam appeared in the passenger seat.

"Makes more sense to talk in here, doesn't it?" he said. "That way you won't have to pretend you're on the phone or something."

"That's actually a great idea."

"What's going on?" he asked, and I thought I detected concern in his tone.

"I've told you this, but I feel like I need to say it again. This isn't going to work if you're not honest with me."

"What now? What do you think I've lied about?" The concern was replaced by a hint of annoyance in his voice.

"I've found out that your business partner had a gambling problem, and he recently lost his financial safety net." My own annoyance was building. "How much *exactly* does he stand to inherit?"

He stared off into the distance for a moment.

"We still owe on the storefront. We are just starting to turn a good profit, but we also just bought two new tour vans and some new equipment. The insurance policy will keep the collectors away and set him up with a relatively clean slate, but he's not going to be rich. I can assure you of that. And I doubt there would be any money left over to pay any debts."

I frowned. Maybe it really wasn't Damian. He hadn't reacted like a guilty man. He hadn't run away like he had something to hide when I tried to talk to him, like Jace had. Following that train of thought, I told Adam what had happened and how Jace had gone to the police and threatened them with harassment.

"Jace is a fussy little pretty boy." Even in spirit form, Adam managed to project the disdain he obviously felt. "But I still don't think he cared enough about Mia to kill me."

"Why would he stalk her if he didn't care?"

"That's a weird question. You know stalking isn't about love or *care*. It's about power. He probably isn't used to his conquests being the one to break things off."

"I wasn't suggesting he loved her, I was saying that he cared about the situation enough to stalk her. Regardless of his motivation, he watched your house enough that you noticed him."

"Yeah, okay." He waved dismissively at me. The motion was little more than a swirl, but it conveyed his meaning with crystal clarity. "In hindsight maybe he was a little obsessed."

"Maybe?" I scoffed. "Did he ever confront you, or was it all directed toward Mia?"

"He made some comments on our Instagram posts, but he was too much of a coward to confront me in person." He seemed to sit up a little straighter. "Which just reinforces that he was too much of a weasel to kill me."

"You seem to be more than determined to argue with me about every potential suspect. So, tell me: Who do you think killed you?"

He vanished. I waited for a few minutes, my anger bubbling up to a low boil. I had a little hissy fit and slapped the steering wheel in a moment of less than ideal adulting and started my car. Adam reappeared in the passenger seat.

"I'm done. Get out or I'll just drive to the edge of your haunt and leave you there."

"I left so I wouldn't blow up again. I'm still working on controlling myself."

Disarmed, I took a breath. "What part made you so angry?"

"I don't know who wanted me dead. But I *do* know that it wasn't Mia. And Damian might not be a candidate for Friendliest Guy of the Year, but he has no motive either. There just isn't enough money in the business policy to kill someone over, and he isn't named in my personal policy. Jace is a twit who probably just moved on to the next conquest, and I cannot, under any circumstances, imagine him putting forth the effort to kill me. And for what?"

"Is Mia named in your personal policy?"

"Well, of course she is," he sneered.

"How much?"

Adam turned away from me. For a moment I thought he might disappear again, but when he turned back, he looked utterly defeated.

"Barely enough to bury me after she pays off our personal debt. I am . . . was"—he caught himself—"in debt up to my eyeballs. We owed on everything. The business. The cars. The house. Hell, we were still paying on Mia's student loans."

"But does she *know* about your policy? Could she have told Jace about the life insurance thinking she would get a big payout? Maybe he thought it would be a payday for him too."

"She knows about my policy, the debt—all of it. She had to sign the second mortgage on our house, and she had to sign on the life insurance too." He still looked defeated, and maybe it was my imagination, but it seemed like he was physically shrinking. "Look, I know it probably seems like we didn't have a good marriage from the little bits that I've told you, but that was *one* bad patch. We came back from it stronger than ever."

I told him about the elderly ghost near his home, and how he had seen Jace multiple times stalking the house, even before Mia had allegedly broken off her affair.

He seemed to be deep in thought, so I let him ruminate on it for a bit.

"I've got to get back to the shop," I finally said.

"I'm willing to entertain the possibility that Jace might have done this," he replied quietly, ignoring what I'd actually said.

At least that was progress. If he was going to let me focus on Jace, I could question him about Mia. He might not think she was involved, but I wasn't blinded by love. I sent a quick text to Nan, to check in, and received an immediate reply telling me to take as long as I needed, that she and Toby were fine. I'd just opened my mouth to ask Adam about Mia's favorite spots and habits when Cady texted me with a reminder about family dinner night that evening.

I cursed inwardly as well as outwardly, but I couldn't figure out a way to get out of it, especially since she'd talked to her Aunt Sugar on my behalf. *That* had probably cost Cady half a day and a promise to stop by in the near future. Sugar meant well, but she frequently subjected Cady to rapid-fire questions about marriage, kids, career plans, and her current weight.

"Everything okay?" Adam gestured toward my phone.

"No. I have to have dinner with my friend Cady this evening."

"If you don't like her, why are you having dinner with her?"

"I love Cady, but her brother is the lead investigator on your case. The one who thinks I killed you."

"Oh. I can see how that might be awkward."

I glanced at the time on my phone. I had a few hours to get work done and wallow in dread before I needed to leave for Cady's parents' house.

"You need to go." It was a statement, not a question, and the sadness in his disembodied voice stabbed me right in the heart.

"I have some time."

I wished I could reach out and touch his hand, comfort him. I almost laughed at the thought. I would have never in a million years guessed that I would want to comfort Adam Brandt.

"I'm sorry to ask," I said, trying to approach the subject delicately, "but can you give me the names of Mia's friends? I'd like to see if they've noticed Jace hanging around, or if he just watched her at your house."

"She had a lot of friends, but her closest friends were Natalie Parker, Jessica Raimond, and Chasity Broussard. It felt like one of them was always at the house for some reason or another. If he was following her, they would know."

"I've got to figure out a better way to talk to people. I've screwed up both times I've tried," I sighed.

Adam turned and stared out the window for a minute, then abruptly back at me.

"How about you tell people that our rivalry was contrived? That we came up with it together for publicity on social media. I mean everyone loves a great controversy. And I just got killed before we could go public with the plan. You could tell them that we were good friends, and you want to see justice done."

"I don't know." I looked at him skeptically. "No one who knew either of us is going to believe that."

"I was a pretty private person. Damian won't believe it, but Mia's friends won't know the difference."

"What about Mia, though? She would know the difference, wouldn't she?"

He nodded. "I guess I didn't think it through very well. I don't really know. There's not much reason for you to play private investigator without telling everyone you see dead people."

"Yeah." Disgusted, I sighed again.

"You could be honest and just tell them you're trying to clear your name."

"I can't imagine Mia is going to want to help the prime suspect in her husband's murder. Same for her friends."

"She'll help you. Just tell her 'Albuquerque.'"

"Say what?"

"It was an inside joke. On our honeymoon in Cancun, we kept running into this old guy from Toledo who kept saying he'd taken a 'wrong turn at Albuquerque.' Every single time we saw him, he'd work it into conversation somehow. So, it became a running joke between us."

I was trying to figure out how that would make any difference if she'd been in on it, but getting her to talk to me might be just what I needed. If she thought I was focusing on Damian, then she might let her guard down enough for me to find out something useful. I'd watched enough true crime to know that most cases are solved by slip-ups and details that the killer overlooked.

"If she's gone back to work, try to catch her at the yoga studio. She's more likely to talk to you there than at home, where she can slam the door in your face."

"Which one?"

"Green Leaf Yoga. Her normal schedule is Mondays and then Thursday through Saturday, so she should be there tomorrow."

"Okay. Good." I nodded. It finally felt like I was organizing my efforts and not just flying by the seat of my pants.

"I have to—"

"I know," he said, cutting me off. "You have to go."

Chapter Twenty-Three

By the time Tess and I talked Nan into going to the house to rest, I was already going to be a few minutes late for Cady's family dinner night. While I was sure that my oldest, dearest friend would forgive me, I didn't want to push the issue, especially since I was supposed to be there as her emotional support human.

"When does the tour start tonight? Did I book eight o'clock or ten?" I tried to pull up my reservations quickly, entered the password wrong twice, and felt like I was going to lose my cool.

"Eight *and* ten," Tess replied.

I cursed under my breath. I'd forgot I'd started adding a later tour when I had enough interest on certain nights.

"Why don't you let me take the first tour?" Tess said with a shrug. "I know the basic spiel, and I know the route."

"You don't have to do that," I protested.

"I know that." She threw the T-shirt she was folding at me. "It wouldn't be any different than the times you have to close the shop and run the tours on your own. Plus, it'll be good practice for me. I need to be ready to go in case you're sick or something."

"I've been meaning to talk to you about that very thing," I said as I retrieved the T-shirt from the floor.

"So it's perfect then. And settled. I'll take the tour tonight."

After thanking Tess enough times to annoy her, I ran to the house. I asked Bryce if he wanted to go with me, to which he replied, "Absolutely not." Couldn't blame him, I wasn't exactly excited about it either. I hastily applied some makeup and braided my hair, deciding that the few minutes I had for minimal effort would have to be enough. I'd worked myself up into a nice little vibrating ball of anxiety by the time I pulled up to the curb in front of the Finches' house.

Rebuilt after Hurricane Katrina, the modern McMansion-style home, while being rather generic, still managed to be cozy and inviting. Cady's most recent stepmother, the one who had immediately preceded her father's current string of girlfriends, had planted flowers and shrubs across the yard and decorated the house with warm colors and homey decor. I missed Brenda, but I understood why she'd left. Mr. Charles Finch, Chuck to those who knew him, was . . . a lot. He was an overgrown man-child who worked too much, played too much, and never seemed to have any sense of adult responsibility. All of that in a package that seemed to be irresistible to women who couldn't pass up a project, especially a project that came with a decent amount of old money.

The Finches had been lucky multiple times in real estate and then used that money in a string of smart investments. I had no idea how much the Finch estate was worth, but it was enough to allow Chuck to dabble as a realtor, website designer, golf instructor, and take up numerous other pursuits over the years. I was pretty sure he was currently working on opening some sort of venue at one of the properties the family owned.

I took a deep breath and grabbed the bottle of wine I'd brought from Nan's collection. She'd warned me never to show up to dinner without a gift, and had selected a bottle of red wine from the rack. I can't tell a sauvignon from a table wine, but I trusted that Nan had chosen well. I almost wished I could chug a bit on my way to the house.

Maybe Dylan will be so busy trying to pin a murder on me that he won't be there, I told myself, although I'm not sure that was more comforting.

I reached up to use the door knocker and nearly grabbed the face of a bouncy blonde woman who had just flung the door open.

"You just have to be Tallulah!" she exclaimed, throwing her arm around my shoulders and dragging me inside.

"Lou." I tried to keep my balance.

"I'm Jenna and we're just *so glad* you're here!"

She squeezed me again for good measure. She was about my height, but she was thin and wiry where I'm broad shouldered and stocky. Her blonde hair was almost white, and her brown eyes were the color of table honey. She smelled faintly of honeysuckle. I wondered if Cady was correct about Jenna being only slightly older than us, because looking at her, I could believe that she hadn't even graduated college yet.

I scanned the room for Cady, hoping for a lifeline to save me from Jenna's iron grip. I could see through the living room onto their massive, well-lit patio in the back. Chuck waved at me with his tongs from beside the grill. At least the food would be worth it. The man could definitely grill a mean steak.

I tried to tactfully release myself from Jenna's grasp, but she continued to herd me along to the kitchen. Cady stood at the island, chopping vegetables, and smiled broadly when she noticed Jenna dragging me along. I smiled back but felt it melt off my face when I noticed Dylan behind her. So much for him being too busy to come.

"Lou," he said with a little chin lift. The stubble on his face only enhanced his chiseled jawline and made his pale blue eyes look even more piercing.

"Detective Finch," I said with as much aloof coolness as I could muster.

"I'm off duty. You can call me Dylan, like you always have." He frowned.

One glance at Cady told me to keep my big mouth shut, so I did. I finally wrenched myself away from Jenna and handed her the bottle of wine.

"Oh, how nice! Thank you! Let's open this right up, shall we?"

She turned her back to us to rummage around in a drawer, and Cady rolled her eyes. Dylan, who had taken a spot next to her, to finish tossing the salad, elbowed her and mouthed, "Be nice." Cady rolled her eyes at him too.

Jenna produced a corkscrew and opened the bottle in a few fluid movements. She smiled the whole time she poured, and I wondered if all of this was as awkward for her as it was for us. At least no one here was accusing her of murdering anyone, so probably not. I did my best to ignore said accuser and happily accepted a glass of wine as Jenna started passing them out.

"It's a little chilly out after dark, but we can light up the firepit." Jenna motioned for me to follow her outside.

"I'll help Cady get this finished and then join you in a minute, if that's okay?" I said.

"Oh," Jenna's smile faded just a bit. "Sure, sure. Just anytime."

Once Jenna was outside and the sliding glass door closed behind her, Cady turned to me, smiling so broadly it looked like it hurt.

"She is insufferable," she said, still smiling. "She must do yoga for her cheek muscles, as much as she smiles." Cady let the smile fall off her own face like she was shedding a mask.

"Give her a chance," Dylan grumbled.

"Why? They never last. You don't dare get attached to any of them because they *always* leave. Not that I'm in any danger of getting attached to *Jenna*. I do really miss Brenda, though."

"Then go see her. It's not like she moved across the country or anything. She'd love to see you."

"Wait—what? You still see Brenda?" Cady whirled around, knife still in hand.

Dylan feigned fear, holding up his hands in mock surrender. Cady rolled her eyes again and put the knife on the cutting board.

"Why wouldn't I still see Brenda? We had lunch last week. Just because she divorced Dad doesn't mean she divorced us."

"I don't know. It just seems . . . awkward."

"It was, at first." Dylan shrugged. "But it would be worse to just forget she was part of our lives for years."

I tried to look anywhere but at Dylan. His loyalty to Brenda wasn't doing anything to extinguish my crush on him. I tried to remind myself that's all it was, a crush. A silly infatuation borne out of proximity and the fact that Dylan is smoking hot. I shouldn't feel anything but contempt for the man who thinks I'm capable of murdering someone, but dang it, that smoldering smile I caught in my peripheral vision made me weak in the knees.

As I was avoiding looking anywhere in Dylan's direction, I noticed Jenna kept watching us through the glass, a wistful expression on her face. I couldn't imagine how difficult it must be to walk into a home that still bore all of the touches of another woman. And to try to make friends with the adult children of her new boyfriend. I honestly felt bad for her.

"I'm going to go say hello to your dad," I said to Cady, still avoiding looking at Dylan.

"You're here for me, not Dad." Cady wrapped herself around my free arm.

"I don't want to be rude." I leaned over and rested my cheek on the top of her blonde head.

She made a noise that sounded like *ugh*, and released my arm. "Fine. Abandon me, then." She pretended to pout. "I'll be out when I finish in here."

Jenna's entire face lit up when I opened the sliding glass doors. She pulled one of the wicker patio chairs up to the firepit, where the fire hadn't really caught on very well yet, and patted the cushion.

"Hello, Mr. Finch. Thank you for inviting me to dinner."

"Lou, you've known me your entire life. Am I ever going to get you to call me 'Chuck' with any consistency?"

"Probably not." I laughed. "But I'll try."

I took the seat Jenna offered just as the struggling fire died out.

"Mind if I try?" I gestured toward the smoking logs.

"No! Not at all. I can't start a fire to save my life."

I got up and used my phone flashlight to find some twigs under the big oak in the back. I arranged the kindling in a little tent, just like my PawPaw had showed me to do on one of our many camping trips, and using the lighter Jenna handed me, I lit the dry branches. I gently blew on them until they glowed red, and the flames danced higher. I piled the logs around the kindling, and we had a roaring little fire in no time. It would have been really nice, except my greatest gift is to attract the smoke, no matter which way the wind is blowing or where I sit. At least she'd loaded it with mesquite logs, so the smoke I was choking on smelled nice.

"So, Cady tells me you found a dead body?" Jenna said, same smile and bright expression as when she greeted me.

I nearly choked on my wine.

Chapter Twenty-Four

"Um, yeah," I said, still sputtering a bit. "It was pretty awful."

"Oh, of course it was! I'm so sorry to bring it up." Jenna shook her head so forcefully that I was afraid it might snap off.

"Who was it again?" Chuck asked, clearly not as concerned about upsetting me as Jenna was.

I looked through the sliding glass doors in the hopes that Cady was about finished inside, but she was moving at glacial speed.

"Adam Brandt. He runs—I mean he *ran*—another ghost tour company in the area."

"That's right!" Jenna suddenly sat up straighter and scooched her chair toward me. "You do ghost tours. That's so exciting!"

"Most of the time it's just a history tour," I said, grateful for the change in subject matter. "But my tours have had some pretty good paranormal captures that have gone semi-viral."

"Can I see one?" Jenna slid even closer. I was afraid she might fall off the edge of her chair.

"Sure." I pulled out my phone and clicked into my saved TikTok videos. I found the video of Mamie's screaming orb and played it for Jenna.

"Was that it?" she asked when the video finished. "The little thingamajig at the end?"

"Yeah," I said, a little crestfallen. In the paranormal community, Mamie's orbs were a big deal. I guess I could see where it might be anticlimactic for someone not familiar with it.

"Oh," she said with one of her huge smiles. "That's really . . . something."

I put my phone away and took another gulp of wine.

"So what happened with the dead guy?" Chuck piped up as he flipped a steak.

"I don't really know," I said honestly.

"Dylan won't tell us anything," he said with a frown.

I thought about texting Cady and telling her to hurry up, but I was afraid that would be too obvious.

"I think it's against the rules for him to talk about an open case."

Chuck waved off the idea with the grill tongs. "Nonsense. We're family, not some seedy reporters or something."

I had to wonder if I'd have been welcomed for dinner if Dylan *had* talked to them about the case.

"So, what do you do?" I turned back to Jenna and seemed to catch her off guard. Her ever-present smile faltered just a bit before she plastered it back on.

"I'm . . . um . . . between jobs right now," she said, and I thought I saw the faintest hint of color rise in her cheeks, but it might have been a trick of the firelight.

"Don't sell yourself short, honey." Chuck abandoned the steaks on the grill to come over and rub Jenna's shoulders. "Jenna is a talented artist."

"Oh, really?" It was my turn to lean forward in my seat. "What's your medium?"

"I dabble in a few different areas." For the first time so far that evening she seemed withdrawn and self-conscious. "A little painting, a little sculpture, some with found objects, some original work."

"I'd love to see your work sometime," I said. I meant it too, regardless of how awkward this evening was turning out to be. I loved art, and hearing about it directly from the artist was even better.

"Really?" Her face lit up again.

"Absolutely."

"I have a few pieces in my studio," she said timidly.

"Here?"

"It's not really a studio, per se. It's a corner I've taken over in one of the guest rooms."

"It looks like we have a few minutes before dinner will be ready." I looked at Chuck for confirmation, and he nodded.

"Cady likes her steak well done." He rolled his eyes. "So you'll have plenty of time while I ruin a perfectly good piece of meat."

Jenna looked suddenly horrified at the thought of showing me her artwork, but she got up, nonetheless. I followed her down the path to the back door of the house and then inside to the guest room closest to the master suite. She didn't look at me when we entered the room. A table sat against the back wall. There were multiple sculptures lined up along its surface. From the doorway, I could see an alligator, a crab, and a snake. As I crossed the room and got closer, I could see that each one was made up of smaller objects carefully, meticulously pieced together to form the animals. The snake was made of spoons for larger scales, pop-can tabs for smaller scales, and various other pieces of hardware for eyes and other features. The crab was an intricate mix of springs, bolts, nails, and what I thought might be pieces of chain link. The alligator was the only nonmetal sculpture on the table, and it was made entirely of driftwood and vines.

"These are amazing," I said as I bent to get a better look.

"You think so?"

"They must have taken forever."

"A while," she said quietly.

As I straightened back up and turned to look at her, I noticed the unfinished painting on the easel and gasped. It was just stunning. She had captured the very essence of the Barlowe Hotel . . . the beauty, the melancholy, the grandeur, all of it shining out from the canvas. I leaned in and studied the brushstrokes and tried to figure out how she'd conveyed all of that in one painting.

"You are extremely talented."

"Thank you," she replied quietly.

When I turned back toward her, she wasn't wearing her usual giant smile. In fact, she looked like she might cry.

"I'm not just saying that. You're really good. You captured the atmosphere of the Barlowe perfectly."

I wanted to ask her *how* she had done it, how she had made the painting look so real, so *haunted*. It wasn't like she would tell me, though, if she shared my ability. I wouldn't tell her if she asked me.

"Thank you. I just tried to imagine what it would feel like to be haunted, and I tried to put that into the painting. It's supposed to be haunted, you know?"

Her insecurity seemed to fade away, and her bubbly demeanor was starting to return.

"I know."

"Oh my gosh! Of course, you know." She gently smacked her forehead with the palm of her hand. "That's what you do, isn't it? Do you tour through the Barlowe?"

"No. That is part of Adam's route." I didn't bother to correct my tense this time. His company was still doing tours, after all.

"I've never actually been inside. I just camped out on the street and watched it for days before I started painting. Took about a million photos." She looked dreamily at her painting. "It seems to breathe, doesn't it? The hotel, I mean. It kind of has a life of its own."

She was definitely more aware than most. Cady was probably going to murder me when she found out that I was coming around to liking Jenna. She was a lot more interesting than I'd expected.

"It does. It has a tragic and fascinating history."

"I've read a lot about it, but I'd like to hear more sometime."

"Here you are," Cady said as she came through the doorway. She didn't bother to conceal the annoyance in her voice.

"All finished with the veggies?" I asked.

She nodded and looked from me to Jenna.

"Oh yum!" Jenna clapped her hands together and made me jump. "I can't wait!"

Jenna passed us and headed back down the hall.

"Sorry. I didn't know she was going to rope you into looking at her stuff." Cady rolled her eyes.

"It's okay. I asked to look at it. She's really talented, Cady."

She stopped and looked at me skeptically.

"I'm not kidding," I said.

"Don't go fraternizing with the enemy, Lou."

"She isn't the enemy. And she sure isn't the worst he's ever brought home. Remember 'Stephany-with-a-Y'?"

At that, we both burst out into laughter. "Stephany-with-a-Y" had been the first one after Brenda left. She was a realtor who used her good looks to wiggle her way into Chuck's good graces, with the hopes that she could get him to invest in some subdivision she wanted to get funding to build. The problem was that she just wasn't very bright, and she ended up not only ruining any sort of relationship she might have had with Chuck, but also earned a restraining order after she started stalking Cady when Chuck kicked her to the curb. It was almost a yearlong ordeal, and she would forever be the bad girlfriend by which all others would be measured, as in "at least she's not as bad as 'Stephany-with-a-Y.'"

We rejoined the others on the deck, and I resumed my efforts to look anywhere but in Dylan's general direction. Cady refilled my wineglass, and I resisted the urge to drain it immediately. I needed to be reasonably sober to host the late tour. Jenna busied herself with setting the patio table, and Dylan was helping his dad at the grill.

"And awkward silence ensues," Cady whispered, and then settled in next to me on the patio sofa.

Dylan took the seat across from us. I frowned. I'd hoped he would stay busy with his dad. I tried to scooch around in my seat and turn more toward Cady without being obvious.

"I'm glad you decided to join us, Lou," Dylan said. He leaned forward and refilled his glass too.

"Always glad to be here." I tried to keep my air of cool indifference, but I think I just sounded cranky.

"I told Cady that I would stay away if my presence kept you from coming."

My head whipped around to Cady before I could stop it. Of course I wanted him to stay away, and of course I would have never told Cady that, but I wished she had *asked*.

"What?" She feigned innocence. "I knew you wouldn't care."

But I *did* care. I also couldn't expect Cady to read my mind, but we'd been friends long enough that she should probably be able to do just that.

"I know things must be awkward for you, given the investigation," he said, his voice low and conspiratorial.

"Well, things weren't awkward until you made them awkward," I lied. I could feel my cheeks burning, and I hated it that I always glowed red when I was angry. Or sad. Or hot. Or mildly inconvenienced.

"I'm not trying to make anything awkward. I'm trying to make you feel better."

"You're doing a lousy job. Why would you even bring it up?" I whispered forcefully. I tried to keep Chuck and Jenna from hearing me, but I wanted Dylan to understand how annoyed I was.

He held up his hands in surrender and leaned back in his chair.

"You're investigating Tallulah?" Jenna said as she took her seat.

So much for whispering.

"I can't really talk about an open investigation."

At least Dylan had the courtesy of shooting me a guilty look.

"You just did, though," Jenna pressed. "I heard you talking about it."

"I wasn't talking about it," Dylan said more sharply. He sat up straighter in his chair.

Cady slapped the coffee table, and I jumped at the sudden crack.

"This subject is officially off limits," she said even more emphatically than her brother had. "We are not going to harass Lou or bombard her with questions."

She stared at Jenna while she spoke, but made a pointed nod to Dylan when she finished.

* * *

"Sorry. I'm too curious for my own good sometimes," Jenna said with a laugh, but she looked genuinely embarrassed.

I felt a little pang of sympathy for her, but not enough to say anything, because honestly, I was just thankful for Cady setting the boundary.

"Who's hungry?" Chuck clicked his tongs together loudly.

After a meal full of uncomfortable questions, thinly veiled barbs from Cady toward Jenna, and Herculean efforts on my part to avoid Dylan, I was extremely thankful to excuse myself to the kitchen to load the dishwasher. Cady had excused herself to answer a few student emails, and Chuck and Jenna went for what they called their "after-dinner stroll."

"You don't have to do that," Dylan said from behind me. I hadn't heard him come in.

"I want to," I said without turning around.

"Very nice of you."

I didn't respond. I hoped he would get the hint that I didn't really want to talk. The irony of that wasn't lost on me. I'd made every excuse under the sun to talk to Dylan Finch over the years. I'd pretended to be interested in football when he'd played in high school. I'd asked about every subject he'd studied in college. I'm sure I'd made a fool of myself more than once. Not that he'd ever noticed. I'm pretty sure he would never even blink if I just disappeared. So the feeling of wanting to avoid him and shun his attention was foreign to me.

"I'm sorry. About earlier. I didn't mean to make things worse."

"Don't worry about it."

Suddenly he was beside me, handing me plates to rinse.

"I got this."

"Lou," he said quietly.

I moved over, away from him, to load the plates in the dishwasher.

"Lou," he said again, and this time he put a hand gently on my arm.

"What?" I said with more of an edge than I'd meant.

"Please know that the investigation is not personal. A lot of what we do means focusing really hard on someone for a while *to rule them out.*"

I didn't know what to say to that, so I just stood there like a moron, staring at the contents of the dishwasher. After a few uncomfortable moments, I reached for the glasses and started loading them too.

"Would you say something? Even if you're furious with me, just say *something*."

I didn't expect the pleading in his voice. Was this the same man who seemed so cold, so clinical, at the police station?

"I don't know what to say." I finally turned around and faced him. I could feel my face burning, and I wasn't sure if it was from anger, embarrassment, or both.

"Tell me you understand. Or tell me you don't. Tell me to take a flying leap off a tall building. Any of those things would be appropriate." He grinned, but his little joke fell flat for me. Logically, I knew he had to follow the evidence, and a dagger from my shop that I couldn't account for was some pretty compelling evidence. But I still wanted him to tell me he thought I was innocent.

"How do you expect me to feel?"

He looked at me, those piercing blue eyes studying me with an intensity that made me squirm.

"I think it would be easier if you were angry," he finally said. "Because this quiet disappointment is heartbreaking."

"If it helps, I *am* angry," I managed, even though his comment nearly took my breath away. I'd never thought he noticed me enough to be *heartbroken* about anything related to me.

"Yeah, that helps." He grinned again and took a step toward me.

I stopped breathing. Stopped thinking. I just looked up into those eyes, dangerously close to mine.

"Oh my gosh!" Jenna gushed from the doorway, breaking the spell. "You two didn't have to clean up in here!"

I turned around quickly and washed my hands. I slammed the dishwasher shut, punched the "Start" button, and retreated back to the patio with Cady.

"Hey, I need to scoot," I said as I flopped down beside her. "I've got to get back to take the late tour."

She gave a disgruntled grumble and patted my knee. "You need to take more days off."

"I'm building a business," I said, patting her hand in return. "Someday, I'll slow down."

I thanked Chuck and Jenna on my way out and nearly set a land speed record getting back to the shop. Tess had everyone gathered for me when I flew through the back door. I was cutting it close because I'd gone to the house first to check on Nan and love on Toby. I really hoped no one responded to my "found puppy" posts because I was hopelessly attached to the little ankle biter. I thanked Tess on my way through the shop and launched straight into my orientation spiel.

The tour was uneventful. Adam waved from the graveyard entrance but kept a respectable distance and didn't interfere. Mamie didn't shower us in orbs (at my request), and Pete was wherever Pete goes in between drunken runs across the street. My group was engaged and interested in the area, and by the time I was bidding them all goodnight, I felt a renewed sense of calm and optimism. That wouldn't last long, however. I had just shut down the iPad and put the cash in the little safe under the counter when the side window exploded, sending glass and debris flying throughout the shop.

Chapter Twenty-Five

Simultaneously, I screamed and dropped to the floor, Tess shrieked, and Toby yelped. When nothing else exploded, I stood up and scanned the room.

"Get down!" Tess hissed from her spot underneath a display table.

I spotted a brick in the middle of the floor among the broken glass and scattered knickknacks from the shelving it had destroyed on the way through the shop. Fury burned my cheeks, and I turned and sprinted through the back door. I ran out into the yard, but I didn't see anyone. To be fair, they'd had plenty of time to escape while I was cowering on the floor. I'm not sure what I thought I was going to do if I caught someone, so it's probably good that they ran away.

"What are you *doing*?" Tess hissed again from the doorway. She was clutching Toby, who strained to get down. "Get in here!"

"There's no one here." I realized I was clenching my fists so tightly my nails were digging into my palms.

She looked around the yard, shivering uncontrollably. "I called the police."

I expected to spend the next several hours with the police, going over details and being impatient while they combed my shop and yard for evidence. What I got was a nervous young cop who acted like I was putting a serious damper on his evening plans. He took a cursory walk around the yard, remarked that the brick was untraceable, and took down our names and contact information. The whole process took maybe fifteen minutes. Granted, in the grand scheme of things, a brick through a window is probably not the highest police priority.

"Do you want me to put some cardboard over that?" Tess pointed to the ruined window.

"Oh no. You go home and get some rest. I'll clean up this mess."

"I don't want to leave you alone." She hugged herself.

"I'll be fine. I'll pepper-spray the hell out of anyone that tries anything." I laughed a little to try to lighten the mood.

She hesitated a moment, but I got the impression she was relieved to be let off the hook. I didn't blame her. This was a lot worse than getting threatening texts. This was up close and personal.

I picked up the brick off the counter where Officer Useless had left it. It *was* a generic brick. But it also looked just like the ones that Jace Klein's company was using to build new trash can bases in the park. I put the brick in the bottom of my bag. I took extra care in sweeping up all of the glass, making several passes with the broom and then again with the vacuum. I didn't want Toby to pick up a stray shard in his tiny pink toe beans.

I wanted something more substantial than cardboard to cover the window until I could replace it, so I headed for PawPaw's shed. Nan hadn't touched it since he died, and I knew I could find something in there. I pulled out two pieces of sheet metal and went to work finding a hammer and nails. PawPaw wasn't much for organization.

"Everything okay?"

I recognized Kenneth's voice from behind me.

"Did you see anyone around the shop tonight? About an hour ago? Someone threw a brick through the window."

"I generally avoid the shop when it's crowded, and I'm sorry to say that I did not notice anyone. That's very concerning, though."

"Believe me, I'm concerned," I said as I finally located a hammer and enough mostly straight nails to hang the sheet metal.

By the time I finally got the window covered, I was absolutely drained. It took everything I had left to walk Toby and stumble into the house. I wanted to go talk to Adam, but I couldn't make myself go down to the cemetery. My exhaustion just got worse as Kenneth berated me the whole time about how dangerous my situation was becoming. The worst part was that I couldn't even argue with him. I *knew* I was in trouble. But the problem was that I was in trouble from every direction. If I quit trying to find out who had murdered Adam, I could be the one to get the blame for it. If I kept poking around, I was putting myself in the path of a killer. It was a no-win situation. As I closed my eyes that night, one thought kept playing on a loop in my head: even if both choices were bad, I was still going to pick the one that gave me a little control.

* * *

In what had become a new routine at the Thatcher household, I found Ronald cooking breakfast while Nan sat at the counter, looking at him with adoration I hadn't seen in years. Bryce sat beside Nan, his open laptop on the counter. Toby wiggled and whined when he saw them. Clearly, he was getting attached to us as well. Fitz, who had been curled up under Nan's stool, hissed and lazily walked away. I hoped he would warm up to Toby eventually. This *was* his house after all.

"Come here, little fella." Nan hopped down and patted her thigh with her good hand.

Toby was only too happy to oblige.

"I'll walk him," Bryce said, and reached for his leash.

It took several tries to get it hooked onto his collar, with all the wiggling and scootching, but he waved me off when I tried to help.

"Dad won't let us have pets. He says they're messy and I won't take care of them."

"A lot of people feel that way." I tried to be diplomatic.

He shot me a scathing look.

"I'll join you." I followed him to the door. "We need to talk."

When we got outside, he let Toby sniff around the porch steps.

"When am I going back?" He squared his shoulders and looked me in the eyes.

"What?"

"No one who says 'we need to talk' has anything good to say. So, I figure you've worked out something with Mom and Dad, and I'm going back."

"That's not it at all," I said, shaking my head. "I just want to make sure that you were serious when you said you wanted to finish the year out down here. If you are, then I'll support you in every way I can. But if you were just trying to shock Mom and your dad, jolt them into realizing how unhappy you are, then I don't want to start World War Three."

He visibly relaxed. "I am serious."

"You're willing to leave your friends behind?"

"I don't have any friends."

The matter-of-fact way he said just snapped my heart in two.

"C'mon, Bryce. I'm sure you have friends," I said, unwilling to believe that my smart, funny, adorable little brother didn't have a single friend.

"I don't. Noah was the last person I had anything in common with, and his parents let him transfer to a private school way back when the bullying started. I can FaceTime him here the same as I can at home."

He followed Toby's latest attempt to track everything that had ever walked through the yard.

"Okay," I said. "World War Three it is. But there are going to be conditions."

"What conditions?"

"I just want you to know that even though I'm supporting you through this, running away was monumentally stupid, and you'd better not think of pulling anything like that ever again. And if we're lucky enough to get them to agree to you staying here, I want you to go to counseling to help you deal with everything that's happened."

He stared off into the distance for a moment before turning back to me.

"That's fair."

Once Toby finally found the perfect spot, we both headed back inside.

"That smells amazing." I pulled up a stool and tried to see what Ron was cooking. "Want any help?"

"No thanks. I'm a solo chef." He grinned. "It's western omelets and biscuits and gravy."

My stomach growled on cue. "You are *not* good for my diet."

He chuckled and handed me a plate with enough food for three people, all of which I intended to eat. In between bites, I broke the news to Nan about the window. I expected her to chastise me or even suggest something drastic like closing the shop until this was all over, but she didn't. She fumed for a moment and then made me promise that I wouldn't let some "murdering jerk" go unpunished. When I picked my jaw up off the floor, she also made me promise to be extra careful and not spend too much time alone.

It was Bryce who was ready to read me the riot act.

"I don't like this," he said in between bites. "It sounds dangerous, and I don't want you to get hurt."

"I promise I'll be as careful as I can," I said, and ruffled his hair.

He jerked away but smiled. He'd always hated it when I did that, which is why I still do it. It's in the contractual brother–sister agreement to always do the things your sibling finds the most annoying. And since I'd moved away before he grew up, I had to make up for lost time.

* * *

Nan insisted on coming to the shop with me, and set to work reorganizing the shelving that had been knocked over the previous evening. I suspected this was part of her campaign to make sure I was not alone.

"I wish you'd just rest. You have a broken arm." I tried to herd her toward the counter and the chair I had placed back there for her.

"Cracked. Not broken. They're probably not even going to put a cast on it."

"Cracked *is* broken," I protested as she dodged my attempts and started sorting the smashed inventory from the salvageable pieces.

"How about I promise to take it easy, and if I get too tired or start having too much pain, I'll go back to the house."

She put her good hand on her hip and looked up at me with the expression that tells me in language clearer than words that this isn't up for debate. I nodded, knowing any further argument would be futile.

"I'm thinking of trying to talk to Jace Klein again." I tried to sound casual, but my heart pounded at the thought of approaching him again. I was almost certain it was Jace who threw the brick through my window. And he was probably the one sending me the threatening texts too.

"I'll go with you." Nan plunked a boxed set of tarot cards on the newly reassembled shelf.

"It's broad daylight," I said nervously. Nan always made me feel like a little kid again. "I think I'll be okay."

"I'm sure you will. But I'm still coming with you. Just give me a minute to go get my purse."

She didn't give me a chance to argue, even if I wanted to. I grabbed a NOLA baseball cap off a hanger and pulled my hair through the hole in the back, hoping that it would change my appearance just enough to get close to Jace before he bolted again.

A few minutes later, I was pulling into a parking spot near Coliseum Park with a tiny puppy and my elderly grandmother. Not exactly the greatest crime-fighting trio. But it did feel good to have someone along with me this time. If anything happened there would be a witness, at least. Nan took Toby's leash and let him meander around, smelling all the interesting scents the park had to offer. He wagged his little tail in complete happiness.

I wished I'd brought the brick with me, although I had no idea what I'd hoped to do with it. There were no identifying marks on it. It wasn't even an uncommon color, something the police officer had pointed out multiple times. It didn't matter anyway, since I'd forgotten it back at the shop. It didn't take long to get to the fountain, even with Toby stopping every few steps to investigate something.

I spotted Jace right away. He was talking to another worker, a tall, slender man who seemed to be gesturing to their work trucks parked farther down the street. I inched closer to them while trying to pass myself off as a sightseer. I snapped random photos as I walked. I couldn't hear what they were saying, but their voices got louder, and Jace started gesturing back. Their body language was clearly aggressive as they alternated pointing a jabbing forefinger at each other. I caught a couple of colorful words lobbed at Jace, who responded by throwing down his hard hat and storming off. I considered following him, but he got into an older Ford Ranger and sped away. I let fly a few colorful words myself at losing yet another opportunity to speak with him.

The man Jace had been arguing with kicked the hard hat Jace had thrown down and ignored the people who turned to look at his angry display. He put his hands on his hips and looked over the work they were doing. It appeared to me that they had been digging an area to build another of the trash can bases the park was installing around the fountain. There was another small crew of men working on the walkway.

"Excuse me," I said to his back.

He turned around and looked me up and down.

"Could you spare a minute?" I hoped maybe I could salvage this situation. I thought he might have some insight into Jace and, since they didn't appear to be besties, that he might share those insights with me. "I'd like to ask you about the man you were just arguing with."

"I don't have time for one of Jace's crazy girlfriends," he said, his disapproval crystal clear on his narrow face.

"I'm not one of his girlfriends." I shook my head and took a step toward him. "In fact, I'm probably the furthest you could get from being one of his girlfriends."

"Then what do you want to know?"

Chapter Twenty-Six

E ddie Dumont took his morning break sipping coffee Nan had the forethought to pack in a thermos for our trip to the park. I swear she could pull anything out of her purse. Eddie had let down his tailgate for me to sit on and pulled a camp chair out of the back seat of his pickup for Nan. He seemed to be comfortable standing while he drank the strong black coffee that was Nan's specialty.

"Ever since that moronic twit started working with us, stuff's gone missing," he said with a scoff.

"Like what?" Nan asked, and elbowed me to refill his coffee cup.

"It was just small stuff, to begin with, a Zippo lighter, a few bucks cash. But after a few weeks, it was tools and any cash he could get his hands on." He ran a hand through his short sandy-brown hair. "Boss doesn't care because Jace shows up and works decent. He's a warm body. So, we've learned to lock our toolboxes and keep our money in our pockets. I hate a thief, though, and I wish he'd get canned, even if we have to work short."

"I don't know if you remember me from yesterday or not, but I tried to talk to Jace, and he ran away."

"No, I don't. But I do remember him taking off for about an hour. I just thought it was another angry husband."

"Funny you should mention that." I leaned toward him from my perch on his tailgate. "The husband of one of his former girlfriends was killed a few days ago."

"And you think it was *that* useless nitwit?"

"The thought has crossed my mind."

He laughed a big, throaty laugh and threw his head back. When he composed himself, he said, "Well, you experienced just how brave he is. He's more likely to turn tail and run than he is to kill anyone."

"The manner of the murder was pretty cowardly," I said, thinking about how Adam had been stabbed from behind, never getting a clear look at his killer. I said as much to Eddie.

"I still don't see him killing anyone. He's a prissy little idiot who whines when he gets blisters on his soft, delicate hands." Eddie took another long sip of coffee, then nodded at Nan. "This is mighty fine coffee, Mrs. Thatcher."

"Thank you." Nan smiled and nodded back.

Eddie turned to me again. "You know he has some harebrained idea about being an Instagram model or influencer, or whatever? Gonna make his millions being a pretty boy on the internet." Eddie was taken with another fit of laughter. "He's always taking shirtless selfies from jobsites."

That would explain the posts I'd seen on his social media.

"Eddie! This ain't social hour. Get back to work." a man I took to be a supervisor yelled from the area where Eddie had previously been working.

"Yeah! I'll be right back. My fifteen's got five more minutes." Eddie didn't bother turning around; he yelled his response while still looking at me.

"Do you happen to know where he was?" I knew it was a long shot, but I had to ask.

"I have no idea where he goes when he leaves here."

"Does he have any friends here? Anyone he goes out drinking or hunting with?" Nan asked. She was better at this than I was.

"Not that I know of. Thank you for the coffee, Mrs. Thatcher," he said, signaling his appreciation with another dip of his head before turning back to me. "Good luck finding out who killed your friend."

I started to correct him but decided against it. I watched him walk back to the worksite. The theft of the tools and money explained why Jace thought I was a cop and had taken off when I'd tried to talk to him. He thought his thefts had finally been reported. And I was back to square one. Again.

I was vaguely aware that Nan was talking to me as we pulled into our driveway.

"I'm sorry. What were you saying?" I turned the key and unlatched my seat belt.

"I was just saying that it doesn't really matter what Eddie thinks of that Jace fella. He could still be the killer."

"I guess. But Adam doesn't think he did it either." The words were out of my mouth before I even realized it. How stupid could I be? I'd never made a slip like that before. Not since I'd made the mistake of telling my mother when I was little. I froze, hoping she hadn't caught what I'd just said.

I realized Nan was staring at me, but I couldn't make myself look at her. I opened the car door and got out as fast as I dared without seeming like I was running away.

"I'm just going to walk Toby real quick before I head over to the shop," I said, still not looking at Nan.

"I'll meet you there," she said to my back. I heard the front door to the house close behind me, and assumed she'd gone to put up the thermos and her purse before joining me again in the shop. I only had a few minutes to collect myself and figure out a way to play off my slip. Shouldn't be too hard, right? I settled on trying to convince her that it was the *evidence* surrounding Adam that suggested Jace was innocent. If she even pressed me on it. Which I hoped she wouldn't.

Toby sniffed around and then plopped down and whined to be picked up. He was still young enough that he tired out quickly, so I grabbed him up, kissed him behind his impossibly soft little ears, and took him inside to his bed. He made the requisite ten to fifteen test circles before settling in with a heavy sigh. I refilled his water bowl, and Nan appeared behind me.

"Oh my god!" I jumped and spilled water down my left leg. "You scared me to death!"

"Sorry about that," Nan said with a chuckle.

I toweled off my leg and filled Toby's bowl again. I wondered if there was enough new inventory in the back to unpack and price— just anything to avoid Nan for a while. Not that it would matter. She never forgot anything.

"You don't have to hide it from me, you know," Nan said gently.

"What?" I squeaked.

"You've always seen ghosts, Lulu Belle. You quit talking about it as you got older, but I've always known."

I felt my breath coming in fast little gasps as my panic set in. I don't know *why* I was panicking, but I couldn't calm myself down either.

"How?" My voice went from squeak to croak.

"The house isn't that big, Lulu Belle. I hear you talking to Kenneth all the time."

I needed to sit down. I backed up until I found the big, comfy chair I keep behind the counter for downtime.

"It's okay," Nan said as she stroked my hair. "But when you catch your breath, I'd love to hear what Adam thinks about all this."

Chapter
Twenty-Seven

I'm not sure how long it took me to rearrange my reality and come to terms with the fact that Nan knew I saw ghosts. And had always known. I'd thought I was being so slick. While Nan didn't have the same abilities that I did, she was more sensitive than I'd ever given her credit for. She could sense the subtle, and sometimes not so subtle, changes in atmosphere and temperature when a spirit was near. She almost always knew when Kenneth was creeping around; even though she'd never voiced it directly before, she'd always complained of a chill when he entered a room. I wondered if he knew she was aware of him. She also told me that her son, my dad, had a lot of imaginary friends as a kid, and she suspected I'd inherited my gifts from him.

It was nearing dark by the time I'd told Nan absolutely everything. It felt so good to finally talk about all of it to someone besides Kenneth. No offense to him or anything, but there was always this annoying little voice in the back of my mind that told me all of it was in my head. That I couldn't possibly see and hear the things

I do, even though I have confirmation of it being real nearly every day. There's always the little kernel of doubt.

"You'd think if he wanted you to help so much, he could at least be helpful himself," Nan said with a frown.

"I don't think he's being deliberately unhelpful." I found myself defending Adam again, and it still felt weird considering how much we'd hated each other when he was alive.

"I think he is," Nan huffed. "He keeps telling you that none of your suspects would have any reason to kill him, even though you've presented some very convincing motives for all of them."

"It has to be hard to think that the people closest to him meant to hurt him," I said, imagining how awful that must be.

"Well, he can't have it both ways." She jabbed the counter with her finger for emphasis. "He can't want you to help and then steer you away from the very people that might have killed him. You tell him that." Another finger jab.

"I've set some pretty clear boundaries."

"You tell him that," she said again, more firmly this time. "I'm not a huge fan of you getting in the middle of this mess anyway. Especially since you're getting threats—and now this." She gestured toward the broken window.

"Yeah, I'm not thrilled about that either. But I am definitely in the middle of it now, so I think I need to figure this out before something else happens." I hesitated to voice exactly how freaked out I was, but I doubted I was hiding it from Nan anyway.

After that, we slipped into an easy routine. Nan would visit with any walk-ins that happened through, tickled all over again every time she made a sale or booked a tour. I took the time to answer online bookings and emails. Interspersed with work, I also did a few Google searches to see if Damian Boyle, Jace Klein, or Mia Brandt had criminal backgrounds. Damian seemed to have had a DUI arrest nearly fifteen years ago and Jace had a drunk and disorderly charge last year. Nothing violent for either of them. I honestly didn't know how the police could do this day in and day out. It was so disheartening to keep turning up nothing.

In desperation, I searched for Facebook groups that talked about police investigation, true crime, and groups of ordinary people who help solve crimes. Unfortunately, most of the crimes they were assisting in solving had helpful components I didn't have, like security footage. There was even a story about a group of automotive enthusiasts who identified the driver in a hit-and-run from the grill that was left behind at the scene. My problem was that the most compelling piece of evidence at Adam's scene, the dagger, pointed straight at me.

* * *

I felt so clueless and out of my element. I knew how to investigate the history of a house or area, and I used my spiritual relationships to help with that. But I was flying by the seat of my pants trying to investigate a murder. I sighed, tried to clear my head, and decided to make an attempt at organizing my thoughts and ideas.

I pulled up a blank Word document on my computer and started a chart for each suspect that included what I knew, what I still needed to find out, their potential motive, and their whereabouts the night of the murder, realizing that I should have started with that last info. If any one of them had a rock-solid alibi, then it would narrow my search. Looking at all the blanks didn't do much to dispel my feelings of defeat and doubt.

"I need to talk to Mia Brandt," I said out loud.

"I'll sit this one out," Nan said. "You just be sure to talk to her somewhere in public. Don't go off alone with some hussy who might have killed her husband." Words I never thought I'd hear coming out of Nan's mouth.

I stifled a laugh. "I'm going to try to catch her at the yoga studio where she teaches classes. If she's following her schedule that's posted on the website, she should be there now."

"Good plan."

I left Toby with Nan, deciding that a puppy might not be welcome at Green Leaf Yoga. Pulling into the parking lot, I already felt a little intimidated. The studio was situated in a newly built strip mall–style building sandwiched in between a smoothie bar and an insurance agency. The entire front of the studio was windows, displaying two small rooms to the entire world. I would hate to try to do yoga in a giant fish bowl. It didn't seem to be phasing any of the women in the classes, though. One looked to be a beginner class, with two instructors moving around the students, adjusting poses. The other class was prenatal yoga, full of baby bumps of every size, and glowing mamas. That was the class Mia was teaching. I recognized her right away. Her jet-black hair was pulled into a high ponytail that swung across her shoulders as she moved among the expectant mothers. Her waist was impossibly tiny, and everything about her reminded me of a Barbie doll in the best way. She was just stunning.

I had looked at the class schedule online, and the prenatal class was listed as lasting an hour. I glanced at the time and saw I only had about fifteen more minutes to wait until she was finished. It looked like she took an hour break before her next class. I hoped I could persuade her to spend at least a portion of that hour with me. I texted Nan to let her know I had to wait for the class to end before I could try to talk to Mia, and received the thumbs-up emoji in response.

I checked Jace Klein's TikTok account while I waited. Surprisingly, he hadn't posted anything since I'd confronted him in the park. Same for Facebook and Instagram. A pop-up reminder dinged and alerted me to my scheduled appointment with Elaine Hastings. I dreaded that. I knew she was going to tell me I had little hope of getting guardianship of Bryce. I'd already googled how hard it was and knew I was facing an impossible battle. I was hoping that bluffing would be enough, that I could hire Elaine to send a strongly worded letter to Mom and Jared, and they would agree to our terms. It was a gamble, but I had to try.

Continuing to kill time, I went back over my strategy for talking to Mia. I hated having to lie to people, but I couldn't tell her that my information had come from Adam. And since I was there to talk about Jace Klein, I had to have a plausible explanation for how I even knew about him. Thankfully, the comments Adam told me that Jace had made on their Instagram posts were still up. I took a screenshot of the most damning of the comments. It was posted below a photo of Adam and Mia cuddling in their porch swing. It appeared that Adam was the one holding the phone for the selfie as he nuzzled Mia's hair. To the left of them in the photo, the corner of a white patio table was visible. Jace had said, *"Nice photo. Did she tell you I bent her over that table beside you?"* I frowned at the screenshot. I wondered why Adam hadn't blocked him and made a mental note to ask the next time I spoke to him.

As the prenatal class wound down, I got out of the car and lurked near the entrance. When the receptionist vanished into a back room, I took the opportunity to go inside. The lobby smelled of lemongrass and something stronger, lavender maybe. The lighting was softer than it appeared from the street, and the whole room was bathed in a warm glow. I felt both relaxed and energized at the same time, exactly how I imagined I should feel in a yoga studio.

I took an out-of-the-way spot by a potted tree and waited for the prenatal class to clear. It didn't take long. When the last mama carried her rolled-up mat through the door, I stepped inside. Mia was sweeping the floor with a large push broom. She made even that mundane activity look elegant. I could definitely see why she had attracted Jace's attention.

"Oh, sorry, I didn't see you there," she said with a little jump. "My next class doesn't start for an hour."

"I know. I was hoping we could talk."

"Do I know you?" She took a step closer to me.

"No, but I knew Adam, and I'm so sorry for your loss." I remembered the shared joke about Albuquerque that Adam had told me I could use to get her to talk to me, but I hadn't figured out a good way to explain how I knew about it, so I planned to save it for an emergency. If I could get her to talk to me in any other way, it would be preferable.

Her face immediately contorted into a mask of grief, and tears welled in her eyes. I hadn't realized she was barely holding it together. She'd seemed so polished.

"This isn't the place," she said quietly, and angrily swiped away a tear.

"I know, and I'm sorry. Would you let me buy you a coffee?"

She hesitated for a moment. "How did you know Adam?"

"Professionally," I said quickly, suddenly realizing that she might think I'd had some *other* kind of relationship with him.

"Oh my god," she said with dawning recognition, "you're Lou Thatcher!"

Chapter Twenty-Eight

Once she realized who I was, I figured Mia would throw me out, refuse to talk to me, or both. So she surprised me when she leaned the broom against the wall and hurried over to my side. Apparently, the police hadn't shared with her that they were looking pretty hard at me for her husband's murder.

"I don't want coffee, but you can buy me a smoothie next door."

She took me by the arm and ushered me out into the lobby. She stopped at the front desk.

"Hey, Selena!" she yelled toward the door where the young woman had disappeared earlier.

"Yeah!" came a distant response.

"I'm going to pop over to the smoothie bar. Be back in a bit."

We moved next door, ordered, and then snagged a booth in the back.

"To be honest, I'm a little surprised you're so eager to talk with me," I said, and took a sip of the best strawberry-mango yogurt smoothie I'd ever had. To be fair, it was the *only* one I'd ever had, but it was still a masterpiece, and Smooth Moves was definitely going to be a new favorite.

"I've spent days crying my eyes out, with all my family and friends telling me that Adam was the best thing to ever walk the earth," she said, tears welling in her eyes again. "I'm actually excited to talk to someone who hated his guts. I think it would be easier to be mad at him for a while."

People deal with grief in a lot of different ways, but that was a new one for me.

"I don't know that I *hated* his guts," I said, squirming in my seat.

"Oh, come on." She waved a manicured hand in my direction. "He made life miserable for you, didn't he? He tried to get your business license yanked—what? Three times?"

"I only knew about the one time," I replied. Maybe I *did* hate his guts after all.

"Well? Tell me all the ways he was awful. Tell me about how he was a smug jerk. Tell me anything except how wonderful he was, because I don't think I can bear that right now."

The raw grief in her face brought tears to my own eyes. If she'd had something to do with his death, she was either the best actress ever or she was feeling some extreme guilt over it. I didn't know how to begin since my planned approach had been to offer condolences and try to talk to her about the night Adam died. As the awkward silence dragged on, I started to get desperate to fill it.

"Look, I don't feel right speaking ill of the dead," I finally said. "And Adam and I had kind of buried the hatchet, so to speak."

She sighed and slumped back in the booth. "I never thought I'd be a widow this young."

"I'm so sorry."

"What *did* you come here to talk about, then?" She arched one perfect eyebrow and fixed me with her piercing green eyes.

I didn't know whether I should beat around the bush a little and work up to it gradually or come right out and say it. I was still warring with myself when she started to get out of her seat.

"I wanted to talk about Jace," I whispered.

She froze. Color started to rise on her pale chest and climbed up her throat, and her breathing quickened.

"How do you know about that?" Her voice was barely audible. She sat back down. All warmth was gone from her expression and demeanor.

"I'm not here to pass judgment or anything like that. I just need to know if he's been bothering you."

"I don't know what kind of game you're playing," she whispered, "but I'm not interested."

She folded her arms over her chest, but she didn't get up to leave.

"I promise, I'm not playing any games. Has Jace contacted you since Adam died?"

She glared at me and fidgeted in her seat.

"You don't have anything to be jealous about. I'm not interested in Jace. You can have him," she finally spit out.

"What? No, that's not what this is about." I shook my head.

"What is it then? If you're not seeing Jace, then how did you know about me?"

"You wouldn't believe me if I told you."

She glared at me again, but she unfolded her arms and took a long drink from her smoothie.

"Has Jace been in contact with you since Adam died?" I repeated, trying to keep my tone gentle and nonthreatening. "Did he ever threaten you or Adam?"

"Yes," she said simply.

My heart raced. But I tried not to get ahead of myself. Just because Jace couldn't let go didn't mean he'd killed Adam. And just because Mia seemed to be genuinely grieving didn't mean she wasn't involved, I reminded myself.

"What did he want?"

"What do you think he wanted?" she scoffed. "I still can't figure out how you know about this if Jace didn't tell you. That would be just like him, to send you here in some stupid attempt to make me jealous or something. You can tell him it won't work. I'm not jealous"—she leaned forward and stabbed at the table with her forefinger—"because I could not care less about Jace Klein. I don't love him. I never did." Her voice cracked. "He was a stupid mistake, and I regret every minute I spent with him."

Her bottom lip trembled. I believed her.

"I think he might have wanted to get Adam out of the way," I said, and then looked around to make sure there wasn't anyone close enough to hear us.

"The police don't think so," she scoffed again. "When they first told me what happened that awful night, I told them it was either Jace or you, but my money was on Jace."

My mouth fell open.

"Oh, don't look so surprised." She smirked. "You all but threatened him on Facebook when he called you out."

"Okay, first of all, I have not *ever* faked anything on my tours. And second, I never threatened him!"

"You told him he would regret it if he kept calling you out," she said smugly.

"I told him he would regret it if he continued to slander me, that I would take him to court. Not that I would harm him in any way," I snapped defensively.

"Libel," she said.

"What?"

"It would have been libel since it was written. Slander is verbal."

I sighed and closed my eyes. This was getting away from me. Fast. "Why are you here if you suspect me?"

"Because I don't. Once I calmed down and looked at it critically, I realized you didn't have anything to gain. It didn't matter what Adam said about you online. In fact, the more he said, the more it just boosted your videos." She took another long drink. "But Jace is capable of anything."

For the second time, I felt my mouth hanging open.

"You must suspect he's dangerous from what you've been asking me."

I nodded.

"He never threatened me—not directly. He showed up at the house multiple times after I ended it, and I think he came to the studio. He sent flowers and gifts begging me to reconsider." She said it with such disgust I couldn't imagine Jace not getting the hint. "Adam thought he saw him outside two days before he died. He chased him down the street and yelled at him that he would kill him if he came back. I think that was the last straw for Jace."

"Did Jace know about me?"

"What do you mean?"

"Did you ever mention me?"

"Why would I mention you?" Mia frowned.

I didn't know if I should tell her about the dagger. She might clam up or, worse, call the police and report me for harassing her like Jace had.

I leaned forward so I could whisper. "I think Jace is trying to frame me for Adam's murder. The part I can't figure out is how he knew anything about me."

"Why do you think he's trying to frame you?" She glanced around like she was suddenly trying to make sure she knew where the exits were. Like she was sitting across the table from her husband's murderer.

I barely took a breath, but I laid it all out for her. Well, almost all of it. I left out the part about talking to her husband's ghost. But I told her the rest, from finding Adam to discovering one of my daggers had been the murder weapon, and finally to how Jace had reacted when I'd tried to talk to him. I couldn't read her expression as she watched me talk.

"You don't know how Jace found out about you, and I'm still wondering how you found out about him," she said flatly, her expression still blank.

I opened my phone and pulled up the screenshot I'd taken earlier and slid it across the table to her. "When I found out about the dagger, I was grasping at straws, so I went through Adam's social media, looking for anything, anyone who might want to hurt him, because I knew it wasn't me."

She shoved the phone back across the table. "Maybe," she said.

"I'm sorry, maybe what?"

"I might have said something about you. When I was with Jace. I don't remember everything we talked about." She stared at the table in front of her, color rising on her neck again.

"Look," she said, suddenly getting to her feet, "I need to get back and get ready for my next class."

"Please don't go," I pleaded.

"I can't do this," she said, but she didn't walk away.

"I'm really sorry, but in addition to trying to frame me, I think he's threatening me too. I've been getting disturbing messages, and someone threw a brick through my window."

She leaned down uncomfortably close to my face. I resisted the urge to push away from her.

"How do you think it feels," she said in a raspy whisper, "to know that it was *my* mistake that got my husband killed?"

"I honestly can't imagine how that must feel."

She straightened back up and glanced at the entrance. "What else do you want to know?"

"Do you happen to know where Jace was the night Adam was killed?"

"Why would I know that?" she snapped.

"Would you be willing to meet with him? I could come along and record anything he might admit to and—"

"Absolutely not. You're insane." She put up her hands between us and turned on her heels.

I jumped up and followed her out. Recklessly, I reached out and grabbed her arm before she could get to the yoga studio.

"You're right." I hated the distress in my voice. "That was a stupid idea. I'm just desperate."

"I'm not getting anywhere near Jace Klein, so I don't know what else I can do for you." She looked down at my hand, and I released her immediately.

"I don't know either, but I'd hoped to talk to you more. Just anything you might be able to tell me about him could help."

She stared at me for what felt like several uncomfortable moments. "Give me your phone."

I didn't question her. I just unlocked and handed over my phone. She punched a few buttons and handed it back.

"That's my number. Text me the rest of your questions."

Chapter Twenty-Nine

I was still kind of numb when I got back to the shop, but even so, Nan required a detailed report of everything I'd found out. Initially, I didn't think I had found out much at all, but the more I told her, the more I realized how important my conversation with Mia had been. I'd found out that someone who knew Jace very well also thought he was capable of murder, and that was perhaps the most important thing. I finally felt like I was focusing on the right suspect and that I had some hope of keeping myself out of a jail cell.

Once I'd answered her twelve million questions, I excused myself to check on Bryce. I couldn't gather my thoughts enough to send my follow-up questions to Mia, so I left that for tomorrow. I found my brother playing chess in the living room with Ron. They both displayed all the seriousness of a high-stakes game.

"Oh hey," Bryce said when he noticed I was watching them.

"Hey," I replied. "I was just going to check on you. Sorry, I've been so busy this week."

"I'm good."

"I'm not. The kid keeps kicking my butt," Ron said with a grin.

"You're getting better." Bryce grinned back. "No one is perfect in the beginning."

I laughed at my initial assumption that it had been Ron teaching Bryce how to play.

"We've got the appointment with the attorney tomorrow," I said. "I'd like you to come along."

"Yeah, I figured I would," Bryce said. "Thank you for not just shipping me back."

"You're always welcome here," I said.

"And you know Lizzie feels the same way," Ron added.

Bryce nodded slightly and stared at his chess pieces.

"If you guys need anything, Nan and I will be at the shop."

I got a thumbs-up from Bryce and a salute from Ron.

I went back to the shop and slipped into autopilot. Foot traffic was busier than it had ever been, and the shop was still full of people when I left with the night's tour. It was a good group, with lots of questions and engagement. I always enjoy those, even though I was distracted and kept thinking about Jace Klein and how I was going to prove he'd killed Adam.

When the last of the customers left, I ran through how to do the end-of-day processes. We left the restocking until the morning. Back at the house, we found Ron had cooked again, and the smell of something I couldn't readily identify made my mouth water. Even if I was struggling with Nan moving on, I could get used to that man's cooking really easily. Ron himself sat in Nan's big comfy armchair reading *The Outsider* by Stephen King. Toby immediately ran to him and begged to be picked up, which he seemed to be happy to oblige.

"What smells so good?" I asked as Nan flopped unceremoniously on the sofa closest to Ron. He reached over and patted her thigh. She smiled at him and squeezed his hand in return. He got up and helped her situate her broken arm on a pillow.

"Chicken pot pie," Ron said. "Nothing special. Just something I thought would warm up nicely when you two came home."

Nan motioned like she was going to stand, but Ron held up a hand.

"You just sit tight," he said. "I'll be right back."

He went to the kitchen, where he pulled out two bowls of the best-looking chicken pot pie I'd ever seen, handed one to me, and took the other to Nan. I settled into the corner chair and devoured mine.

"I'm worried about Bryce," I blurted out while I was deciding whether or not to lick the bowl.

"Kid's actually pretty well adjusted, considering," Ron said, looking up from his book.

"It's the 'considering' part I'm worried about. I have no legal grounds to keep him here. The law doesn't view crap parenting as actual abuse. But I can't stand the thought of him having to go back there."

"We'll just have to make sure he doesn't," Nan said.

"We can't kidnap him." I put my bowl on the side table and rubbed my temples. "I'm meeting with the family law attorney tomorrow to see if we have any options at all."

"That's a good place to start," Nan said. "Just see what she says, and we'll go from there."

I nodded. "I'm exhausted. I'm going to turn in."

"Just throw that in the dishwasher, and I'll run a load when Lizzie's finished." Ron gestured toward my bowl.

Yep, I could get used to having Buff Santa around.

I extricated Toby from Ron's lap, where he had settled again while we ate, and headed upstairs. I didn't hear any sounds coming from Bryce's room, so I didn't knock. When I put Toby down in my room, he immediately found his chew toy, and the fight was on.

"I couldn't help but overhear what you told Elizabeth about your encounter with Mia Brandt," Kenneth said as the temperature in my room dropped a few degrees.

"Good, because I don't think I have it in me to recount all that again tonight."

"What do you think about it?"

"What do you mean?" I asked. My exhausted brain felt foggy and at least two steps behind.

"About what she told you. Do you think she was involved?"

"If she was, then she is an amazing actress." I flopped down on the bed.

"She probably is."

"What?"

"She kept her affair a secret, didn't she?"

"Well, yeah. But grief is harder to fake, and she is definitely grieving," I argued, but I was replaying her responses in my head. Had she said or done anything suspicious?

I needed to see Albert Fortier again. I needed to find out if Mia had been seeing Jace since Adam was killed. He could at least tell me if she'd been meeting him at the house. I also needed to talk to Eddie and see if Mia had been visiting Jace at work. If they were smart, they would be more discreet than that, but it was at least a direction. My efforts had been all over the place, and it finally felt like I was getting somewhere.

There was a soft knock on the door. Kenneth and I both snapped to attention.

"Come in." I sat up on the edge of the bed.

"Hey, Lou," Bryce said timidly. He cracked the door open just a few inches and poked his head inside.

"You can come in," I urged.

He opened the door wider, and Toby bounded over to him, little tail wagging so fast it was a blur.

"I was wondering if Toby could sleep in my room tonight?" He bent down and picked him up, much to Toby's delight. "I've always wanted a dog."

"Sure, he can." I smiled. "He gets up really early for a walk, though. His little puppy bladder barely makes it till sunrise."

"I'll set an alarm. I don't mind."

The thought of being able to sleep in almost overrode the twinge of sadness at giving up my little buddy. Almost. But the ear-to-ear smile on Bryce's face made the sacrifice worth it. He tucked Toby under one arm and gathered up his bed, toys, and leash with the other.

"Goodnight, Lou."

"Goodnight."

*　*　*

I didn't even remember settling into bed when my alarm woke me up the next morning. I missed Toby, but not getting up at first daylight or before was glorious. I silenced my alarm, yawned, and pulled up the business account to triage any bookings that came in overnight. There wasn't anything that needed immediate attention, so I clicked over to my own social media for a change. I reposted a few tour videos from guest tags, answered a few questions, and scheduled a new round of Facebook ads. I was just about to get up and figure out what to wear when aggressive knocking on the front door rang out through the house. Someone had to be hammering that door with a fist for it to be that loud on the second floor.

Frowning, I grabbed the closest T-shirt and jeans and dressed as quickly as possible. Kenneth floated through the door backward, something he had always done when he wasn't sure if I was dressed or not.

"It's Laura and Jared," Kenneth said, his back still to me.

"I'm dressed." I angrily shoved my feet in my sneakers. The involuntary bristle I felt at my mother's name unnerved me. "They've come for Bryce," I said, even though that was obvious.

I flung the door open and sprinted down the steps. Nan and Ron were already at the door when I got there. Ron had subtly angled himself between Jared and Nan. Jared seemed to be jabbing his finger in Ron's chest. Bold move since Ron towered over him by at least a foot. Ron seemed completely unbothered by the angry little man growing redder in the face by the minute.

"Where is he?" my mother asked as soon as she saw me approach.

"Hi, Mom," I said sarcastically. "So good to see you."

"Drop the attitude, Lou." She stepped in between the two men and tried to come inside, but Nan stood in her way.

"I think we can all discuss this like adults, can't we Laura?" Nan smiled menacingly.

"There's nothing to discuss, Elizabeth. Bryce is *my* son, and I'm here to get him."

I cursed under my breath that they couldn't have waited *one* more day so I could have met with the attorney and armed myself with the knowledge of our potential options.

"Why don't you both come in, and I'll fix us some nice tea?" Ron said with a broad smile.

"I don't want any damned tea!" Jared's voice was just slightly raised, but it was dripping with rage. "Get my son *right now*."

"I'm right here, Dad," Bryce said from behind me.

"Go get in the car, Son. Your mother will get your things."

"No." Bryce stepped around me to look his father in the eye. Toby stopped wagging and looked from Bryce to Jared and back again. I'm sure the little guy was wondering why our normally happy home had suddenly gotten so tense.

"Excuse me?" Jared stood taller and puffed out his little chest.

"It is ridiculous to stand here in the foyer and argue." Nan moved forward, between them. "Let's at least have a seat and *talk like adults*," she repeated. "Please join me in the sitting room."

We all followed her in an uncomfortable momentary truce. Nan took PawPaw's chair, and Ron sat closest to her on the loveseat, a united front. I took the floral chair on the other side of Nan, and Bryce pulled a hard-backed chair over to sit near me. We all faced Mom and Jared, opposite us on the sofa.

"You have to understand that this is a tense situation," Jared started, flashing that used-car-salesman smile.

"Jared has had to take off work, and this has all just been awful. I haven't slept in days," Mom said, dabbing at her eyes.

She was certainly laying it on thick. I doubted there were any tears to dab at.

"Well, Mom, it's too bad you didn't feel the same urgency about the bullying Bryce was dealing with."

"There was no bullying," Jared scoffed while Mom stared daggers at me. "You can't get offended at every little thing. You've got to toughen up, Son. Be a man."

Bryce sat up straighter beside me. "I *was* bullied, Dad. They put dead fish in my locker. They stuffed trash in my backpack." Jared shook his head and waved his hand dismissively at his son. But Bryce continued. "And that was just the beginning. They posted horrible comments on all of my posts, and when I shut down all of my profiles, they made a page called *Bryce Is Queer* and invited everyone to make horrible posts about me."

Bryce was getting more animated as he spoke, until he finally stood and passed Toby over to Ron. Jared stood as well, leaving Mom to sob dramatically on the sofa.

"And then, when the cyberbullying wasn't enough, they hid outside my room and took pictures of me in my underwear and posted them everywhere. And when that wasn't enough either, they started beating me up."

My heart broke. While Mom was pretending to cry, actual tears welled in my eyes, and a lump formed in my throat.

"So, yeah, I am *not* going back to that," Bryce said, his hands balled into fists at his side.

"You make yourself a target," Jared said with obvious disgust.

"You are not going to blame him for this." I stood too. All of the anger and resentment from my childhood bubbled to the surface.

"This is fun and all, but we're done. Get in the car, Bryce."

"Can I go to private school?"

"We're not paying for private school," Mom interjected, her theatrics forgotten. I did note that her eyes appeared clear and dry.

"Then I'm not going."

"It's almost cute that you think you have a choice," Jared sneered.

"He does have a choice." I returned his sneer.

"Okay, enough of this crap. I'll just call the police and let them settle this."

"Call them." Ron stood beside me, and I was never so thankful for that mountain of a man. "I'm sure they'll be really interested to hear Bryce's side of things."

Jared made a show of taking his phone out of his pocket.

"I can make a phone call too, Dad. I can call the newspaper at home and give them an exclusive interview about how the gay son of a local councilman faced horrendous bullying, and that councilman did nothing about it."

Jared froze. No, he did more than freeze. He looked like he'd been kicked in the gut. I tried to hide my own reaction.

"I doubt that it will end your career," Bryce continued. "Missouri is pretty bigoted as a whole, but it would definitely put a dent in your reputation. Plus, what will all the other councilmen think about you being the father of a gay son?"

A whole range of emotions flooded over Jared's face. Mom just clamped her hand to her mouth and shook her head.

"Don't threaten me with lies," Jared finally said when he found his voice again.

"I'm not lying, Dad."

Jared backed away from his son. Mom jumped to her feet.

"You know what?" Jared said to me. "You can have him. See if you can do anything with him."

"Jared!" Mom gasped.

"He's not moving to Mars, Laura," Jared turned his contemptuous gaze on her. "It might be nice to have some peace and quiet for a change."

I couldn't help but look at Bryce after that comment, and the obvious pain it caused made me furious.

"I'll have our attorney send you guardianship papers," I said, trying to keep the tremor out of my voice.

Jared turned around and glared at me.

"Absolutely not!" Mom squawked.

"I can't enroll him in school or take him to the doctor without legal guardianship, unless you want to just abandon him here." I gave up trying to keep my emotions in check, and my voice was as shaky as I felt.

"Fine," Jared said without looking at Bryce.

He turned and flung the front door open. Mom hesitated for a moment, but she followed him without another word. When they were both gone, I turned around to Bryce and expected to find him as heartbroken as I was, but he was smiling. He rushed over and wrapped me up in a bear hug so fierce I could hardly breathe.

"Well done, kiddo," Ron clapped him on the shoulder.

When Bryce released me, he turned to Nan and stared at the floor.

"That wasn't really how I wanted to come out to you," he said quietly.

"Oh nonsense. Nothing to come out about." Nan waved him off with her uninjured hand. "You just make sure you don't settle for some boy who doesn't treat you right."

I pulled Bryce in for another hug.

"We need to leave by nine thirty," I reminded him. "We still need to see the lawyer and get the guardianship in place."

"Oh, that doesn't give me much time to get breakfast fixed," Ron said cheerfully as if he hadn't just witnessed our ridiculous family drama.

"You don't have to fix every meal," I said.

"I love to cook." He shrugged. "And I like taking care of people."

Ron put Toby down on the floor, and I heard Fitz hiss from somewhere behind me.

"Poor Fitz. I hate that he's so upset about the puppy," I said.

"He'll settle down," Nan said.

I tried to find where he was hiding, but being pressed for time, I gave up after a few minutes. We hurried through waffles and bacon, but by the time Bryce joined me in the car, I was afraid we were going to be late. Bryce was quiet, but he seemed to be taking the rejection of the morning remarkably well.

"You okay?" I asked as I navigated some tourist traffic.

"Yeah." He shrugged.

"That was pretty rough this morning." I tried to urge him to open up a little. I was going to need to get him into counseling as soon as possible. He was a great kid, but what I'd just witnessed was *a lot*, and I hadn't even dealt with my own trauma, so I had no idea how to help Bryce navigate his. Even if he didn't yet realize it was a trauma.

"Honestly, I'm just relieved right now."

"Fair enough. I'm just here if you want to talk about it."

I pulled into Elaine Hastings's tiny parking lot and fought the feelings of nausea that had plagued me all morning. This was, without a doubt, the right thing to do, but it was such a big thing to assume responsibility for another human being.

"Are you ready?" I asked him.

He nodded. He looked contemplative, but he didn't appear to be as nervous as I was. As we walked toward the door, I felt Bryce slide his hand into mine the way he used to when he was little. I gave it a reassuring squeeze.

Her office had clearly been a residential house at one time. Maybe she even lived there, but I doubted it. I couldn't imagine an attorney living at the same place they saw clients. Even though I would hope that a family law attorney would see fewer criminals than one who specializes in criminal cases, I wasn't sure about that. The one-story, white, ranch-style house was tiny, probably less than a thousand square feet. On the front door, her name was painted on the frosted glass in large print: "Elaine Hastings, Attorney at Law."

Bryce ducked behind me as I opened the door, which signaled our arrival with a melodic chime. I expected a receptionist, but there was no one in the lobby, if the tiny space could be called a lobby.

"Take a seat," came a voice from the office just to our right. "I'll be with you in just a moment."

We did as we were told. The chairs in the lobby were comfortable, with blue upholstery, rounded backs, and narrow armrests. Bryce slouched in his and pulled out his phone, frowning when he clicked it open.

"They shut off my service," he said quietly.

"Are you kidding me?" I jerked my own phone out of my bag to check if we were just in some freak dead spot or something, but I had full bars. I fumed all over again.

"I'll add you to my plan," I said, shoving my phone back in my bag.

"Tallulah Thatcher? Pleased to meet you." Elaine Hastings extended her hand.

I stood and shook it. She was several inches shorter than me, even in her pretty navy-blue heels. They matched her very expensive-looking suit perfectly. Her auburn hair was cut in a very flattering pixie that accentuated her high cheekbones.

"And you must be Bryce." She turned to him and shook his hand as well. "Come into my office, and we can get started."

I began by updating her on the morning's events. When I'd initially made the appointment, I'd thought we were going to be fighting to keep Bryce in Louisiana. All of that had changed, and now the focus was getting guardianship as fast as possible so I could assume the care and feeding of a teenage boy. She shifted focus seamlessly and outlined all the steps we needed to complete, which involved filing documents and requests in both Missouri and Louisiana. She assured us she would get to work right away and petition for expediency at every opportunity, but cautioned us that could still take months.

She told me that she would take over contact with Mom and Jared and work to get the necessary documentation to allow us to enroll him in school. When I vented just a bit of my anger, she warned me to keep things civil with Mom and Jared so they would continue to cooperate with us. I wanted to finally cut ties with them completely. Bryce was the only reason I'd continued to have anything to do with them, and now that he was here, I didn't see any reason to keep subjecting myself to them. But I could hang on long enough to make it legal.

After I wrote a check for a significant portion of the money in my checking account, we left Elaine's office. I needed to figure out what else I wanted to ask Mia, go back and talk to Albert, and try to catch Eddie at the jobsite again. And I hadn't had a chance to go back and talk to Adam either. But I put that off in order to run by the cell phone store and add Bryce to my plan. Thankfully, his phone was compatible with my carrier, so the transition was pretty straightforward, and I didn't have to fork over another huge chunk of change.

"I'll send Mom my new number," Bryce said as we got back in the car.

I wanted to tell him not to, but remembered Elaine just warning me not to do that. So instead, I simply nodded. I couldn't help but think that if Mom had wanted to stay in touch, then she wouldn't have canceled his service immediately after leaving our house. We lapsed into an easy silence on the way home, each of us consumed in our own thoughts.

It was almost lunchtime when we got back home. We pulled in to find Nan and Ron, who had Toby tucked under one arm, walking around the backyard, talking with a man holding a clipboard. There was a white truck parked behind Ron's with a "Quality Fencing Solutions" decal on the side. Bryce and I joined them. From the last bits of their conversation I overheard, I gathered that Nan was getting a quote for a fence so Toby could have the run of the yard.

"Does this mean you're going to keep him?" Bryce asked. He reached out and took Toby from Ron, and the little puppy was so happy he wiggled all over.

"Of course, we're keeping him," Nan said.

Bryce turned to me expectantly. "Can he stay in my room?"

It looked very much like I was losing my little buddy, at least part of the time anyway. But I couldn't resist. And as busy as I was at the shop, he would get more attention from Bryce in the evenings anyway. I nodded and Bryce looked like he might burst with excitement.

"C'mon Toby, let's go do some homework." Bryce hugged him gently. "Until I can transfer down here, I'll just keep working online. I don't want to get too behind."

"I think that's a great idea." I was so proud of that kid. "I'm going to open up the shop, but you're welcome to come over anytime you want to."

"Thanks. I'll come over when I'm finished."

Nan gave Ron a quick kiss and followed me to the shop. I inhaled deeply when I opened the doors, taking in the sweet vanilla scent. Once inside, I turned to ask Nan if she would watch things for me while I ran around the city like a mad woman, trying to find out if a potential killer had an accomplice, but she spoke before I could.

"Go," she said, waved me on. "Do what you need to do, and I'll hold down the fort here. I'm getting pretty good at this."

"You read my mind."

I grabbed my notebook from under the counter and stowed it in my bag.

"Before I forget, the attorney said we should all play nice with Mom and Jared, at least until the guardianship is official."

"I always play nice." Nan put on her most innocent smile.

"Sure." I gave her a wicked side-eye.

"How are you? That had to be difficult this morning," she said. Concern replaced the silliness.

"I'm fine," I lied. "I'm worried about Bryce, though. I've had longer to deal with them than he has."

"I'm glad you're both here now," she said warmly. "We can all work on healing together."

I circled the counter and hugged her fiercely. "I love you so much," I whispered into her hair.

"I love you too, Lulu Belle."

* * *

I parked down the street from Adam and Mia's house. I didn't risk doing a drive-by to see if she was home, so I tried to creep down the sidewalk as nonchalantly as possible. I was still leaning around a shrub, trying to see into her driveway, when Albert spoke behind me.

"Back so soon?"

"Oh, hi. I was hoping to see you while I was here."

"I haven't haunted anyone, I promise!" He looked horrified.

"I'm here about Mia Brandt again," I tried to reassure him. "I am never going to try to banish you. I don't even know how."

He seemed to believe me, because he visibly relaxed.

"That man you saw lurking around," I said as I glanced around to make sure no one was watching me. "Has he been here recently?"

"Oh yes," he said.

"How recently?"

"I don't have a great sense of time anymore." He shrugged. "I didn't have a great sense of time when I was alive, and now it's much, much worse."

"Was he here in the last few days?"

"Maybe."

"When he was here, did he just watch the house, or did he go inside?"

"Oh, he just crept around outside. I don't think she even knew he was here."

I shuddered at the thought. Adam had been watching me too, for different reasons, but it still made my skin crawl.

"Did you ever see him go into the house? Did it ever seem like she was aware of him?"

"I don't think so. He just watched them, sometimes just her, but sometimes both of them."

"Thank you, Albert. You've been very helpful."

Very helpful might have been a stretch. I needed to know if Jace had been there since Adam died, and I still wasn't sure. It wasn't really important that Jace hadn't been in the house. That wasn't where Adam had been killed, and I already knew about Mia's affair.

"There was something I wanted to ask you the last time you were here," Albert added eagerly.

"What?"

"How can you see me?"

I laughed nervously. I never knew how to answer that question. No one ever seemed to be satisfied with the truth, which was that I had absolutely no idea.

I settled on, "It's a gift I've always had."

He seemed to be considering that information.

"Thank you for your time," I said as I turned to go back to my car.

"Sure." Albert's face brightened. "Come back anytime."

I left and tried to decide if I should see Adam or try to catch Eddie. It was getting late in the day, so it would make more sense to leave my visit with Eddie for tomorrow. Adam it was, then.

After a couple of circles around the cemetery, I found Adam lurking under an oak tree. I pulled into the nearest parking space, and I hadn't even shut the car off yet when he appeared in the passenger seat.

"What's going on?" he asked immediately.

"I'll get to that in just a minute. But first I want you to know how messed up it was that you were *stalking me*. I need you to acknowledge that."

His form faltered for a moment, shimmering like a mirage.

"Yeah, it was. I wish I could go back and change it, and not just because it got me killed, but because it was wrong. You're an honest, genuine person, and you didn't deserve all the crap I gave you."

I was speechless. I'd expected him to argue. I'd expected to have to fight for an apology.

"Lou?"

"Yeah." I snapped back to attention. "I just—I mean . . . thank you."

"You don't have to thank me for an apology I should have already made."

"I came here to tell you that I believe Jace killed you." I told him everything I'd found out so far. He listened quietly and intently, not speaking until I finished.

"I guess just follow your gut. I can't imagine him doing something like that, but what do I know?"

"I'm going to try to keep you updated, but I have a lot going on right now. In addition to being the main suspect in your murder, I've working on getting guardianship of my little brother."

"They don't seriously consider you a suspect," he laughed.

"Adam, they executed a search warrant on my business and home."

"Still, surely it's just to rule you out, right?"

"That's what everyone keeps saying, but it still feels like I'm in real danger of getting framed. I didn't even think that happened in real life."

"You can stop anytime it gets too dangerous. I know I begged you in the beginning to make sure they found my killer, until you agreed, but it's not worth it to put you in danger."

"I think it's too late for that," I said.

Chapter Thirty

Dylan was waiting for me when I got back to the shop. He leaned casually on the counter, talking to Nan.

"Did they forget something when they executed the search warrant?" I said, making sure my voice was dripping with contempt.

Something flashed for just a second on Dylan's face. Had I hurt his feelings?

"I came by to check on you." He stood up straighter and adjusted his jacket.

"I probably shouldn't talk to you without an attorney present," I said, but I dropped the contempt. I didn't want to be a *complete* jerk, but I was also aware that he could use anything I might say to him against me.

"I don't want to be the enemy," he said. He paused as he passed me in the middle of the center aisle.

"Look, I know you have a job to do, and I know it's not your fault I'm caught up in the middle of this." I tried to keep my wits about me as I looked up into those pale blue eyes. God, he smelled good. "But the fact remains we *are* on opposite sides of things right now."

"I can understand why you feel that way," he said quietly, a sad look overtaking his handsome face, "but I have always been on your side. I always will be."

He turned quickly back to Nan. "Good day, Mrs. Thatcher."

I crossed the room and shoved my bag under the counter.

"Are you ever just going to ask that boy out?" Nan put her good hand on her hip.

"Nan!" I gasped, and instantly felt my face get hot.

"You've had a crush on that boy your entire life. Just get it over with and go on a date."

She looked at me, and it made me squirm.

"Now is exactly the time," she called after me. "He obviously cares, or he wouldn't have come by like this."

I tried to ignore her and sort inventory, but she followed me.

"He doesn't care about me like *that*," I argued. "He cares because I'm Cady's friend. Nothing more."

"When this is all over, why don't you test out that little theory?"

"For the same reason I never have: because of Cady. It would be awkward and weird, especially if it didn't work."

"You forget I *know* Cady, and she is the last person on earth who would make a fuss about it."

I sighed an exasperated sigh and continued to sort T-shirts into piles separated by size. Nan sighed too and left me to it. I managed to find enough little projects to stay busy until the first tour guests started filing in. I let my brain rest, pushing any thoughts of murder and suspects out of my mind, and just focused on movement, action.

My tour group that evening was lively and fun. They laughed, cracked jokes, and asked great questions. So when we made it to Mamie's haunt, I worked the word *rabbit* into my discussion of folklore and superstition to signal her that she had full freedom to dazzle them in any way she saw fit. I heard her haunting giggle in response, even though I couldn't see her.

As I continued talking about the New Orleans history surrounding lucky rabbit feet, which includes a colorful story about how the rabbit had to be dispatched in a graveyard on a full moon by a specific type of person at midnight, Mamie got to work. I was the first to notice the tiny orbs, more numerous and smaller than she usually produced, but I tried not to draw attention to them. I wanted one of the guests to notice them without my help.

I thought at first that they were minuscule versions of the screaming skull she'd already created, but I should have given her more credit than that. Finally, one of the young women in the group elbowed her friend and pointed to the display. Heads began to turn, and soon all eyes were on the orbs. Several guests scrambled to get their phones out to record. I hoped they succeeded.

There was a haunting, melancholy melody accompanying them, just barely loud enough to register. It was almost a sigh on the breeze, but somehow musical and menacing. The orbs themselves were so small it was hard to focus on their features. They resembled diaphanous jack-o'-lanterns, with little glowing pinpricks for eyes and a jagged, ripped line for a mouth. They floated around us like dust motes, lulling us into a reverie. Then, suddenly, the orbs swirled violently, threateningly before they screamed and appeared to melt, midair, into a million flecks of light, like glitter. It was over in a matter of a few seconds, yet we all stood looking at one another, transfixed. Me included. Mamie never ceased to amaze me.

"*What* was that?" asked the young woman who had first noticed the orbs. She had long, brunette hair that hung in beachy waves over her shoulders.

"This area is becoming quite the hot spot for orb manifestations," I said when I found my voice. "I'm so glad you were all here to witness it."

It took a while, as it always does after one of Mamie's productions, to get everyone moving along again. And for the rest of the tour, everyone was abuzz with trying to figure out if they'd captured photos and videos. I kept to my usual stories and histories, but I doubted anyone paid any attention. I sneaked in a little wave at Adam on our way by, and he waved back, a sad smile on his flickering features.

* * *

It didn't take long to shut down after the tour since I'd already restocked all afternoon. I'd managed to talk Nan into going home when I'd first returned, but she sent Ron over to walk me home. He pulled up a stool and sat at the counter. I'd planned to take my nightly walk and talk to both Adam and Mamie. I needed to thank her for the spectacular show she'd put on tonight.

"Anything I can help with?"

"I'm pretty much finished. I just want to sweep back here."

"Good tour tonight?"

"It was," I said, and paused my sweeping to lean on my broom. "So, you and Nan . . ."

A broad smile bloomed across his face, pulling his white mustache up at the corners. He stroked his beard and nodded. "I'm hooked," he said. "I worship the ground that woman walks on."

"She's happier than I've seen her in a long time," I admitted. "She hasn't told me much about you, though."

To be fair, I hadn't asked either.

"What do you want to know?"

"How did you meet?"

He laughed. "I got in line behind her at the grocery store. There was just something about her. When I'd checked out, she was still in the parking lot, so I asked her out." He got a faraway, dreamy look on his face.

"I lost my sweet Alice almost ten years ago, and I never thought I'd find anyone else I wanted to spend my life with. But Lizzie . . . Lizzie's special."

"Do you have kids?"

"We had one precious boy, Paul." Pure, raw grief overtook his face. "He had Down syndrome, and we lost him to heart complications far too young."

"I'm so sorry. I shouldn't have pried."

"Of course you should. You're entitled to know anything you want about me. And it hurts, but I like to talk about Paul. He was a kind, gentle soul, and my world is better for having loved him."

Tears welled in my eyes. I was struck by the difference between Ronald and Jared. I would bet real money that Jared had never said anything so heartfelt about Bryce. I covered up my sudden burst of emotion by finishing up my sweeping.

"Thanks for walking me all the way home," I said, laughing as I locked up.

"It's a long trip. Lizzie was worried." Ron smirked back. "But seriously, you ever need anything, you let me know. If I catch someone trying to hurt anyone in this family, they'll regret it."

"I'm glad you're here," I said, and even though I meant it, I surprised myself by saying it out loud. Before he had a chance to respond, I ducked inside and sprinted up the stairs. I lingered outside Bryce's room, and Kenneth appeared in the hall.

"He's asleep. Took the little mongrel out for a run and then crashed out."

"Mongrel?" I raised an eyebrow.

"Adorable, but mongrel nonetheless."

I yawned and looked wistfully toward my room.

"You should sleep."

"I need to go thank Mamie for a spectacular show she put on tonight."

"I'll bet she would understand. Get some rest for a change."

I opened my mouth to argue but snapped it shut again when I realized all I wanted was to curl up and go to sleep. I wanted to forget all about murderers and suspects. I wanted to go to sleep and wake up and find that all of this was over.

Chapter Thirty-One

I n what had become our new morning routine, I ate breakfast with Nan, Bryce, and Ron while Toby chewed our shoes and Fitz fumed from the periphery.

"What's on the agenda today?" Ron asked as he cleared away the dishes.

"I thought Bryce and I would help Lou at the shop," Nan said, reaching across the table to squeeze Bryce's arm. "After he finishes his schoolwork, of course."

"Of course." Bryce playfully rolled his eyes.

Ron looked expectantly at me.

"I have a few errands to run this morning, but I shouldn't be long."

"We'll be here when you get back," Nan said with a knowing wink.

I made a beeline for Mamie's haunt. I chose to drive so I could use Adam's suggestion to speak to her in my car. She took to the idea immediately and asked a million questions about cars and how they work, only about half of which I was able to answer without the help of Google. Kenneth had been correct about Mamie understanding I had needed to rest, but she was practically vibrating with excitement

209

by the time I pulled up our tagged videos from the previous evening. The comments did not disappoint, especially the lively debate between one man who was one hundred percent sure the orbs were an elaborate hoax, and the video poster who kept insisting she was there and that there was no way it could have been faked.

"I love it when they quarrel," she said when I'd finished reading the entire back-and-forth.

"I'll keep you updated as more come in. I'm expecting that one to get a lot of interaction. That was a pretty epic show you put on."

"You believe so?"

"It was amazing!"

"I always wonder if it is enough," Mamie said.

It was so endearing when she became shy and unsure of her ability to stun the socks off my guests.

"If it's any more, I'm going to have to put health disclaimers in my reservation agreement," I said, laughing. "You'll give my guests heart attacks!"

Mamie laughed and then looked very serious again.

"How is your investigation coming along?" She looked at me intently.

I sighed. "I think I finally have a clear direction. But I don't know. Seems like I just hit a roadblock at every turn."

"You must persevere," Mamie said fervently. "It is selfish on my part, but I am quite attached to you."

"I am quite attached to you too, Mamie." I wished I could reach out and hold her hand. "I'll figure this out, one way or another."

* * *

With a renewed sense of determination, I left Mamie and drove straight to Coliseum Park. I circled on foot a few times, trying to stay inconspicuous, to see if Jace and Eddie were there, which they were. If Jace noticed me, he didn't let on. He seemed to be leaning on his shovel more than using it, and he pulled his phone out of his back pocket every few minutes and looked at the screen.

I circled again, and by that time Eddie had moved some distance away from Jace to unload supplies. It looked like they were finishing up their work, so I was glad I'd come back when I did. I positioned myself on the other side of a parked truck so I wouldn't be easily visible to Jace, but Eddie noticed me right away.

"Comment ça va?" he said with a big grin. He had cement dust on his forehead where he'd wiped his arm earlier.

"I'm good. Would you mind answering a couple of quick follow-up questions?" I glanced nervously back in Jace's direction.

"Sure," he said, and took a few steps forward to join me beside the pickup.

"This is Mia Brandt." I pulled up her Instagram photo on my phone. "Has she come to see Jace Klein here in the last week? Maybe after work or on his lunch break?"

"Not that I've noticed. But I don't pay much attention to him, to be honest."

"Okay, thank you. I really appreciate your time."

"You could make it up to me," he said with another broad grin, this one a little crooked. It suited him. So did the faint wrinkles at the corners of his eyes.

I cocked my head a little to the side but didn't respond.

"You could have a drink with me Friday night," he continued. "I clean up pretty good."

A smile tugged at the corners of my lips. I looked at Eddie Dumont in a whole new light, and I could imagine how well he cleaned up.

"I run tours all weekend, unfortunately," I was forced to say.

"Name the night, then. I'm flexible." He leaned on the truck casually. "But 'no' is also a choice, if you're not interested." There was no challenge in his voice or demeanor, and it was really refreshing. Plus, he wasn't the brother of my best friend, and there were no messy entanglements to worry about. Eddie wasn't hot in the same way Dylan was hot; he was more rough and rugged, but it worked. It was the look that Jace was trying for in his lumberjack thirst traps, but Eddie accomplished it effortlessly.

"My days off are kind of all over the place, but I don't have anything scheduled Monday, and I'd love to have a drink with you." I suddenly felt self-conscious and wished that I'd put more effort into my appearance, but he *had* already asked me out despite my lack of fashion sense or any makeup save for a little bit of mascara.

"Monday is perfect."

He took off his leather gloves and reached into his pocket for his phone. We'd just finished exchanging phone numbers when I jumped at a loud cursing behind me. I turned around and came face to face with Jace Klein.

Chapter Thirty-Two

"What are you doing here?" Jace asked, his voice low and menacing. "Are you following me?"

"Not everything is about you," Eddie said, moving up beside me. "She's here to see me."

"I don't believe you."

"I don't care what you believe, Genius," Eddie laughed. "Go back and lean on a shovel."

"What's that supposed to mean?"

"We all know you're allergic to work. Wouldn't want those soft hands getting a callous."

Jace got red in the face and rocked back and forth like he was about to throw down.

"I don't know what's going on back here, and I don't care," an older man said, joining our little party. "But you two need to get back to work, and you need to move along." He pointed at me.

"Sure, I'm so sorry." I nodded at the foreman.

"I'll call you and we can work out details," I said to Eddie, and ignored Jace.

"Looking forward to it."

I walked away quickly but glanced back as I left. Jace was jabbing his finger into Eddie's chest, but Eddie just looked amused at the whole situation. The foreman yelled at them again to get back to work, and they separated. Eddie pulled on his gloves and went back to the sacks of cement. Jace stormed angrily toward the fountain.

I was downright giddy on my drive back to the shop. I hadn't been on a date in forever, and I was more than ready for some fun distraction in my life. I tried to think about what to do next to figure out whether Jace was guilty, but my thoughts kept snapping back to Eddie. I really needed to get out more.

Nan was sitting behind the counter when I got back. Bryce had joined her and was playing with Toby on the floor. Toby's little puppy growls and yips were too cute for words.

"Hey, you two." I bent down to pet Toby, and Bryce handed me the tug rope.

"Watch out. His little teeth are like needles."

"No joke. They're brutal."

"No customers yet today," Nan said, looking up from the game of Candy Crush she was playing on her iPad.

"It's early yet for foot traffic. They usually start trickling in closer to dark."

I heard Tess's keys jingle as she tried the back door. "It's unlocked," I called out.

She burst through the door in her usual swirl of pleasant chaos.

"Hello, Thatchers!" she sang as she slung an enormous tote full of creepy puppets onto the counter.

"And one Monroe," Bryce raised his hand high enough for her to see it over the counter.

"Hello, Thatchers and one Monroe!" she sang again.

"What do we have here?" Nan asked as she opened the bag of horrors, I mean *puppets*.

"I've almost got all the finishing touches on these guys for the upcoming show. I thought I could work on them between customers."

"Oh, cool." Bryce stood up and pulled one of the blue fuzzy demons out of the bag. I fought off a shudder as its lifeless, beady eyes lolled over in my direction. "Can I help?"

"I'd love some help!" Tess said enthusiastically. Then she leaned over and cupped her hand next to her mouth. "Between you and me, your sister is afraid of the puppets."

"Why on earth are you afraid of these adorable things?" Nan asked. She pulled a yellow feathery thing out of the bag and held it up.

"I'm not *afraid* of them," I protested. "I just don't *like* them. The same way some people don't like clowns."

"Sure, Boss." Tess clapped me on the shoulder and winked at me.

I gave her a scathing look, and she winked at me again.

She and Bryce set up on the little desk behind the counter, with overflow on the folding table I kept in the storage room for unboxing and sorting inventory. Nan took her spot back on one of the stools behind the counter and I took the other one as far away from the puppets as possible.

I opened the reservation bookings and checked my schedule. But I was quickly distracted and found myself clicking over to Facebook to see if Eddie Dumont's profile was unlocked. It wasn't. But his profile picture was of him, leaning against a wooden fence with a beautiful shepherd mix dog sitting next to him. There were four comments visible under the photo. Two of them were emojis, heart eyes smiley face, and the flame emoji. A third said "nice photo Bro" from someone named Allan Dumont. And the fourth was from someone named Theresa Monterey that said, "You and Murphy are looking good." Any man who has pets that appear to be as well cared for as the blue merle shepherd in that photo automatically goes up a few notches in my book. I clicked out of Facebook and went back to the chart I'd created on my laptop. Adam had proved that he wasn't the most objective in helping me look into his family and friends, either because he really believed they weren't responsible or because he couldn't admit it even to himself. I needed someone who knew Adam but wasn't plagued by the doubts Adam had about my suspects, someone who could look at the evidence objectively and help me sort through it. I scrolled through my text messages and clicked on Lucas Wells's number.

Hi, it's Lou. I was wondering if you had some time to talk?

I put my phone down, not expecting an immediate reply, but it dinged as soon as my hand left the PopSocket.

I can be there in 30. Or if that doesn't work, I'm free at 7 too.

I glanced at the time.

I have a tour starting soon, but I can meet tomorrow.

I watched the little dots at the bottom of the screen.

Why don't I just come by after the tour?

My tour for the evening was a light one. Initially, a family group had booked half the available openings, but they'd canceled because of illness, and I'd failed to repost the spots. When I'd discovered my mistake, I'd posted them right away, but only one other person booked, bringing the tour total to six, down from my usual ten. I could take some extra time to make it cozy and memorable. But even though it was a small group, the tour would still last until ten PM or later.

I won't get finished until after 10.

Again, he replied quickly. *I don't mind at all. Love to help. See you tonight then.*

I typed multiple messages, but everything sounded wrong somehow so I ended up just sending a thumbs-up emoji.

I was still trying to decide if I should signal Mamie to dazzle my little group with whatever new orbs she'd imagined up, when the guests started checking in. While I hadn't noticed her name on the booking, I recognized the pink-haired Granny Ghost Hunter right away. She stood in line behind another guest, waiting for Nan to scan the QR code on her phone, generated by the booking site. When it was her turn, her eyes lit up as I joined Nan at the counter.

"Welcome back," I said with a smile.

"Hello, dear. I found some very interesting things on my camera the last time I was here, and I was hoping to see if I could capture anything else."

"I love it when people come back."

"Oh good." She looked relieved. "I was hoping you wouldn't mind."

"Of course not! I hope you won't get tired of hearing me tell the same stories, but you're welcome to come back as many times as you want."

She patted my hand. "Thank you, dear. Here's to hoping that we have an active evening."

I moved with her down the counter as another guest checked in with Nan.

"Just out of curiosity, what did you catch?"

"Joan," she said extending a hand.

"Lou." I shook her offered hand, strong and weathered. She reminded me of Nan; age had done nothing to dim her fierceness either.

"There was some interesting shadow play near the cemetery. I'm not entirely convinced it's a capture. Our group has already dismissed it, but I just wanted to come back and see if there's anything else," she said sheepishly.

"Can I see?"

"Sure!" Her whole face lit up.

She pulled out an older model Nikon digital camera and clicked back through the images. She pulled up a photo of the cemetery gates. I recognized the slightly zoomed-in view of Lafayette Cemetery No. 1 from our route that passes by that very spot. I'm ashamed to admit that I didn't see anything when I first looked at the photo. I see that a lot. People will send me photos they took on their tour, showcasing a blurry leaf or a speck of dirt on their camera lens, and they are absolutely sure they've captured a paranormal image.

"You don't see it, do you?" she asked, but she didn't seem disappointed by my lack of recognition.

"I'm sorry."

"Look here." She pointed to the long shadow cast by an oak tree. It stretched into the street. I squinted, but I couldn't see anything in the shadow. It was just a shadow.

"Okay, now look at this one." This time she pointed to the shadow cast by a random pedestrian walking past the tree. "The shadows are cast in opposite directions." There was a triumphant look on her face.

I let out a little gasp as it finally dawned on me.

"The group thinks that the anomaly was caused by a passing car or some other trick of the light, but I can't find any evidence of that in any of the photos before or after this one. The shadows are opposite only in this one." She clicked through the photos to show me, and sure enough, she was right. There was nothing off about the shadows in any of the others.

"That's not even the most interesting thing," she said as she took the camera back. "This photo of you isn't like anything I've ever seen before."

I held my breath as she turned the camera screen back toward me. There I was, in the right side of the frame, the cemetery across the street behind me. But there was something else too. A blob-like thing that was both behind me and in front of me at the same time.

It was more solid, more corporeal behind me, with just a suggestion of form in front of me, but it was unmistakably there.

"I think it's ectoplasm," she whispered conspiratorially. "That's why I wanted to take another tour. I think you might be the key to this."

I studied the photo more closely and tried to remember that single moment captured on her camera. Was that when Adam was screaming at me? Had Joan gotten a photo of Adam materializing? It would make sense. He'd been completely unhinged, and the energy he must have been channeling would have been immense. It could very well have bled over into the physical world.

Nan motioned to me in my peripheral vision that everyone in the tour group was now checked in.

"I'd love to talk more after the tour," I said. I wondered if it was Adam making the shadows wonky too. Ghosts can affect reality in some strange ways sometimes, even when they're not a raging lunatic.

"If everything goes well, maybe we'll have even more to talk about." She grinned and crossed her fingers.

The tour group was engaged and friendly, and although I was really enjoying the guests, there was a chill in the air, and I felt jumpy and apprehensive. I kept getting the feeling I was being watched, even though that would mean someone would have to be following me. It was absurd to think that, really. Or at least that was what I kept telling myself. Every chance I got, I would scan the area for anyone I recognized . . . like Jace or Damian. But they weren't there. It was just my imagination running away with me.

Once again, Adam kept a respectful distance from my tour. I nodded to him to let him know I appreciated it, and he smiled at me before fading away. Joan snapped a photo every few seconds, most of which were aimed in my direction. I tried not to cringe at the thought of all those pictures of me.

Although the group was friendly and engaged, and Mamie flooded the area with some stunningly delicate orbs, I don't think anyone but Joan was a hardcore ghost enthusiast. I'm pretty sure Joan was the only one who even tried to get a photo of Mamie's orbs, a fact that was not lost on her. She'd even blasted an orb right into one guy's face, and he managed to miss it.

We finished a little earlier than I'd originally thought, which worked out well since I'd forgotten I had made plans with Lucas after the tour, and I still wanted to visit with Joan. The group didn't stay long in the shop after we returned. Ron, who had joined Nan while I was gone, helped me talk her into going home to finally get some rest. Once they were gone, I invited Joan to join me at my little desk in the back.

"I haven't had a chance to go back through very many of tonight's photos," she said as she pulled up my spare chair. "I may have gone a little crazy. Thank goodness for digital cameras!"

"No joke." I laughed. "Would you like some tea or coffee? I have a kettle in the back."

"Oh no, I don't want you to go to the trouble."

We sat side by side and clicked through her photos, looking for anything out of the ordinary, paying extra attention to the ones near the cemetery, where she'd captured the first photos. I was just about to give up on there being anything to see when she pulled up an image of the sidewalk by the main entrance. It was early in the evening, at the beginning of the tour, and a fair number of pedestrians were still visible in the streetlights.

When I recognized the face looking back at the camera, I gasped so loudly Joan jumped.

Chapter Thirty-Three

"What is it? What do you see?" Joan leaned over the screen, scrutinizing what had caused my reaction.

I leaned in too, disbelieving my own eyes. But there was no denying it. Adam looked back at me, waving, with a wistful smile. He had a slightly fuzzy, unfocused look, but otherwise, there was no indication that he was a ghost.

"I'm so sorry." I smiled apologetically. "I thought I saw my ex, but it's not him. I feel silly that I still think I see him everywhere."

She looked at me skeptically but didn't press me further. She resumed clicking through the images while my mind raced. Why was Adam so clearly visible in that photo? It was even more likely that the earlier picture she'd captured was Adam as well. But why? I've never seen any other ghost so clearly photographed. Not that I'm an expert in the field, but I'd wager I've seen more spirits than even the most seasoned ghost hunter. Maybe it was because he was a "young" ghost. Adam was definitely the newest spirit I'd ever met.

Joan finally reached the end of her reel and leaned back in her chair.

"Well, save for ex-boyfriend doppelgangers, I didn't get squat this time."

"Tell you what," I said, and got up from my chair. I grabbed one of my brochures off the counter and scrawled a note across the front. "Next tour is on me if you can stand to hear all my stories for a third time."

"You don't have to do that, dear." She shook her head.

"I want to."

She smiled as she took it. I hoped she would cash it in. I enjoyed her company, and I was definitely curious to see if she would be able to catch more photos of Adam. We said our goodbyes, and I started the nightly wind down. Tess spoils me. She always has the daily totals tallied and everything ready to shut down by the time I get back from the tours. I vowed that when all of this was over and I could breathe again, I would propose that she come on full-time, maybe as a partner. We were good together, and I hoped she wanted to expand as much as I did.

I heard the door open in the silent shop and turned around. I expected to see Lucas Wells, but it wasn't Lucas. Jace Klein stood in the doorway, framed by the darkness outside.

"Can I help you?" My voice cracked.

"I don't know. *Can you?*" he sneered in a singsong taunt. "Can you help me by leaving me the hell alone?"

He took a step into the shop and shoved the display of Haunts & Jaunts souvenirs onto the floor. Keychains skittered against the wall, and mugs shattered as they hit the hardwood. Toby startled in his little bed and looked to me for reassurance. I bent down and grabbed him before he ran away. I started to inch toward the back door.

"I just wanted to talk to you," I said softly.

"About *what?*"

Another couple of steps and he kicked another display over, this time sending books, bookmarks, and stickers flying across the floor.

I winced as some of the dust jackets on the New Orleans history books tore in the chaos.

"About Mia Brandt," I said, still inching toward the back door. If I could just get outside, I could duck into the shed. If I couldn't barricade myself inside, I was sure I could find something in there I could use as a weapon. What on earth had I done with my phone?

"Well, here I am," he said, his arms spread wide, a maniacal smile plastered on his face. "What do you want to know?"

He punctuated that question by shoving over both tables of T-shirts and sweatshirts. At least they wouldn't break when they hit the floor. I couldn't say the same for my display tables and shelves, though. He was destroying my entire shop on his way to do the same to me. So much for Adam's assessment. *This* Jace Klein was more than capable of violence. Toby squirmed in my arms, I'm sure sensing both my fear and Jace's anger.

"You know you almost got me fired," he sneered again when I didn't answer.

I wanted to say that I hadn't made him run away like a little coward, but I thought better of it before it dropped out of my big mouth. Antagonizing the threatening maniac wouldn't be the smartest move I could make.

"I'm sorry." I tried to sound sincere. I wondered when he had been in my shop to take the dagger he'd used to kill Adam. It could have been anytime, though. It's impossible to watch everyone at once. Not that it mattered at the moment; I just couldn't keep my mind from racing a mile a minute.

As if he'd read my mind, he sidestepped to the shelf where the occult supplies were displayed. I was thankful that I'd pulled the inventory of decorative daggers after Dylan told me that a dagger had been the murder weapon. But there were some very pointy crystal wands on the shelf that could definitely be stabby in the right hands.

I decided to take my chances at escape while he was still a good distance away. I turned on my heel and sprinted the few steps toward the back door. I hadn't counted on Jace being cat quick or accounted for him jumping the counter instead of going around it. He was between me and my only means of escape before I even got a hand on the doorknob. My heart was pounding in my ears, and I could barely hang on to Toby, who seemed to be as terrified as I was.

"Where do you think you're going?"

Jace reached toward Toby, and I jerked him out of his reach. Acting purely on fear, instinct, and a deep desire to *not* end up as a ghost myself, I hauled off and kicked Jace in the shin with all the force I could muster. It wasn't nearly as impressive as I'd imagined, because I had been aiming for his crotch, but true to my usual lack of coordination, I missed. Still, it had the desired effect, and he stumbled backward, cursing. I didn't waste any time grabbing the door, but Jace slammed it shut as soon as I opened it. He raised a hand, and I instinctively ducked and braced myself for the blow, but it never came.

I opened my eyes to find Jace being hauled backward.

"Are you okay?" Lucas Wells asked as he continued to pull Jace toward the counter.

"Yes," I answered breathlessly.

Jace regained his balance and squirmed out of Lucas's grasp. He whirled around and swung at Lucas, but Lucas easily ducked the clumsy blow. I saw my phone lying on the little table where Joan and I had looked at her photos, and dove for it. Toby continued to squirm, but I held on tight. I dialed 911 and started rattling off my address and requests for help, like an auctioneer on crack, as soon as the operator connected.

When Jace realized that I was on the phone with the authorities, a look of horror washed over his face. He turned and sprinted for the open front door just like he had the day I'd tried to talk to him.

"Stay here," Lucas said, and took off after him.

I didn't have any intention of chasing Jace, but I nodded anyway. The 911 operator kept asking me if I was there and if I was okay. I kept answering her, but I was only sure about one of those things. There, yes. Okay? I had no idea.

Chapter Thirty-Four

After several very long minutes, Lucas jogged through the front door.

"That jerk is *fast*," he said with a nervous laugh. He nodded toward my phone. "Police on their way?"

"Yeah, hopefully soon."

And then, as if on cue, we heard sirens approaching. I cringed, knowing the commotion would wake Nan and Ron. I couldn't see the house since the broken window was covered with sheet metal, but I imagined the lights flicking on as two cruisers pulled in at the front of the shop, their flashing lights casting pulsing shadows over everything.

I disconnected the 911 call and shoved my phone in my pocket. I was grateful to have two free hands to wrestle with Toby.

"Who was that guy?" Lucas asked.

"Jace Klein. He was having an affair with Adam's wife."

"How did you find *that* out?"

"Police Department! Make yourself known!" came a booming male voice just outside the front door.

"I'm Lou Thatcher!" I yelled back. "I'm the one who called! My friend Lucas is in here too, but he's not the one who assaulted me!"

The officers entered through the open front door, guns drawn. I put up one hand and held Toby in front of me to show the other hand was full of puppy. Lucas raised both his hands above his head. The male officer, a tall Black man, holstered his weapon and crossed the room to the counter. His female counterpart followed suit, but she was slower to cross the room, taking in all of the destruction.

After Officers Will Brooks and Saylie Evans introduced themselves to us, I had just started to tell them what happened when Nan and Ron burst through the back door.

"Lou? Lou!" Nan called frantically, not giving me time to answer in between her yelling out my name. "Tallulah!"

"I'm here. I'm fine." I waved my hand to get her attention.

She completely ignored the police officers and pulled me into a crushing hug, nearly squishing Toby in between us.

"What is going on here?" she demanded when she was finished squeezing the life out of me.

"I promise I'll fill you in, but right now I need to finish up here."

She nodded. But I thought she might cry when she looked around the shop. Instead, she stood a little straighter, pulled her sweater a little tighter, and then took Toby from me. His little tail thumped against the plaster splint on her wrist.

"I'll be home as soon as I can." I squeezed her shoulder, and she nodded again.

Ron turned back to me on his way out the door. "Just call if you need anything, kiddo."

"Thank you. I will."

Officer Evans took Nan and Ron's contact information before they could get out the door.

"Back to the events of the evening." Officer Brooks seemed to be trying to get me to focus again. Thankfully, these two seemed more committed to figuring out what had happened than the one who'd responded when my window had been destroyed.

"I had just closed up for the night when—"

"Lou!" Dylan burst through the front door almost as frantically as Nan had torn through the back. He flashed his badge at the officers but never took his eyes off me. "Are you all right?"

"I'm a little shaken up but okay."

He looked Lucas up and down.

"This is Lucas. I'm pretty thankful he showed up when he did. He kept Jace from—" I couldn't finish that sentence. I didn't want to think about what he'd stopped Jace from doing.

Officer Brooks used his flashlight to continue looking around the shop while Officer Evans went back outside.

"Walk me through what happened," Dylan said.

So, I did. I recounted everything from when Joan left to the moment the two police officers had arrived. Lucas told them about the few moments when he had given chase, when Jace proved to be too fast and sped away in his truck. Dylan listened intently; concern written all over his face. When I finished, I really thought he was going to offer comfort, or at the very least, some basic human decency.

"Maybe you'll take this seriously now," Dylan said coldly.

So much for comfort and decency.

"I *am* taking this seriously. I have *always* taken this seriously. Especially the part where you accused me of murder."

He sighed and pinched the bridge of his nose. "I never accused you of anything. I merely pointed out that we would follow the evidence. But the fact remains that none of this would have happened if you weren't playing Nancy Drew. You keep doing stupid things and making reckless decisions. How am I supposed to keep you safe if you keep insisting on behaving like there aren't consequences?"

"Cady doesn't expect you to 'keep me safe.'" I used my fingers to make air quotes.

"I don't worry about you just because you're Cady's best friend," he said quietly.

My breath caught in my chest and I suddenly had a belly full of butterflies. Did that mean what I thought it meant? Was I reading too much into it because I wanted to believe I was more to him than his sister's friend? Or did he just mean he was worried in that whole "protect and serve" way?

"I gave my contact information to that officer." Lucas pointed toward Officer Brooks. "Do you need anything else tonight?"

"No. If we need anything else, we'll be in touch."

I took a step back and leaned on the counter, grateful that Lucas had broken the awkwardness.

"And you," Dylan pointed at me. "Just stay out of this. Keep your head down, and stay safe."

I couldn't think of a witty response, so I just crossed my arms and glared at him. Thankfully, he turned then and left. Without looking back, I should add. Whatever moment I thought we'd shared had just been wishful thinking. And as I stood there fuming, I felt stupid for even wanting to have a moment with that infuriating man.

"Want to reschedule?" Lucas's question jerked me out of my internal conflict.

"Yeah, I think that might be a good idea. I'm exhausted." Just admitting how tired I was made me yawn. "Thank you so much for everything."

"Call me tomorrow," Lucas said with a smile. "We can hash it all out over coffee."

I gave him a thumbs-up.

"Come lock the door behind me. We don't know where Jace went, and he seemed like he was crazy enough to come back."

"Yeah, no joke." I shuddered as I thought about that.

I locked the door after Lucas left and then went to the back and locked that door as well. I wasn't ready to go to the house and repeat everything I had just told Dylan, so I started cleaning up Jace's mess. I separated the intact items from the casualties and wondered if I could file for the loss on my insurance. After all, that was one of the reasons I paid for insurance, wasn't it? Then my exhausted mind started making weird connections. Like, what if Jace knew about Adam's life insurance, and what if it was more than Adam had thought it was? Money is always a huge motive in murder cases. He might have thought he could weasel his way back into Mia's life. Or maybe she was in on it all along. Surely, now that Jace Klein had committed an actual crime Dylan would have to take a harder look into him. If threatening and vandalism were serious enough crimes to get Dylan's attention, that is. He seemed to only want to pay attention to the things that pointed to me.

I went to the back room to get the broom and dustpan but stopped where I'd thrown my bag. I knew inside that bag was a notebook where I'd written down everything I'd learned so far and moved Jace to the top of my list of suspects. After tonight, he was my *only* suspect. I was a bundle of nervous energy, and against all good sense, all I wanted to do was go talk to Adam. I wanted to tell him how wrong he was about everything and find out if he knew something, anything, that might help nail Jace to the wall.

I reasoned to myself that it was safer to drive over to Adam's haunt than it was to walk since I doubted the police had caught that maniac Jace Klein yet. I texted Nan that I needed to do something before I came home, and while she didn't seem thrilled with the idea, she said they would be waiting for me when I got home. I told her how much I loved and appreciated her, and she responded with what has become our personal code, the heart emoji and the bell emoji. "I love you, Lulu Belle."

I drove slowly past the cemetery, looking for any sign of Adam. At this late hour, finding a parking spot wasn't a problem, so I pulled in under a streetlamp where I could still see the cemetery walls. I waited for Adam to show up, but since I could hardly sit still, I moved the car several times. I finally gave up and got out. I clutched my jacket and spent a ridiculous amount of time trying to see behind me. But that's just the thing, there's *always* a "behind you," no matter how many times you spin around like an idiot.

"You're extra jumpy tonight."

I recognized Adam's voice before I figured out where it was coming from.

"Well, I have good reason to be." I looked up at Adam, perched on the cemetery wall like the Cheshire cat.

Concern immediately replaced the smirk on his face. He dissolved into a fine mist and then appeared in front of me.

"What's wrong? Did something happen?"

"You could say that," I said, hugging myself against the chill in the night air, which was exaggerated by Adam's presence.

"Are you going to tell me?" he asked impatiently.

"Jace attacked me tonight."

"He *what*?"

I recognized the look of rage building on Adam's transparent face. I'd seen it several times recently as he struggled to contain his emotions. I was in the middle of telling him everything that had happened when he held up his hand to stop me.

"That's it. You have to stop. This is far too dangerous for you to keep going. I don't want you to keep taking risks like this anymore."

"I'm already in the middle of it. I think it's too late to stop. Jace knows who I am and where I work, and he's already proved he's capable of violence," I said pointedly, making sure Adam understood I was saying *I told you so.* "I need to make sure he's arrested, prosecuted, and sent to prison."

"I never meant for you to be in danger. I've been so selfish."

"At least your friend is willing to help. Honestly, if it weren't for him, I'm not sure what would have happened." I shivered again.

"*My* friend?"

"Yeah. Lucas Wells. I was meeting him at the shop after my tour. He was going to help me go through what we know about your, uh, case. He got there just in time and chased Jace off."

"Lucas Wells is *not* my friend."

Chapter Thirty-Five

"What do you mean he's not your friend?" I could feel my heartbeat speeding up again, adrenaline spiking as my anxiety peaked.

"Lucas Wells was a creepy little thief. I caught him stealing from guests at the Barlowe and went straight to the manager."

"Wait, it was you? He said Damian got him fired for messing up tour reservations."

"Reservations? He didn't have anything to do with our reservations. He was a bellhop." Adam paced a few steps in front of me on the sidewalk. Well, he floated angrily, anyway. "I was filming during one of our ghost tours through the staff hallway. It's supposed to be one of the more haunted areas in the Barlowe. When I was reviewing the footage later, I realized I had caught that little worm stealing out of a guest's luggage while he was waiting for the elevator."

"Oh my god," I whispered. I felt like all the oxygen had been sucked out of the air around me, and I couldn't catch my breath. "He lied about everything."

"For a few weeks he followed me everywhere, begging me to help him get his job back, but I wasn't about to help that sniveling little thief."

"How long ago was that?" I asked, breathlessly.

"I don't know. A month or so?"

"Was Lucas mad enough to kill you?"

Adam's head snapped back toward me, his eyes wide and pan-icked. It took just a fraction of a moment for me to realize he wasn't looking at me. He was looking *behind* me. I whirled around just in time to see Lucas Wells raise his hand above his head, knife glinting in the streetlight.

Instinctively, I threw my arms up in defense, even though my flesh would be no match for what looked like a large Bowie knife.

"Lou!" Adam yelled from beside me, and in a blinding flash of light, he managed to push me out of the way of Lucas's blade. Much like he'd done with the leaves to entertain Toby, Adam shoved me down the sidewalk.

I recovered quickly, but Adam was a different story. He was barely keeping his form.

"Run." Adam's voice was little more than a whisper carried on the breeze, and then he was gone. I didn't have time to think about what that meant, if he had somehow extinguished the tether that kept him in this world by exerting himself so much to save me.

"Who were you talking to?" Lucas turned toward me, his momentary confusion gone as fast as it came. "I heard you talking to someone about me."

I looked around. Homes were lining the streets so close, but so out of reach.

"Help!" I screamed as loud as I could manage. My throat felt raw with the effort. "Help!"

No lights flicked on. No one came running out of their house to see what was going on. I was on my own. I pulled my phone out of my pocket to call 911 for the second time in less than twenty-four hours, but I fumbled it like some ditzy girl in a horror movie. It skittered across the concrete sidewalk and landed at Lucas's feet. He laughed, a hyena laugh that reminded me of the Joker's, and bent to pick it up. I was too far away to kick him in the face, and I'd left my freaking pepper spray in my car. I was *all* of the horror tropes I hated all rolled into one huge disaster of a human. If—no, *when*, I lived through this, I would never make fun of another girl in a movie that stumbles, drops her keys, or ends up in some stupid situation she never should have been in to begin with.

I watched helplessly as Lucas tossed my phone over the cemetery wall. I could hear it whack crypts or trees or both, even over the sounds of the city. I doubted it had survived that fall even if I could get away from Lucas, get over the wall, and manage to find it.

"You need to shut your mouth," Lucas hissed, a menacing sneer on his thin face.

I took a measured step backward away from him and rummaged in my pocket for anything I could use as a weapon. I really needed to start carrying a pocketknife. And pepper spray. And not leave either of them in my freaking car.

"Because if you don't cooperate, I'll carve your grandmother up like a Christmas turkey." He laughed at his own little joke.

He must have noticed the look of horror on my face because he smiled again. "Got your attention now, don't I?"

"I'm not falling for your empty threats." I glanced around, trying to gauge whether I could bolt or not, and where I could hide if I did.

"Oh, they're not empty, *Lou*." That awful sneer was back. It twisted his thin face into something awful, like a funhouse mirror. "Your *Nan*, isn't that what you call her? That stupid little nickname"—he hissed the words like even saying them was offensive to him—"is currently zip tied in a location where she will never be found if something happens to me. I snatched her right off the little floral clawfoot chair in your living room. That oaf of a man she's seeing might never wake up."

I gasped; the sudden intake of air caused me to choke. But he had won. I wouldn't do anything that would put Nan in any more danger than I already had. My heart ached at the thought of her tied up, cold and scared, somewhere this monster had put her. I was surprised at the level of anger rising in my belly. I wanted to do unspeakable things to this man. No, not a man—this subhuman *thing* that had already taken one innocent life.

"Now that I have your full attention, you're going to walk in front of me. And if we pass anyone, you're going to smile and keep walking. Because remember, if anything happens to me, if you signal anyone, your grandmother will get to die slowly over several days without food or water."

"I got it." It was my turn to hiss. He might have me at a disadvantage, but I didn't have to like it. "Where am I going?"

"Just walk. I'll tell you when I want you to do something else."

I walked down Sixth Street toward Prytania, toward Mamie. I could just make her out, under the light of the streetlamp, wringing her hands.

"Lou!" she called. I nodded slightly, trying to make my movements subtle so Lucas wouldn't catch on. "What can I do?"

She sounded so desperate. But I couldn't respond. Lucas had already warned me about signaling someone.

"You never answered me," Lucas said.

He shoved me from behind, and I stumbled a few steps.

"About what?" I asked between clenched teeth.

"Who were you talking to?"

"Adam," I said truthfully. No point in lying now.

He laughed that hyena laugh again, and it sent chills down my spine.

"Part of this deal is your honesty. *Who were you talking to?*"

I don't think I had ever heard anyone sound so menacing, so . . . predatory. And I'd met some pretty scary spirits over the years, but none of them compared to this monster.

"I *am* being honest. I come here to talk to Adam, back here where you killed him, to talk things out."

"Oh, I didn't kill him," Lucas said with another shove to my back. "He killed himself when he betrayed me."

"Lou!" Mamie cried. I didn't think her haunt extended this far toward the cemetery. She'd always told me she didn't like the cemetery, that it was a reminder of the rest that was denied to her, so I'd never pressed her on how far her haunt reached in this direction. But here she was, halfway down the cemetery wall, farther than I'd ever seen her before.

"Stop," Lucas commanded. "Climb over the wall."

"What? No!"

"You will if you want your *Nan* to see another day."

"Why don't you just kill me in the street like you did Adam?"

"Because I almost got caught." He grinned like we were discussing some silly prank and not an actual murder. "You almost got a good look at me. And you probably would have if you hadn't tripped over Adam's body."

I felt sick to my stomach.

"Oh god, Lou, what can I do?" Mamie cried.

"Climb over the wall *now*."

I grabbed the iron railing and pulled myself onto the concrete half wall that flanks the entrance. The gate itself was chained shut since the cemetery was closed at this ungodly hour. I considered the fact that for just a few seconds, Lucas and I would be separated by a wall and I could run and hide among the crypts. I scaled the wall with no problem at all, but on the other side, I hung my jacket on the ironwork, fumbled, and crashed to the ground with a meaty thud. Lucas had jumped over before I even caught my breath.

"I wasn't going to kill you, you know," he said as he stared down at me on the ground. "I tried really hard to get you to back off."

"You mean you tried to frame me," I choked.

He laughed again. Apparently, this was all just *super* amusing for him.

"Yeah, but you would have been alive in jail. *Stand up.*"

He loomed over me, his face in shadow. He looked even more like a stick insect, standing over me, with his long arms and legs and the way he cocked his head slightly while he gestured with the knife. Mamie was also hovering over me, wringing her spectral hands, a mask of worry on her pale face. I started to haul myself up, and then I got a wild idea. As I got my feet underneath me, I glanced up at Mamie and said, "Rabbit."

Chapter Thirty-Six

M amie knew exactly what I was asking for, and she whirled around in Lucas's face, hitting him with volley after volley of screaming orbs. She held nothing back, and it had the desired effect. He stumbled away from the onslaught, swatting at the screaming balls of light. It gave me enough time to bolt into the cemetery, propelled by a speed I hadn't even realized I possessed.

I ran to the area where I thought Lucas had thrown my phone, but I couldn't find it, and I had no time to comb the area. I ran out into the cemetery, trying to stay ahead of Lucas long enough to get out of there and get some help.

"That was a fun little parlor trick."

I could hear Lucas from my hiding spot behind a tall, ornate crypt. His voice wasn't raised, so that meant he was closer than I'd hoped. If I could just stay out of his sight, I had a shot at making my way to one of the entrances, where the concrete and brick walls are much shorter and it's easier to climb over the ironwork fencing on top of the smaller sections of the wall.

"I'm not going to ask how you managed to pull that off," he continued. "Why couldn't you just leave this all alone? Why did you care? Adam was a jerk to everyone. He didn't have to get me fired.

I wasn't stealing anything from those rich maggots that they would ever miss."

He was getting closer. I could hear the crunch of leaves and twigs under his boots.

"Why does everyone always have to kick me when I'm down? I didn't deserve any of it. And then he treated me like I was just an inconvenience when I asked him to help me get my job back. You know I'm about to lose my apartment?"

I carefully backed up until I was in the path again, scanning the area for my next hiding spot the best I could in the dark.

"This has been fun, but if you don't come out, I'm just going to have to go take my frustrations out on your grandmother."

I froze.

"Or maybe I'll pay a visit to that friend of yours, Cady. Or even better, that pretty black-haired one with the tattoos. She was so helpful that day when I took the dagger."

I've never hated anyone, except for maybe Jason Carter in the third grade when he put bubblegum in my hair, but I one hundred percent hated Lucas Wells.

"You win," I said, and walked toward where I'd heard his voice.

"It's about time," he said with another laugh.

I was getting really sick of listening to that dirtbag laugh. I held onto the anger, stoked it, and let it fill me. Anger was better than the fear that I was about to die, that I was willingly giving myself up so my family and friends might be okay. But I had no guarantee he wouldn't go ahead and hurt them anyway. Now that I thought about it logically, he had no incentive to set Nan free once he killed me. She would be a loose end. He was armed with a knife, which meant he had to get close to me to use it. If I could just find a nice, long oak branch . . .

"There you are," he sneered as he rounded a tall white crypt.

He held a shiny revolver out in front of him. So much for needing to be close to me to kill me.

"Aren't you afraid that'll draw too much attention?"

He shrugged. "Not really. I'll be gone by the time the police get here."

He raised his gun hand to aim at me, and my heart pounded in my ears. I wanted to shut my eyes so I wouldn't know when the end was coming, but I couldn't seem to make my body cooperate. As the revolver was almost level with my chest my eyes were drawn to a figure rising above Lucas from behind.

Adam.

My heart leaped that he was okay—well, as okay as a ghost stuck in our world can be. He looked at me, smiled, and then engulfed Lucas in a blinding flash of light that finally caused me to close my eyes.

When I opened them, Lucas looked like he was battling . . . himself. His movements were erratic, jerking, and he stumbled back and forth while his head whipped from side to side. He dropped the gun at his feet and clapped his hands over his ears. And then he was suddenly completely, impossibly still. Not a single muscle moved, and I couldn't tell if he was breathing or not.

I felt like I needed to get the gun out of his reach, so I took a step toward it. I kept my eyes on Lucas, ready for him to spring to life and dive for the gun. I took a few steps toward him, when suddenly his mouth fell open.

"Get out of here, Lou."

The sound came from Lucas's mouth, but it didn't move. It was coming from *inside* him, and it was Adam's voice.

He didn't need to tell me twice. I turned on my heel and sprinted for the nearest gate. I was over the wall and back out on the sidewalk before I looked back. I'd taken several turns through the crypts so

I couldn't see Lucas, but I still had the horrible feeling that he was going to jump out at me from every shadow.

"Are you well?" Mamie appeared at my side. "I have been so worried."

"I'm okay, but I've got to call the police. I don't know how much time I have."

"I believe they have already been alerted," she said.

"How?"

She pointed down the sidewalk to a figure hidden in the shadows under a massive oak tree. Maybe someone had heard my original screams for help. I didn't have to wonder for long, because when she stepped out of the shadows, I recognized Joan and her bright pink hair right away. Granny Ghost Hunter to the rescue. I rushed toward her.

"Joan! Did you call the police?"

As the words left my mouth, a wailing emanated from the cemetery that made the hair on the back of my neck stand up. It was a primal keening, unlike anything I'd ever heard. Joan looked as terrified as I felt, and as we both stared at the brick and cement wall, afraid whatever was screaming on the other side might burst through, the sound blended with the approaching police sirens before dying away.

Chapter Thirty-Seven

The responding police officers quickly ushered Joan and me a safe distance away and instructed us to wait for more officers to arrive. It didn't take long, and soon the entire area was crawling with law enforcement. An older officer with salt-and-pepper hair approached us as others fanned out around the cemetery. Now, lights flicked on in the surrounding houses, and people started looking out their windows.

Officer Marcus Daniels introduced himself and offered us both blankets that he'd pulled out of his trunk.

"Which one of you called 911?"

"That was me." Joan raised her hand.

"Do you live around here?" he asked.

"No. I do paranormal investigations, and I had recently gotten an unexplained photo during one of Lou's tours." She gestured toward me. "I was hoping to catch something tonight, so I was wandering around taking photos and some videos. That's when I saw the man kidnap her with a knife. He forced her into the cemetery, and I called 911."

He looked from Joan to me, and I couldn't tell if he believed us yet or not.

"He told me he kidnapped my grandmother, Elizabeth Thatcher," I said desperately, and rattled off my address. "Please, I don't know where he took her, but he said he kidnapped her from our living room and hurt her boyfriend, so there might be evidence there. You've got to find her!"

He talked into his shoulder radio, and I heard dispatch confirm that they would send someone to my house. Once the adrenaline started to wear off, I felt sick to my stomach with worry over Nan.

"She's a witch!"

All three of us snapped our heads toward the screeching voice across the street. Several uniformed officers surrounded Lucas Wells and sort of dragged him along with them.

"She put some kind of spell or something on me! You have to believe me! She's a witch!"

"Sure, buddy, sure," one of the officers said with a laugh.

Joan shuddered beside me, and I put an arm around her. She smiled up at me.

"I have most of it on video"—Joan held up her camera—"up until he took her into the cemetery and I couldn't see them anymore. I might have gotten something on the audio, though, because I kept filming, just in case."

"Joan, you are amazing." I hugged her tightly.

It took what felt like forever to recount everything that had happened and everything that led up to what happened. I was nearing the end of my story and still hadn't figured out how to explain how I'd gotten away from Lucas when Dylan came running down the street. He flashed his badge to the uniformed officer.

"Are you okay?"

"I'm fine," I said quietly. "But I don't know about Nan," I told him what Lucas said he'd done. "Can you find out if the officers found anything at the house? And if Ron is okay?"

"Is the suspect in custody?" he asked Officer Daniels.

"Yeah. I think they may be ready to transport to holding," he responded, and hooked his chin toward one of the police SUVs.

"It's not Jace," I said, correctly assuming who Dylan thought was in the back of that SUV.

He turned to look at me, confusion replacing the concern.

"It's Lucas Wells. He murdered Adam."

Saying his name made me wonder where Adam was. It didn't appear he was still possessing Lucas from the way Lucas had behaved when he saw me. And it would seem that Lucas hadn't realized what Adam had done anyway. I scanned the area but didn't see Adam anywhere.

"The man from your shop earlier? The one who chased Jace Klein away?"

"That's the one," I said.

Dylan nodded, then turned and walked over to the SUV where Lucas was held. He opened the door and bent over to look Lucas in the face. I couldn't hear what Dylan was saying to him, but Lucas's expression went from smug to terrified in just a few seconds. Then Dylan straightened up and slammed the door. The SUV pulled away, carrying Lucas away from us.

"Let's get you two out of the cold, and you can fill me in," Dylan said as he ushered us toward his car. "I'll find out what's going on at your house."

Neither of us argued. We could hear Lucas yelling as the SUV pulled away with him inside. As it departed, I noticed Adam in the middle of the street. I smiled and nodded to him.

"Thank you," he yelled above the din. "Thank you so much, Lou."

"No." I shook my head as I mouthed the words. "Thank *you*."

Dylan had allowed Joan to turn over her camera for evidence and go home from the scene. She promised she would check in on me in the next few days. After Dylan put me in the passenger seat of his car, he left for several long minutes. When he returned, he told me that the police officers that Officer Daniels had sent to my house had found Nan and Ron safe and sound. They reported that they were worried about me, but they were both just fine.

"Lucas lied about that too," I said, and tears threatened to well in my eyes. "I fell for everything he said, hook, line, and sinker."

I spent the next several hours at the police station. Once we arrived, Dylan let me call Nan to let her know that I was all right. After receiving a sound butt chewing, I got off the phone and recounted the night's events again. Dylan was mostly silent while I talked, only offering a head nod or an occasional "Go on."

When I finished, he just got up and left. I pulled the police-issued blanket around my shoulders and leaned back in the uncomfortable chair. Exhaustion had caught up with me, and all I wanted to do was sleep. It was only a few minutes before Dylan returned, though. He brought me a large coffee and a ham-and-cheese croissant. The coffee, even though it appeared to have been brewed in-house, smelled heavenly, and I was thankful for the warm goodness and comfort.

"Thank you," I said, and closed my eyes for another sip.

"I'm really glad you're okay," Dylan said quietly.

"Me too," I said, my eyes still closed. "Cady would never forgive you if you let me get killed," I added with an exhausted laugh.

"Let me take you home."

"I'd appreciate that."

I couldn't keep myself from nodding off on the short trip from the police station to my house. I felt tired all the way to my soul. I knew that I would have to tell my story yet again when I got home, because telling Nan that I was too tired to talk would *not* be acceptable. When Dylan pulled in behind Ron's pickup, I took a deep breath and tried to ready myself for Nan's gentle wrath.

"When I got the call this evening, I was really scared that I'd missed my chance," Dylan said as he turned the car off.

"What chance?"

My tired brain thought that maybe he was talking about the chance to catch Adam's killer.

"Look, you've always been Cady's friend." He glanced sideways at me while he spoke. "And there was a time when I just considered you another annoying little sister."

"Gee, thanks. I'm super flattered," I said dryly.

Whatever pep talk he thought he was giving me was falling pretty flat, and I needed to get inside, where Nan could tell me how much I'd worried her and let me give her an abbreviated version of the night's events. And then I could crash for the ten to fifteen·hours of sleep I desperately wanted.

"What I'm saying is that time passed, and I no longer saw you *that way*, but you were still my little sister's best friend." Dylan finally turned toward me in his seat.

I nodded.

"You're not making this easy for me." He laughed and ran a hand through his hair.

"What am I not making easy for you?" I was fast getting tired of whatever game he was playing.

"Lou, I'm trying to tell you that I'm attracted to you."

I couldn't be sure in the dim light from our security lamp, but I got the impression that Dylan Finch was blushing. Meanwhile, I had ceased to breathe, think, or move in any way.

"I have been since high school. But the timing has always been wrong, and honestly, you've never seemed to care for me much. But tonight made me realize that I don't want to go one more day without telling you that."

I tried to speak, but I only made some weird mewling sound when I opened my mouth.

"I'm sorry." Dylan turned away abruptly. "I've put you in an uncomfortable position. You don't have to say anything."

He opened his car door and started to get out, but I grabbed his arm. I have no idea what came over me, but I finally found the capacity to speak.

"Dylan Finch, I've had a crush on you my entire life."

The biggest, goofiest grin spread across his face.

"Really? I thought you hated me."

"I thought you hated me too."

"So, where does that leave us?" He reached up and brushed a strand of hair out of my face.

My breathing quickened as panic overtook me. I'd just agreed to have drinks with Eddie Dumond. And I wanted to have drinks with Eddie. But I'd wanted a chance with Dylan my entire life.

"Are you all right?" he asked, and then he must've read the look on my face, because a dawning recognition washed over his. "Oh. I get it. You're seeing someone."

"I'm not really *seeing* someone. We haven't even gone out yet, but—"

"But the timing is still not right," he said, and he looked genuinely sad about it.

I searched for something to say, looking hopelessly at him and praying that the only chance I'd ever had with him wasn't slipping away.

"Let's get you inside before she comes out to get you," he said, and then pointed at Nan, who was staring at us from the window.

"Dylan, I—"

"Lou," he interrupted, "you don't owe me an explanation." He reached over and squeezed my hand and then got out of the car.

I opened my door, fully expecting to argue with him, but Nan, Ron, and Bryce all rushed out to meet us, and I didn't get the chance.

Chapter Thirty-Eight

Rather than reschedule the tours for the next day, Tess took over and let me chill at the shop. I didn't have any major injuries, but I was sore from my face-plant off the cemetery wall, and mentally I just needed a few slow days. The day after Lucas tried to kill me, six large boxes were delivered to the house. At first, I thought there had been some sort of mistake, but I soon realized our mother had boxed up all of Bryce's belongings and mailed them to us. I made an appointment for Bryce with a counselor that afternoon. I made one for myself too. He told me neither of them were returning his phone calls. I needed someone to help him navigate that kind of abandonment. Even though he continued to insist he was okay, there was no way that wouldn't affect him.

Ron and I helped Bryce rearrange the guest room that evening and make it fully his. I wanted him to have a nest, a sanctuary to call his own since he was losing the only home he'd ever known. I wanted to drive to Missouri and shake my mother until her teeth rattled and force her to understand the mistake she was making, but I knew it wouldn't matter. If she were capable of realizing that, Bryce would have never had to run away in the first place.

The next morning, I woke up later than I had in years. Everyone had already eaten breakfast, but true to his caring nature, Ron had left me a plate warming in the oven. I devoured it before I found the note Nan had left me.

Lulu,

We'll probably all be out when you get up—breakfast for you in the oven. Ron took Toby to the vet for shots and stuff, and Bryce went with him. I'm going to that blasted follow-up appointment. Check in later.

Love you lots,
Nan

At odds over what to do with myself when left to my own devices, I decided to visit my dearly departed friends. I started with Albert, after a quick drive-by to make sure Mia wasn't home. I still didn't want her to find me lurking around outside her home. I found Albert trying to scare a couple of squirrels who were raiding a mushroom-shaped birdfeeder.

"Hey, Albert," I said over the short chain-link fence.

"Blasted squirrels," he grumbled. The offending rodents were either completely ignoring his efforts, or they weren't animals that see ghosts.

"I just wanted to thank you for all your help. They caught Mr. Brandt's killer last night."

"Oh! That's wonderful news!" He clapped his hands together in a gesture I'm sure he made a lot when he was alive. In his current form, there was no sound associated with it. "Was it the man you asked me about?"

"No, it wasn't him." I pulled out my phone to show him a photo of Lucas Wells. Being in police custody hadn't afforded him with the time to lock down his Facebook profile, so I found a photo easily.

Albert studied the photo carefully.

"I don't understand," he said, his ghostly eyebrows knit together. "That's the one I told you about."

If there was ever a moment in my life where everything crashed to a halt with that screeching record sound, this was it.

"No," I said, just as confused as Albert looked. I pulled up Jace's photo. "This is the man I asked you about."

"Oh yeah. That one was here once. But that other one was here *all the time.*"

Lucas.

Suddenly, everything made sense. Lucas had been stalking Adam, not Mia. I hadn't shown Jace's photo to Albert when I talked to him previously because I'd let my assumptions blind me. I'd just been *so sure* Jace was guilty. Adam had seen Jace once. The rest of the time it had been Lucas.

"Are you all right?" Albert waved a wispy hand in front of my face.

"Yes, I'm just a little tired," I said with a smile. "I really appreciate your help."

"Of course." He returned my smile. "Could I ask you a favor?"

"Sure. I owe you, after all."

"Would you mind getting those dadgum squirrels out of that feeder?"

After scaring off two very persistent tree rats, I bid Albert farewell and went to see Adam. He appeared in my passenger seat before I even got parked.

"How are you? Are you okay?" He peppered me with questions the minute he appeared.

"I'm sore but okay."

I parked under a mossy oak. I didn't waste any time in telling him what I'd just found out from Albert.

"That little weasel," Adam said in a tight, clipped voice. "I should have killed him when I had the chance."

"You don't mean that."

"No," he admitted. "But it felt good to say it."

"How were you able to . . . overtake him?" I hesitated to use the word *possess* because it creeped me out in a way I couldn't put into words.

"I don't know how any of this works." He shrugged. "I was hoping you could tell me."

"We're both in trouble then, because I'm no expert." I stared off into the distance. "I don't know how you're able to move leaves, like you did for Toby, but you can't affect people the same way. I mean, except for what you did with Lucas."

"Speaking of the little guy, where is Toby?"

I told him about Bryce, how he'd fallen in love with the puppy, and kind of unloaded about my horrible relationship with my mother. He listened politely through the whole diatribe.

"Sorry. I guess I needed to get that off my chest."

"Anytime."

"Something else that's been bothering me: I also have no idea why I was able to affect you that day when you scared Toby."

"Maybe we're just connected a little more since you were there when I died," he said quietly.

"Maybe so."

"Look, I have no business asking you for anything else, ever," he began tentatively.

"Adam, I promise I won't stop coming to visit."

"No, that's not it. I mean, I want that too, but that's not what I was going to ask."

"Sorry. What is it then?"

"Can you help me write a letter to Mia and then make sure she gets it?"

Tears welled in my eyes. "I'd be honored to."

Adam must have been thinking about what to say for some time, because he didn't need much time to dictate a letter that made my heart ache. He thought of nearly every detail, having me type the body of the letter, which I ran home to print, and then brought back for him to sign. He held his hand over mine and I matched his movement to sign the letter. He said it wasn't perfect, but it was good enough.

"I just can't figure out how to get it to her. There's no reason for you to have a letter from me."

"Leave that to me. I have an idea."

I drove straight to the police station after I left Adam's haunt. I gave my name to the desk sergeant, and I didn't have to wait long for Dylan to appear.

"Is everything okay?" he asked, his brows furrowed in concern.

"I need to ask a favor," I said. I was suddenly self-conscious and found it hard to look him in the eyes. "Can we talk outside?"

He nodded and opened the doors for me.

"I need you to give this to Mia Brandt. It's from Adam. I can't tell you how I got it," I said so fast I sounded like an auctioneer. "Can you please just tell her you found it in his things?"

He arched an eyebrow and looked at me skeptically.

"I'm not in the habit of lying to victims' families."

"Please," I pleaded. "I know I'm asking a lot, but it's important."

He took the envelope with obvious hesitation. "Am I allowed to know what's in it?"

I hated to share the very private letter with Dylan, but if that's what it took to get it to Mia, then it would be worth it.

"See for yourself."

He opened the envelope and quickly read the letter, his face growing more solemn with each line.

"I'll make sure she gets it."

"Thank you." I shifted from foot to foot anxiously. "About the other night . . ."

"Like I told you, you don't owe me any explanations."

"I'm not trying to explain," I protested. "I actually wanted to ask you something." I stood a little straighter, feeling bold and a little reckless. Nearly getting killed seemed to have given me a confidence boost. And reading through Adam's letter made me realize I didn't want to have regrets. None of us know when our time will come, and I didn't want to end up as a ghost with a lifetime of missed chances.

His brows furrowed and he cocked his head ever so slightly, like I'd just asked him a question in a language he didn't understand. I took his silence as a cue to keep going.

"Do you want to have dinner next week?"

"I thought you were seeing someone."

"I told you we hadn't gone out yet." I felt my confidence waning. I watched him for a moment, desperately wanting to figure out something to say that didn't sound stupid or desperate, but I failed. His phone started ringing before I could even say something stupid.

"I have to take this," he said apologetically. "If it's meant to be, the timing will work out eventually."

"Sure, no problem. Maybe I'll see you at family dinner night sometime soon," I said with a laugh.

Good lord, Lou. Smooth.

He nodded as he took the call and headed back inside. The sting of rejection, even a hopeful rejection, left me deflated and confused. Hadn't he just confessed that he was interested in me?

"Can I help you?"

I jumped at the uniformed officer who had apparently walked up while I was lost in my thoughts. He looked concerned.

"No thank you. I was just leaving." I smiled at him and tried to look less like I'd just been gut punched.

He nodded, but he watched me while I got in my car and drove away.

* * *

Everyone appeared to be home when I pulled into the driveway. I took a deep breath and pulled up the letter on my phone. I read through it again and wiped away the tears welling in my eyes.

My darling Mia,

Where do I even begin? If you're reading this, I'm gone. But please know that wherever I am, I'm still loving you. Nothing will change that, not time, not space, not even death. You were always the light that made my life worthwhile.

I have a favor to ask of you. Please, whatever you do, move on. Find someone who worships you as much as I do, as much as I always will. Do all those things you put off because I was too busy or too distracted to do. Live your life while you're here, because no matter how long you have, it's too short. Just do that for me, Mia. Live, love, and be happy. And if you get the chance, come see me where I died. I'm told that's where spirits might stay. Tell me about your life, but don't make it a habit.

Don't hang onto my memory so hard that you forget to fulfill my request. Live, Mia. Just LIVE *to the fullest.*

All my love, always.
Adam

As I read that last line, the tears turned to sobs, and I let myself have a good, cleansing cry.

Chapter Thirty-Nine

The weekend was a blur. I managed to sneak away long enough to thank Mamie for her role in saving my life and promised that I would keep her up to date on any online drama about her videos. Cady spent the whole weekend at the house, and it was like a high school sleepover. We binged two full series on Netflix, ate way too much junk food, and laughed so much that by Monday, my ribs were sore. She taught Bryce how to make her famous hamburger queso and joined me on Saturday night's tour.

By the time she left Monday morning, I was the best kind of exhausted. After helping her carry her numerous and varied belongings to her car, I went back to bed and slept until Kenneth woke me in the early afternoon. He ignored my grumbling.

"Don't you have a date tonight?"

Apparently, he'd been eavesdropping when I'd told Cady about getting drinks with Eddie. Although with the way she'd squealed at the news, it would be no surprise if the whole neighborhood hadn't heard.

"Yes, *later*." I pulled my comforter over my head.

"You need to shower. You're a mess."

"Thank you, Kenneth. Always appreciate the ego boost."

Kenneth made a noise like a heavy sigh, which was always funny since he had no breath to sigh.

"Who is this guy you're going out with?"

I told him about Eddie.

"Humph," he said when I was finished. "And you like him?"

"Um, yeah, or I wouldn't have agreed to go out with him."

"Well, this is the perfect opportunity for another tarot lesson," he said, and made a show of pointing toward the deck on my vanity. "Let's see what the cards have to say."

I groaned.

"C'mon. Chop chop."

"Can you just haunt me normally? Open a cupboard every once in a while? Make creepy noises in the dark?"

Kenneth rolled his eyes. "Shuffle the cards."

With another huge groan, I got up to grab the deck and shuffled them. I laid out the cards on my bed in what Kenneth said was a five-card love spread. I flipped over the first card, which was supposed to represent what my prospective partner might bring to the relationship. It was the ten of cups. A couple stood in the foreground, their arms open wide. Two children played to their right. Above them were ten cups floating in the air in a kind of arch. I studied the card.

"Well? What do you see there?" Kenneth prompted. "What does that card say to you in relation to the position in the spread?"

"Why are the cups floating in the air? That doesn't make any sense."

Kenneth made a sound like *ugh* and crossed his arms. He gave up by the third card when I asked him again how on earth two sphinxes represented goals on the Chariot card. He threw his hands in the air and vanished. Left to get ready in peace, I showered and found my most flattering pair of jeans. I paired them with my favorite gathered cropped sweater top that flattered my figure in the best way. I finished the look with low-heeled, slip-on boots.

I glanced over at the deck of cards and pulled the next one off the top. I don't know what the next position in the spread was supposed to be, but for the first time I knew exactly what the card was telling me. The eight of cups stared back at me, and the symbolism was crystal clear. The eight cups were stacked in the foreground, a gap in the top row. *Something has been missing.* Behind the cups, a cloaked figure has turned his back and is walking away toward mountains in the distance, *letting go and moving on with his life, heading toward new possibilities.*

I'd spent my entire life chasing the *idea* of Dylan Finch. Why? Sure, I had to admit, even to myself, that the man was ridiculously good-looking. I mean, he was really hotter than anyone has a right to be. But was that it? Was that the only reason I'd pined for him, daydreamed, and wished for something more? I considered how he'd treated me throughout the investigation, accusing and cold at times and really only supportive after it was clear I wasn't a murderer. Sure, some of it could be explained by the fact that he was in a tough spot. But could all of it be excused?

I looked back at the card. I realized, in that moment, I was ready to walk away from the old and welcome the new. Maybe Dylan was right, and if we were meant to be, the timing would work out eventually. But for the first time in my life, I admitted to myself that it was okay if it didn't. It was time for me to move on from teenage crushes. I tucked the card in the deck and put it back into its velvet bag. Before heading down to my car, I checked myself in the mirror one last time. I liked what I saw there: resilience, determination, and—most of all—happiness.

Acknowledgments

Thank you to everyone who made this book possible.

My fellow writers at Pitch Perfect—you are the most supportive and understanding group anyone could ask for. Special thanks to Jodi Lasky, E. Marie Robertson, and Rebecca Paddock.

As always, thank you to my amazing agent, Jill Marsal. I still can't believe I get to say I have an agent!

Thank you to the team at Crooked Lane Books. To my editor, Jennifer Hooks, I've said it once, but I'll say it again, you make the editorial process feel like a celebration of growth, and for that I am truly grateful.

Thank you to my readers! Without you, I'd still just be talking to myself.